Endorsements

"In the pages of *No Greater Love*, as I ran, hid, fought, escaped virtually through apartheid-era South Africa, I caught a glimpse of God's heart. His hatred of injustice. His compassion for the oppressed and grieving. His forgiveness for the repentant. And, oh, such love! No greater expression is there of heaven's own immeasurable love than that a man lay down his life for another. This read is far more than just a great fiction plot!"
—Jeanette Windle, author of *Betrayed* and *Veiled Freedom*

"With raw truth and gritty realism, Kathi Macias has once again written a riveting fiction masterpiece that tackles a difficult societal issue...your heart will be drawn into this amazing story of God's transforming grace."—Kelly Kiggins-Lund, Philadelphia Christian Books Examiner

"In this first book of her "Extreme Devotion" series, Macias proves herself to be a masterful storyteller, mixing complex characters with a riveting plot, and showing how God calls each of us to be closer to Him."—Cheryl C. Malandrinos, The Book Connection

"A gripping book that will challenge your thinking and move your heart."—Shelly Beach, Christy Award–winning author of *Hallie's Heart* and the sequel, *Morningsong*

"Macias has created a heart-wrenching tale of prejudice, racial battles, and fear during the South African apartheid. Delicately woven into the story is the theme of love's ultimate sacrifice...."—MaryLu Tyndall, author of *The Red Siren*, *The Blue Enchantress*, and *The Raven Saint*

"Kathi Macias has created a sweeping epic about a land alien to too many, but more important is the crucial nature of the story and its monumental implications. You'll feel as if you were there."—⬚⬚⬚⬚ ⬚⬚ ⬚⬚⬚⬚⬚⬚ coauthor of the "Left Behind" series

More New Hope books by Kathi Macias

More than Conquerors

Mothers of the Bible Speak to Mothers of Today

How Can I Run a Tight Ship When I'm Surrounded by Loose Cannons? Proverbs 31 Discoveries for Yielding to the Master of the Seas

Beyond Me: Living a You-First Life in a Me-First World

No Greater *Love*

Book 1 in
the "Extreme Devotion" series

Kathi Macias

NEW HOPE
PUBLISHERS
Birmingham, Alabama

New Hope® Publishers
P. O. Box 12065
Birmingham, AL 35202-2065
www.newhopepublishers.com
New Hope Publishers is a division of WMU®

Library of Congress Cataloging-in-Publication Data

Mills-Macias, Kathi, 1948-
  No greater love / by Kathi Macias.
    p. cm.
  ISBN 978-1-59669-277-0 (sc)
  1. Race relations--South Africa--Fiction. 2. Interracial marriage--
South Africa--Fiction. 3. South Africa--Fiction. I. Title.
  PS3563.I42319N6 2010
  813'.54--dc22
                                    2009043829

ISBN-10: 1-59669-277-4
ISBN-13: 978-1-59669-277-0

N114126 • 0410 • 5M1

To my Savior, whose great love for me
is beyond my comprehending;

To my husband, Al,
with whom I share a lifelong love;

And to those throughout history
and around the world even today
who exhibit the greatest love
by laying down their lives for others —
thank you.

Multiplied thanks and blessings
to Alan Lester of South Africa
(http://www.graceunlimited.co.za/),
whose advice/input on this manuscript
was invaluable to its completion and authenticity.
Thank you!

Prologue

1989 WAS NOT A GOOD YEAR TO FALL IN LOVE— at least not in South Africa, and certainly not with a white man. Chioma had fought it with every ounce of her being, but there it was, literally, in black and white.

Chioma hated whites, and that included Andrew—except that Chioma also feared she was falling in love with him. And that made her dilemma even worse.

But at least she had never admitted to him—or anyone else—how she felt, nor did she have any intention of doing so. And yet, the way he looked at her, she couldn't help but wonder if he knew—and if he felt the same about her.

It was ridiculous, of course, even to think such a thing about a white man, someone who represented everything she despised. But if it were true, she could only hope he would never be foolish enough to say anything about his feelings—to her or anyone else. Not only would a relationship between them be nearly impossible, but it would be dangerous as well. And Chioma already had enough danger in her life; she certainly didn't need to look for more.

Though the family still clung to many of their ancestral apartheid beliefs, they had been willing to give work to two young orphans.

Chapter 1

IT WAS HOTTER THAN USUAL THAT SUNDAY AFTERNOON in January 1989, as Chioma and her younger brother, Masozi, trudged home on the last leg of their rare excursion into town, toting their sparse purchases in knapsacks thrown over their shoulders. It had taken the siblings months to save enough out of their meager wages to make the all-day trip worthwhile, and even then Chioma wondered at the wisdom of venturing away from the farm and its relative safety. For the city of Pretoria, despite its original name of *Pretoria Philadelphia*, showed little brotherly love to anyone with skin the color of Chioma's or Masozi's. Chioma had long believed that the city whose streets were lined with royal purple jacarandas, which bloomed every spring and thrived in the valley's fertile land, had rightfully earned its reputation as the capital of apartheid South Africa, a beautiful land marred by the ugliness of a system that enforced a cruel and unequal separation of the races.

Chioma cut her eyes sideways, too hot to expend any more energy than necessary by turning her head but wanting to see how Masozi was holding up. Since disembarking the crowded, noisy bus, they had already walked for nearly an hour, and they still had at least that much longer ahead of them. And though the blistering sun had finally begun its slow descent behind the Magaliesberg hills, it had not yet offered them any respite from its punishing rays.

Masozi's pace was steady and measured, as was Chioma's. She could see where the road dust had settled on his partially bare, muscular legs, clinging to the sweat that oozed from his pores. Chioma had collected her own layer of dirt, but her calf-length dress, made of coarse, cheap cotton, covered much of it.

"Are you okay, brother?" she asked. "Do you want to stop and rest?"

Chioma could not see Masozi's head without lifting her own, but she could imagine its curt, side-to-side shake as he answered. "I'm fine. I'm fifteen now, remember? Nearly a grown man. I'm strong, and I don't need to rest."

Chioma stifled a smile. She had anticipated his answer, but his determination to be her protector, though a year younger than she, served only to endear him to her even more. Masozi had been forced to grow up far too soon. But then, she reasoned, nearly everyone she knew had been forced to accept responsibility beyond their years in an effort to survive. Without father or mother, Chioma and Masozi's situation would have been more difficult than most, had they not stumbled upon their live-in jobs at a large dairy farm owned by an Afrikaner family named Vorster. Though the family still clung to many of their ancestral apartheid beliefs, they had been willing to give work to two young orphans and thankfully treated their employees as decently as most and better than some. They also paid their workers what was considered to be more than a fair wage, though Chioma doubted any of the whites in South Africa would want to try living on such an income.

We have no one but each other, Chioma reminded herself, clenching her jaw to obliterate the memory and its accompanying pain. *Just Masozi and me—and the cause. That's all we have left...*

The thought reinforced her need to stop and rest—for both of their sakes. They still had more than two hours before they would be considered late in returning to the farm and in danger of being out after dark, so a fifteen-minute respite couldn't hurt.

She spotted a small stand of trees, interspersed with spurts of bright yellow King Proteas, less than a hundred yards ahead, and set her course to lead her brother there and convince him to stop amongst the national flower. Ironically, the same country that enforced the laws of apartheid also had a law protecting this lovely plant.

"Maybe you don't need to rest," she said, her eyes fixed on her destination, "but I do. Fifteen minutes under one of those acacias, and I'll be ready to go again."

Masozi grunted his agreement, and Chioma knew her carefully worded suggestion had kept his fragile masculine pride intact. Neither said anything more until they had thoroughly checked the area below the acacia karoo's branches for thorns, then dropped to the ground in the welcome shade and deposited their knapsacks beside them.

Masozi removed the water bottle he wore on a leather thong around his neck and offered it to Chioma. She took a long, welcome drink and handed it back to him, then leaned her head against the rough bark and closed her eyes. She sensed Masozi had done the same, as the high-pitched hum of the *sonbesies*, or beetles, an ongoing South African phenomenon throughout the month of January, lured her to slumber.

Chioma sighed. For as long as she could remember, she and Masozi had been inseparable, even when they were children, living in their parents' shanty, listening to their father's stories of Nelson Mandela, the ANC, and the massacre at Sharpeville. The one thing Chioma couldn't understand was why Masozi wasn't as passionate about the cause as she. Her father's stories had birthed the fire in her; his murder, as well as her mother's, had sealed it to her heart. But for now, revenge was only a dream. Unless their situation changed drastically, survival was the best they could hope for.

Chioma had not meant to fall asleep, but the anxious nudge from her brother and the loud, angry voices snapped her back to attention.

Where had they come from, these three young white men who stumbled around Chioma and Masozi's resting place in what was obviously a drunken state, cursing them and accusing them of stealing the contents in their knapsacks from good, honest, hard-working Christians like themselves?

The reference to Christians made Chioma want to spit in defiance, as she had heard many references to the white man's God from the Afrikaner *dominee* who owned the farm where she and Masozi lived and worked. But wisdom and experience told her to hold her tongue, even as she lowered her eyes to avoid their gaze and berated herself for having fallen into such a deep sleep that she had not sensed the approaching danger.

Sneaking a peek from her downcast stance, her eyes moved from the ranting trio to their truck, just as a fourth man emerged from the passenger side of the cab. The tall figure stepped out and moved quickly in their direction. Chioma's heart caught as she recognized the familiar face, and she dared to breathe a tentative sigh of relief. Andrew Vorster, the only son and heir of the farm where she and Masozi were employed, would certainly not allow any harm to come to his servants.

"What's going on here?" Andrew asked, the question coming across as more of a demand than an inquiry.

In the four years Chioma and Masozi had been with the Vorsters, they had become quite familiar with and even fluent

14

in the Afrikaner tongue. Chioma had seen Andrew many times during those years, though she had never spoken directly to him—and she had never heard him speak in such a tone. He had, in fact, always been polite yet firm with his employees and had never allowed any of them to be mistreated. She wondered now how much of the tone he exhibited in his speech at this moment was as authoritative as it sounded, and how much was merely bravado. Her life and Masozi's might well depend on the answer to that question.

At the sound of Andrew's voice, his companions stopped their swaying and cursing, and looked at him blankly, as if wondering who he was and where he had come from. To his credit, Andrew stood his ground and kept his gaze steady, though he moved it from one man to the next with slow precision.

The three men, however, were not so easily cowed. Inebriated though they might be, they slowly regained their limited wits and rose to counter Andrew's challenge.

"What business is it of yours, Vorster?" demanded the largest of the three, his eyes glinting as he took a step in Andrew's direction. "What do you care what's going on? You thinking of sticking up for these no-good thieves?"

Chioma detected only a flash of indecision before Andrew responded. "Who said I was sticking up for them?" he asked, his voice a bit less confrontational now. "And who says they're thieves?" He shrugged. "Looks like a couple of kids taking a nap along the side of the road. Why should that concern us?"

The big man spoke up again, taking another step toward Andrew. "Kids? You call them kids? Look at them. They're no kids, and they were doing more than taking a nap if you ask me. I say they're thieves, on the run from the law. And they got no business out here. None."

Before Andrew could respond, the other two chimed in with their agreement.

"That's right," said the one with a beard. He spat on the ground and leveled his eyes on Masozi. "Thieves, they are!

15

You can tell by looking at them. No-good thieves, I'm telling you."

"Oughta be hung," said the third man, his voice slurred. "Up to no good, and that's a fact."

"We are not thieves!"

Chioma stiffened, a cold chill snaking up her spine despite the lingering heat. Why had Masozi opened his mouth? He knew better, knew that to contradict a white man in a situation like this was like poking a deadly viper. What was he thinking? When would he learn to keep his mouth shut, the way she'd had to when—

The big man turned and glared down at them, as the other two approached Masozi and yanked him to his feet.

"What did you say, boy?" demanded the bearded man. "Were you talking to us?"

The flash of terror on Masozi's face as Chioma lifted her head enough to look directly at him told her he had come to his senses, though it might well be too late. If she didn't move quickly, her brother wouldn't have a chance.

"Mr. Vorster," she cried, jumping to her feet and daring to look directly at the man who was her only hope. "Please, you know us! Tell them we work for you, that we wouldn't steal, that we were coming home from town with our purchases, that we had permission. Please, *baas*, please!"

Andrew turned to her, shock registering on his face, as he squinted his eyes in an obvious effort to identify Chioma.

He doesn't know me, Chioma thought, stunned. *Four years Masozi and I have lived and worked on his farm—in his house!—and he doesn't even recognize us.* Her sense of terror returned, as all hope of deliverance evaporated under her employer's confused gaze.

"Chioma?" Andrew's voice scarcely registered in her brain as he said her name. All she knew was that he had spoken it—her name. *Chioma.* He knew who she was! They were going to be all right.

She nodded. "Yes, Mr. Vorster. Yes, *baas*. It's me, Chioma. And my brother, Masozi. We work for you, remember? For your pa. For your family. It's our day off, and we have permission to go to town, so long as we're home before dusk."

Andrew held her gaze for a moment, then turned to his cohorts. "Let him go," he said, his tone of authority having returned as he fixed his eyes on the two who held Masozi. "Now."

Masozi's captors hesitated, while the big man took yet another step in Andrew's direction and glared as he spoke. "Why should we listen to you, Vorster? They might work for you, but we don't. We're free men."

Chioma saw Masozi's jaw twitch, but he said nothing, nor did she. This was no time to lose control. She could only hold her breath and hope that Andrew's will was stronger than his companions'.

At last the big man broke the silent gaze that had locked between him and Andrew Vorster. He stepped back and turned toward Chioma's brother, nodded at the two who held Masozi, and said, "Let him go. He's not worth the effort."

The bearded man complied, but the other one appeared angrier than before, as he gripped Masozi's arm with both hands and threw him against the acacia's trunk. Even at fifteen, Masozi was taller and more muscular than his assailant, but it happened too fast for the teenager to be able to fight back or even to brace himself before being slammed into the tree.

The crack as Masozi's skull connected with the trunk ripped through Chioma's heart like jagged lightning. She opened her mouth, but she had no idea if any sound came out, though she thought someone was screaming. Oddly, it sounded like her mother, but she had been dead since just before Chioma and Masozi had found their way to the Vorster farm. Who, then, was screaming? Could it be Masozi himself? Could he have survived the blow that Chioma was sure had cracked his skull? Or was it simply the ongoing cry of the *sonbesies*, mourning the loss of yet another son of South Africa?

The questions swirled around her, even as her vision slipped away and the hard earth came up to meet her. Her last conscious thought, as she fell amidst the protected flowers of her beloved country, was a desire to sleep, dreamlessly, with no hope of awakening, to join her ancestors and their gods in peaceful, welcome oblivion...

❖❖❖

Andrew lay in the dark, staring at a ceiling he couldn't see and wondering how any of them would face the impending dawn. How, indeed, had they even survived the previous day? How had so many circumstances come together in just the right configuration at just the right time to have produced such a wrong outcome? And why hadn't God intervened to stop it?

He squeezed his eyes shut in an effort to stem the seemingly never-ending flow of hot tears that had plagued him since he locked himself away in his room, drawing the heavy drapes and flopping down on his bed without even removing his boots. Surely the Almighty could have prevented the tragic encounter on the roadside; it would have been nothing for Him. Hadn't He noticed Andrew's efforts — puny and futile as they were — to rescue the teenagers and diffuse the situation? Why hadn't God helped him? Why had He allowed things to go so terribly and tragically wrong? Surely God knew Andrew hadn't meant for it to turn out this way...

The crack of the boy's skull against the tree — Andrew would never forget it. Or the look on his sister's face. Chioma, was it? Yes, Chioma and Masozi. He had seen them around over the last few years, and though they were young, it seemed they were good workers. He had even heard his mother mention once that she suspected they were orphans, and Andrew was glad his family had taken them in and given them jobs and a place to live. But apart from that, he had paid them little mind—until now. Until today. Until it was too late. And the guilt was pressing on his heart until he thought it would burst from the pain.

Andrew opened his eyes and let the tears flow freely down his face and into his ears, as the girl's large, dark eyes—astonished, horrified, accusing—swam before his own. What could he say to her? What could he do to make her understand that he hadn't meant for things to happen as they did, that he was sorry, that he had wanted to help? And why was it so important to him that she know? Why did this young woman, with skin the color of creamy, pale coffee and eyes that appeared as limitless pools of grief, weigh so heavily on his heart?

He groaned, remembering his father's assurance that Andrew had done all he could, that sometimes tragedies occurred and they couldn't be helped. But his father's words weren't enough. In fact, they hadn't been enough for a very long time now, and the sound of Masozi's skull being split against the tree had forever sealed that fact in Andrew's conscience. Something at the very core of his father's apartheid beliefs and his Christian faith was in direct conflict and no longer rang true for Andrew—and he was determined to identify and expose it for the fallacy it was.

❖❖❖

Chioma had thought she knew pain. She was sure she had endured the worst the world had to offer—and survived. Now she realized she had been wrong. Seeing her parents murdered because they dared to fight against the tyranny of apartheid was a nightmare Chioma would carry to her grave, but it didn't begin to compare to seeing her only brother destroyed before her very eyes.

True, Masozi was still alive—for now. Breathing, anyway. But he would never walk again—never run or jump or dance; never marry or have children, or fight for the cause; possibly never even speak or cry or laugh. His neck was broken, and the doctors said there was nothing that could be done for him. *Nothing.* Chioma wondered if those same doctors might have offered a more encouraging prognosis if Masozi were white.

What would she do now? How would she care for him? Andrew had assured her that his family would take care of Masozi for the rest of his life—such as it was—and that she would always have a job with them. Was she supposed to be grateful for that, grateful to the one whose companions had so cruelly smashed her only living relative into a tree? Though she desperately wanted to keep Masozi alive for as long as possible, simply because she couldn't bear the thought of losing him, she knew in her heart that her brother would prefer death over the kind of life he would now live—assuming he awoke and recovered at all.

For now, all Chioma could do was sit beside his bed, the one Andrew had instructed the other servants to construct in the closed-in shed attached to the back of the main house. True, it was better than the bedroll on the floor of the shack where Masozi had slept before his spinal cord was severed, but at least then he could still get up and move. Now he would never move from this place again, unless someone carried him. And that was the worst kind of existence Chioma could imagine.

Prior to this day, Chioma had thought her hatred of the white man couldn't get any deeper. Now she knew otherwise. Despite Andrew's feeble attempts to stop his friends from hurting her and Masozi, as well as his obvious efforts to assuage his guilt over his failure to stop the assault, Chioma swore she would never trust a white man as long as she lived. She also made herself a promise that if Masozi died, she would spend the rest of her days avenging his death on any white man, woman, or child who dared to cross her path.

❖❖❖

"You mustn't let it get to you, son." Anana Vorster's voice was as soft and gentle as her pale blue eyes, and Andrew wanted desperately to believe her. But he also knew, deep down, that his mother felt nearly as badly as he about what had happened. As strong and unbending a role model as Andrew's father had been throughout Andrew's twenty-one years of life, his mother had been just the opposite—not weak, of course, but soft and tender, kind and loving. She was the one Andrew ran to when he was hurt or confused—precisely the reason he had sought her out on this warm Wednesday evening. Now they sat beside each other, in matching wicker chairs, on the sweeping veranda that encircled the front of their home. The sun had nearly set, and a welcoming breeze ruffled their hair as they turned just enough to face one another as they talked.

"Yes, Ma," he said, still gazing at her lovely face and wondering, as he often did, if he would ever be as blessed as his father to find such a loving and godly wife. "I know you're right. But—"

"But it keeps playing over and over in your mind," his mother said, interrupting him as she reached out and took his hand in hers, the feel of her skin reinforcing the softness that exemplified her personality. "I know, son. I know. You want to go back in time, to do things differently, to change the outcome...but you can't." She sighed, and Andrew thought he saw a mist form in her eyes before she blinked it away. As kind and gentle as she was, Anana Vorster was not one to allow herself to give in to tears easily, though Andrew remembered a time when it seemed she would never stop crying.

Apparently she was remembering that same time, for she confirmed it with her words. "It was like that for me when Gertie—" Anana's voice broke for a moment, and Andrew waited while she regained her composure. "When Gertrude died." She finished her sentence, then sighed again before continuing. "All I could think of, day and night, was 'If only I had been there,' 'If only I had not left her in the first place,' 'If only I had been a better mother...'"

When her voice broke this time, Andrew leaned across the arm of his chair and pulled her into an embrace, sensing more than feeling the shudder she suppressed. "Oh, Ma, don't say that. No one could ever be a better mother than you. What happened to Gertie was an accident. It wasn't your fault—"

Anana pulled back and locked his eyes into hers, a lone tear trickling down her cheek. "Nor was what happened on the roadside on Sunday your fault, Andrew. You must accept that, my son, or the guilt can get you into serious trouble." She paused, and when he didn't answer, she added, "Do you understand what I'm telling you, Andrew?"

He knew he should say yes, though he really wasn't sure what she meant. Serious trouble? What sort of trouble? But he could hear his father approaching, his heavy boots announcing his arrival as he strode purposely through the kitchen toward the front door.

"Yes, Ma. I understand. And...thank you."

Anana nodded, as the door swung open and Pieter Vorster stepped out onto the veranda to join them.

Squinting her eyes against the blazing sun, she lifted her head long enough to catch Andrew staring at her.

Chapter 2

CHIOMA REFUSED TO CRY, EVEN AS THE LAST shovelful of dirt was dropped onto Masozi's crude grave. There would be plenty of time for tears later, when she gathered together with the other servants for their own service of mourning throughout the night to come. But not now — not today, here, in the presence of the enemy.

Far worse even than her brother's death was seeing and hearing her *baas*, Pieter Vorster, standing over Masozi's lifeless body, serving in the capacity of *dominee*, or preacher, as he prayed to the white man's God and proclaimed what he called the "gospel," or "good news," of Jesus Christ. Pieter Vorster, Andrew's father, often referred to himself as a "minister of the gospel," and attendance at his Saturday evening services was mandatory for all employees living on Vorster property — meaning his black and coloured servants, whom he quite obviously considered heathens in need of salvation. Chioma and Masozi hadn't missed one of the senior Vorster's sermons since they came to work for him, but Chioma had never found any good news in the many words he preached. The Afrikaner *dominee* spoke loud and long about love and forgiveness, but Chioma had never experienced anything close to love from anyone of the white race, and she therefore saw no reason to forgive them for their many sins.

Squinting her eyes against the blazing sun, she lifted her head long enough to catch Andrew staring at her, and the look of pity on his face sickened her. She dropped her eyes quickly, refocusing on the dirt being dropped on her brother's grave—dirt from the white man's farm, though on a plot of land specifically set aside by the *dominee* as a burial spot for his servants. Chioma had heard it said that Pieter Vorster was a kind and thoughtful man to do such a thing, as most Afrikaner farmers did not want blacks buried on their land where the deceased's family members might later return and lay claim to the property because their ancestors were buried there. But Chioma was convinced the *baas* had done this thing only to make himself appear generous, and that he had purposely chosen a spot at the far edge of his property to keep the bones of what he considered the inferior blacks and coloureds as far from the main farmhouse as possible.

Chioma's blood boiled at the hypocrisy she sensed from this family. How dare Pieter Vorster act as if he were doing her a favor by burying her brother on the outskirts of his land? And how dare his son look at her in pity? How dare either of them act as if he cared that Masozi was dead! Maybe Andrew had stepped in and tried to stop the tragedy, but it hadn't worked, and it was his friends who had committed the act—his friends who called themselves Christians but considered Chioma and Masozi heathens. If Andrew Vorster thought she was in the least grateful or indebted to him, he couldn't be more wrong. She decided at that moment that if she ever found herself alone with him and had the chance, she would kill him without the slightest hesitation.

Still, she couldn't help but wonder why Andrew had attempted to stop the confrontation. Was it strictly business, because he didn't want his father to lose two of his best workers? Or was it possible there was a spark of human kindness within him that spurred him to try to save an innocent life?

No! She squeezed her eyes shut, holding back the stinging tears that refused to abandon their assault. The white devils had no human kindness; if they performed what appeared to be an act of kindness, there was always an ulterior motive. How many times had Chioma seen that truth proved out? That she stood here alone, every member of her family dead and buried because of the white man and his hypocritical beliefs, was testimony enough to that tragic fact. She couldn't allow herself to weaken in her commitment to one day be a part of overthrowing the apartheid system, no matter how kind any white man might pretend to be.

She was, after all, her father's daughter...and he had taught her well.

❖❖❖

Her chance for revenge presented itself much sooner than she expected. After Masozi's "Christian burial," the servants had been sent back to work, having to postpone their customary night of mourning until their duties to the white man were completed. After all, the death of one coloured teenager was certainly not important enough for a full day of lost production. A large farm with crops and dairy cattle required constant attention, and it was enough that the servants were excused from work on Sunday.

Chioma, however, had been afforded the consideration of a little extra time after the ceremony; it was, after all, her only remaining relative who had been buried. Pieter Vorster had therefore told her to take a few more minutes to "collect herself" before returning to work with the others. And so she had wandered off to a secluded spot behind the one-room shack she shared with her roommates, Mandisa and Mbhali.

A few minutes to collect myself—another great kindness from the white man, Chioma sneered silently. *However will I repay such bountiful blessings?*

Reaching into the large front pocket of her apron, she pulled out the one thing that remained of her former life, the only thing besides Masozi that she'd had with her when she and her brother had watched her parents murdered and then run for their lives. She fingered the small black journal, grateful she had carried it with her since her father had taught her to read; otherwise, it, too, would have been lost.

Gently she opened the cover, lovingly turning the pages that bore her father's ragged script, even as those same pages rehearsed the struggle for which he had eventually given his life. As always, the sight of his handwriting and the memory of his voice as he recounted these same stories brought a fresh threat of tears to Chioma's eyes.

Sharpeville…

Chioma closed her eyes, glad her father hadn't lived long enough to hear of some of the more recent tragedies, as their people continued their struggle to regain the rights that should have been theirs by inheritance. As the daughter of a faithful ANC comrade, she knew what it was like to face resistance on all sides—not only the Afrikaners and, to some degree, the other South African whites, but even people of their own color, such as the hated Zulus…

She nearly dropped her beloved book when Andrew walked up behind her, shocking her as he touched her elbow to announce his presence. Chioma's eyes flew open and she spun around, heart racing, fully expecting to join her brother in death at any moment, only to find herself staring into the sky-blue eyes of the tall young man who had attempted—however unsuccessfully and for whatever self-serving purpose—to rescue her and Masozi from his companions. What was he doing? Had he forgotten the apartheid prohibition of even touching someone of another race? In the four years she had worked on the Vorster farm, not once had she had physical contact with one of her employers. Even as she stuffed her journal back into her pocket, she dropped her eyes from his, but not before being struck by his odd yet strangely attractive features—and being disgusted with herself for thinking such a thing.

"What do you want?" she spat, casting off all caution and lifting her head to glare at him, even as she felt her eyes flash with the anger that emanated from her heart. "I'm not doing anything wrong. Your father has given me permission to take a few extra minutes to 'collect myself.'"

The flicker of pain and surprise in Andrew's eyes appeared genuine, but Chioma closed her mind to the thought. He was there for a purpose, and whatever that purpose might be, it wasn't for her good. And her words of defiance and disrespect would certainly not help the situation. But at that moment, rage won out over terror, and she held his gaze with contempt.

"I—" Andrew's voice cracked, and he cleared his throat and tried again. "I'm so sorry, Chioma. So... sorry."

Chioma. He had said her name again, as if he had known it all these years. As if he cared about her in some way. But she knew better. She also knew not to further push the boundaries of their relationship, which she fully understood was nothing more than master and servant, *baas* and hired hand. She had already far overstepped her bounds, but it was too late to undo the damage now.

Swallowing her pride and diffusing her anger, as she had so many times throughout her relatively short lifetime, she dropped her eyes and spoke in the most contrite tone she could muster.

"Forgive me, *baas*. I didn't mean to be disrespectful. I appreciate all you've...done."

For a moment neither of them spoke. Then Andrew cleared his throat once again. "It wasn't enough...or your brother would still be alive."

Warily, Chioma raised her eyes. She still didn't trust his motives, but at least his words were true. She wanted to scream at him and tell him that of course it wasn't enough, but she didn't. Instead she simply said, "Thank you." Then she waited, lowering her gaze to just below his eye level.

She saw the almost imperceptible movement of his Adam's apple as he swallowed, and for a brief instant she was tempted to believe that he truly was sorry about Masozi's death. But only for an instant.

Andrew spoke again. "Is there...anything I can do for you? Anything you need, or—?"

Chioma wondered what it would be like to recite to him a list of the many things he could do for her—for her people—and of the many things they needed to recompense them for the years, the generations, of degradation, disenfranchisement, and cruelty. But she just shook her head, wanting the conversation to end so she could return to work with the others.

Then she spotted it—a pitchfork, lying in the brush less than a foot away. She could wait until he turned to leave, then grab it and plunge it into his back. There was no one around to see her, no one to stop her. She could do it. It would be so easy...

"Chioma!"

The familiar voice came from behind her. It was Mandisa, no doubt coming to offer her comfort. The fifteen-year-old, whose name meant "sweet," was taking a big risk to leave her work and come in search of her friend. But Chioma knew that Mandisa, too, was grieving, as she had considered Masozi her "man" and hoped they would someday marry. Now that would never happen, and Mandisa was expected to carry on with her duties as if Masozi's death were nothing more than an inconvenient interruption.

Andrew's eyes broke from Chioma and looked past her, to a point in the distance. Chioma turned and watched Mandisa approach, seeing the look on her friend's face turn to puzzlement and alarm upon seeing Chioma and Andrew together.

"Forgive me, *baas*," she said, her voice quavering. "I didn't mean to leave my work, but . . . I was worried about Chioma, and—"

"I understand," Andrew said, interrupting her nervous apology. "Please, take all the time you need—both of you. I'll leave you two and . . . get back to my own work."

Chioma was surprised to hear the tremor in Andrew's voice, as if he were the one who had been caught shirking his duties, rather than she and Mandisa. The sense that his words were sincere assailed her again, but she steeled herself against the possibility of such a destructive thought.

"Thank you, *baas* . . . Mr. Vorster, sir," Chioma said, turning back to her employer as she spoke, "for your . . . kindness."

Andrew's eyes held hers, though she fought to pull them away. She knew she shouldn't be looking directly at him, and yet . . . What was it about this white devil that beguiled her? Whatever it was, she was determined not to give in to its lure.

When she said no more, Andrew nodded at each of the girls, said, "Well . . . all right, then," and turned on his heel and walked away.

Chioma reached out and took Mandisa's hand. "Thank you for coming when you did. You may have saved a life today—his or mine, maybe both. Whatever the outcome, mine would have been over."

❖ ❖ ❖

The wind was hot as Andrew rode the fence line, absently checking for worn spots and potential problem areas. He needed to stay busy, needed to keep his mind off the attractive, angry young woman whose eyes flashed with emotion he couldn't read—and probably wouldn't want to if he could. What was it about her that so drew him? Her grief and loss, certainly, for which he felt more than slightly responsible—but there was more. Rebellion, perhaps? How better to defy his father's authority and apartheid beliefs than to associate with one of the servants? Considering that might be a real motive for his behavior, he didn't feel very proud of himself at that moment.

He drew his mount to a halt and sat up straight, resting his hands on the saddle horn and gazing out over the fertile land he so loved. It had been less than two weeks since he and his drinking buddies had come upon the pair, sleeping in the shade of the acacia tree at the side of the road. Why had they stopped? Why couldn't they have kept going and left the two young people to rest on their journey? And why hadn't he tried harder, done more to stop the violent, senseless confrontation? Andrew was beginning to understand why his mother had been so adamant in insisting he stop blaming himself or thinking about what could have been.

Less than two weeks, and yet it seemed his life had changed forever. The Christian faith he had grown up with, already questionable in his mind, had suddenly become reprehensible to him, inextricably tied to the practices of apartheid. And his father, the man he had loved and respected throughout his lifetime, seemed a hypocrite of the worst kind.

All because of Masozi, a black boy whose name, aptly and prophetically, meant "tears," and who was now buried in the ground on the edge of the property Andrew called home. Ever since, the dead boy's sister, Chioma, haunted Andrew's every thought, stalked his every move, challenged his every belief.

He cursed and slammed his fist against his leg, causing the bay mare to bolt, nearly unseating him. What was happening to him? In all his twenty-one years, he had never felt so out of control, so lost and vulnerable and . . . guilty.

Exactly what his mother had warned him about. And he didn't like the truth of her warning or the way he felt one bit.

❖❖❖

"Are you two going to cry all night again?" Mbhali demanded, as the three young women lay on their mats in the stifling, semi-darkened shack they called home. The room's only window was open, but no breeze ruffled the ragged, once-white curtains. "Because if you are," Mbhali added, "I'm going outside where I can get some sleep."

Chioma eyed the dim outline of her older roommate, the strikingly beautiful eighteen-year-old whose name meant "rose" but whose personality spoke more clearly of thorns.

"Sorry," Chioma sniffed. "I know you need your sleep. We all do. It's just that Mandisa and I have lost—"

"I know what you and Mandisa have lost," Mbhali interrupted. "You lost a fifteen-year-old slave, a coloured boy with no future. Your brother, Chioma—I understand that. But you, Mandisa? What was he to you? A future husband? Ha! What could he give you that would be any different or any better than what you already have? Could he even offer you hope? No! And that is the real sadness, more so even than his death."

The antagonistic young woman paused for a moment and then shook her head, her face hard as she continued to address the two mourners. "When are you going to figure out that this is as good as it gets—unless we do something about it?"

Chioma raised her eyebrows. She much preferred Mandisa's sweet personality to Mbhali's abrasive one, but deep down she knew Mbhali was right. If they didn't do something to change their situation, as Chioma's father had told her for years, then they were accepting the hand fate had dealt them—and it was a losing one. The very fact that Mazosi's death had already been ruled an accident and no one was even going to be arrested for it was proof enough of that.

"I loved him," Mandisa said, her voice breaking with the declaration. "And he loved me. He was a good man."

Mbhali snorted. "Was! He *was* a good man—or at least a good boy. And what profit did it bring him—or anyone else? Where did it get him? Buried in the ground, that's where! Dead and buried, like thousands and thousands of our people. And what would have happened if he'd lived? He'd have been a cripple, dependent on someone to carry him everywhere he went. Is that the life you'd want for him? The gods—if indeed there are any—did him a favor by letting him die."

Chioma hated hearing her brother talked about in the past tense, and she hated hearing the words that she knew brought more pain to Mandisa's tender heart. But she couldn't deny the truth that Mbhali spoke. Chioma, too, was glad that Masozi hadn't lived as a cripple, had never awakened from unconsciousness and seen the pity on the faces staring down at him.

Yes, Mandisa was sweet and gentle, a good and faithful friend and one whom Chioma loved dearly. But Mbhali was a warrior, with a fearless heart and a determined will, and if there was one thing Chioma needed at this point in her life, it was a warrior at her side. She must discipline herself to follow in Mbhali's footsteps and not get sidetracked by Mandisa's sweet nature...or the questionable kindness of a white devil.

Chioma. She thought of her name and wondered, as she had so many times through the years, why her parents had labeled her so inappropriately. She could understand Masozi's name, as tears were a familiar phenomenon to her people. But

Chioma—"God is great"? She nearly snorted with contempt. If there was anything great about the gods, she had yet to see it, and certainly didn't expect to any time soon.

Experience had taught Andrew that the longer it took to get started, the worse it would be.

Chapter 3

ANDREW GRITTED HIS TEETH, KNOWING HE WAS IN for another of his father's famous lectures, designed to build backbone and drive out the devil at the same time. The younger Vorster had been raised on lectures and sermons, and for most of his life had done his best to live up to his father's high expectations. But lately the hypocrisy he saw between the words his father spoke and the lifestyle he lived was fueling the rebellion that had long lain dormant in his heart.

Pieter Vorster paced, his brow furrowed and his stride steady, never missing a beat. When Andrew was young, he had counted his father's paces, knowing he would never start speaking before he reached at least one hundred steps. The elder Vorster had passed that number some time ago, and Andrew expected the angry monologue to erupt at any moment. Experience had taught Andrew that the longer it took to get started, the worse it would be. But even his years of experience hadn't prepared him for the onslaught that came in the form of a still, small voice.

"Why, Andrew?" Pieter's voice was scarcely audible, though it slowly rose to a more normal decibel level. "What could I possibly have done to cause you to shame me so? And your ma... Even if you don't care about me, have you no regard for her feelings?"

Andrew didn't have to feign ignorance; he truly had no idea what his father was referring to or why he was asking him such questions. His eyes were fixed firmly on his father, who had stopped pacing now and stood looking down at his only son, obviously waiting for an answer.

"I'm sorry, Pa. I don't understand."

Pieter's bushy blond eyebrows shot up. "You don't understand? Well, of course not. If you did, you would show respect to the family name and avoid such shameless behavior. Do you know how quickly the gossips pick up something like this and how fast and far it can spread? And once the damage is done..." His voice trailed off, as he shook his head in what appeared to be a combination of disbelief and disgust.

Shameless behavior? Gossip? What was his father talking about? Andrew did a quick mental review of the past few weeks and could think of nothing except the tragedy at the side of the road. He and his father had already discussed that incident, immediately after it happened, so what else...?

The light came on as Andrew remembered his brief encounter with Chioma after the burial of Masozi. Had someone other than Mandisa seen them together that day? Likely so. Andrew's father had always cautioned him against "fraternizing" with blacks and coloureds, whether they worked for the Vorsters or not.

"We certainly don't mistreat our help, regardless of color," Pieter Vorster had explained many times. "But we don't fraternize with them either. God expects us to maintain the proper order of creation—the blacks and coloureds keep to their own, and we do the same, just as the good Lord intended. Otherwise we'd have chaos, and we know the Bible says that God is not the author of chaos or confusion. The races can only stay pure if they don't mix, and it's up to us as the superior race to maintain that purity. Certainly we show Christian charity to all races, and we do our best to lead them out of paganism and into the truth by preaching the gospel to them, but that's where our responsibility to them ends."

So that was it. Andrew had committed the unpardonable sin of "fraternizing" with nonwhites.

"If this is about Chioma, I—"

"Chioma!" His father's voice was nearly a roar now, as he interrupted Andrew midsentence. "So now you're on a first-name basis? When did that happen? Am I to assume the girl now calls you Andrew?" He paused, drawing his brows together as fire shot from his hazel eyes. "Is there anything else I should know, any other clandestine meetings besides the one behind the servants' quarters after that unfortunate boy's service?"

Clandestine meetings? Was he joking? But Andrew knew his father didn't say anything he didn't mean. He wasn't one to joke, or even laugh much, claiming that too much frivolity and jesting were tools of the devil to keep people from the important work of the kingdom.

His father was still staring at him, and Andrew knew he was expected to answer. For the life of him, he couldn't think of a thing to say—at least, nothing that would be acceptable to Pieter Vorster, farmer, *dominee* of the gospel, and respected head of his family.

Andrew loved his father, but his respect for him had been eroding for some time now. This confrontation wasn't helping.

"I don't know what to say, Pa," Andrew said at last, doing his best to keep his voice firm and even. "I'm not even sure what you *want* me to say. I can only assure you that I did nothing wrong. I simply wanted to comfort that poor girl after her brother's death. You know I tried to stop it, but—"

"Of course you did." Pieter's stance relaxed, and the fire in his eyes dimmed, as his voice returned to a more normal level. "And I'm proud of you for that. It was the right thing to do—the Christian thing. But, son, don't take this beyond where it needs to go. That girl is not your responsibility, nor is her brother's death. It was simply an unfortunate accident that couldn't be prevented. We've given the boy a proper burial, and now it's time for everyone involved to move on—including you." He paused a moment, and when Andrew didn't respond, Pieter's voice took on an icy edge. "She's coloured, Andrew. However attractive you may find her, don't even think about crossing that line."

His warning hung in the air between them, as Andrew gazed up at his father, studying him as he wondered just how close love and hatred could actually get before becoming indistinguishable. His father may have been referring to the line marked by race, but Andrew was more concerned about the line that divided his own feelings—and what he might do about them.

An even bigger concern at the moment was why his father's words about Chioma evoked such an emotional response within Andrew. After all, he was an Afrikaner, and he knew his place. He was white; Chioma was coloured. Nothing else needed to be said. As much as he hated to admit it, his father was right—again.

He nodded and forced himself to speak. "Yes, sir. I understand. I...wasn't thinking about how it might look. It won't happen again."

Pieter Vorster's lips formed a tight, thin smile, and he reached down with his right hand. Andrew responded, and as their hands clasped together, the father pulled his son to his feet and into a bear hug. "I knew you'd see it my way, Andrew," he said, pounding the younger man on the back with his free hand. "You always do. You're a good man, son. A good man."

Andrew swallowed, wanting to believe his father's words but still struggling with the emotions that warred in his heart.

❖❖❖

Even with the overhead fan running at top speed, the bedroom was a bit stuffier than Anana liked. As she lay in bed, next to the man she had married nearly a quarter of a century earlier, she wondered how they had become so close when, indeed, they were so different.

"Are you awake?" she whispered, knowing full well that he was or he would be snoring loudly enough to ruffle the sheets.

When he grunted his answer, Anana reached over and found his hand, tucking hers inside his large, calloused one and smiling at the comfort that existed in such a small gesture.

"What is it?" he asked finally, though he didn't move, and Anana knew they were both staring at the unseen ceiling.

She wondered if she should tell him what was on her heart, or just leave it to be worked out with time. But this man was her partner, the one with whom she had produced two children, even if only one had lived to adulthood. They had never had secrets between them—at least, as far as she knew—and this was no time to start.

"I'm worried about Andrew."

Without asking for specifics, he responded. "The coloured girl."

"Chioma. Yes."

"Don't be. I talked to him about it today. He understands."

She swallowed, wanting to believe him. But her heart was still troubled.

"Stop worrying," he said, squeezing her hand. "Andrew will be fine."

A picture of Gertie—chubby cheeks, sparkling blue eyes, heart-shaped smile—flashed through her mind, and the ever-present threat of tears burned hot behind her eyelids. She mustn't give in, for once she did, she knew she would never be able to stop.

Locking down the tears once again, she scooted closer to Pieter, who pulled her into the crook of his arm as she lay her head on his broad shoulder. *Thank You, God*, she prayed silently, *for this good man You have given me for a husband. Thank You for this place of refuge.*

But long after Pieter Vorster's breathing had turned to rumbling, Anana stared into the darkness, praying for her son and for the unreasonable fear that gripped her each time she thought of him...

❖❖❖

Chioma dared to watch him ride by on the bay mare that had been his mount for as long as she had lived on the Vorster farm. She hated herself for staring at his broad shoulders and the rock-hard muscles in his suntanned forearms, but she seemed unable to tear her eyes away. Though she grudg-ingly admired the way he sat tall in the saddle and his appar-ent fearlessness of the animal beneath him, she refused to believe that what had appeared to be kindness on his part was not fueled by some perverse, ulterior motive. Instead, she steeled her heart against him and spat on the ground beside her after he had passed, as if dismissing her feelings with her spittle.

Andrew's blue eyes had flickered in recognition, and he had given her a curt nod as he rode past, but he hadn't spoken a word of greeting—nor had she. Though they had encountered one another several times in the last few weeks, nearly always locking eyes before quickly looking away, they hadn't conversed since the day of Masozi's funeral. Chioma told herself that was exactly the way she wanted it, but her heart contradicted that thought as she watched him ride off, and self-hatred roiled within her.

"Lusting after the *baas* again?"

Chioma spun around to find Mbhali standing at her side, a sneer marring her otherwise lovely features.

Chioma felt her face grow hot. "I wasn't lusting! I was just…watching him and thinking how much I hate the whites—especially him!"

Mbhali's eyebrows arched over her large, dark eyes. "Really? And why is that? Because he tried but failed to save Masozi? Because he tried but failed to comfort you after the funeral?" She shook her head. "When are you going to learn, Chioma? Don't you have enough troubles, enough heartaches, without looking for more?"

"What are you talking about?" Chioma protested. "I'm not looking for anything—not from the likes of him, anyway!"

Mbhali pursed her lips and studied Chioma for a moment before speaking. "Good. I hope that's true, because trouble is always on the horizon for the likes of us." She lowered her voice conspiratorially. "You know, my cousin Themba brought me a message the other day. The word is that Nelson Mandela has been diagnosed with tuberculosis. Our people won't take it well if he dies in prison."

Chioma felt her eyes widen and her heart stop. Mandela? Tuberculosis? No, it couldn't be! He was their savior, their hope for freedom and a better life! Her father and mother had devoted their lives to that cause—even to the death—and now Mbhali was telling her it might be over, that the man she had never met but revered her entire life might die without ever being freed from prison!

"No," Chioma said, feeling the fire in her belly build until it flashed from her eyes. "It can't be. Nelson Mandela can't die—not in prison, not like this."

Mbhali smiled. "Ah, that's what I wanted to see—a reaction, some indignation, determination and dedication to the cause." She grabbed Chioma's arms. "Listen to me, Chioma. Themba is helping to organize our people. We must fight, however and wherever we can—in small bands and on the run, if need be. The time is short, but the more chaos we cause and the more we disrupt the government's ability to function, the better our chances. We can't let the cause die with an old man in prison. Some say this news of Mandela is a blessing in disguise, that it will force the government to let him go. I say, forget the laws and the government; apartheid must be overthrown, and we must be a part of making that happen!"

Mbhali's face was close to her own now, and Chioma knew her friend was serious. She nearly shivered, remembering the rumors she had heard about Themba leading raids on some of the more remote farms, stealing whatever he could find and killing those who tried to stop him. He was a wanted fugitive who left no doubt that he was dedicated to the cause and would do whatever was necessary to see it succeed.

Chioma had met Mbhali's cousin once, when he snuck in during the night to see Mbhali, and Chioma knew from that moment on that she would never forget him. Themba was a tall, strong, handsome black man with muscles like thick ropes and eyes like steel, and whose name meant "hope." One of the things Chioma remembered most about Themba was the scar that ran across his chest, from his right shoulder to the left side of his waist. Mbhali had told Chioma that had the sword slashed him in the opposite direction, it would have cut through his heart and killed him. But the gods had protected him, Mbhali insisted, so that he could help lead the fight for their people.

The very sight of Themba had frightened Chioma—not so much because she was afraid he would harm her, but because she was afraid she would follow him anywhere he asked. And so, to prevent him from asking, she had avoided him the next time he came to visit Mbhali. But how long could she avoid him? How long could she avoid her destiny, continuing to work on the white man's farm while her people suffered and Nelson Mandela, the man in whom she had long placed her hopes and dreams, might even now be dying in a prison cell?

Her eyes locked with Mbhali's, and she knew the commitment was made. She had no idea where this commitment would take them or how it would end, but she knew her days of working for the Vorster family were nearly over. Her destiny lay ahead of her, and her heritage demanded that she fulfill it. With Masozi dead, what loyalties were left to tie her to the white man's farm? It was in her best interests to get away from the Vorster home and everything that tied her to it...as quickly as possible.

Andrew was a white man, and she was
coloured. End of story.

Chapter 4

CHIOMA FLUFFED THE PILLOWS AND TUCKED IN THE crisp white sheets, closing her mind to the image of the man who slept each night on the four-poster bed. This was her job—nothing more. Along with Mandisa and Mbhali, Chioma had been cleaning the Vorsters' home for several years now. She had changed this bed—and the others in the big house—countless times. Why did it feel so different this time?

She shook her head, trying to dispel the thoughts that seemed ready to pounce each time she let her guard down. Andrew was a white man, and she was coloured. End of story. Her mind knew that perfectly well. If only her heart would get the same message.

Thinking of Masozi or her parents and the way they were murdered at the hand of white devils sometimes helped, but not for long. She even tried to concentrate on the fact that Andrew had been with those who killed her brother, but sooner or later her thoughts shifted to the fact that he had tried to stop the killing. True, he had failed, but at least he had tried.

Why? That was the question that plagued her most. Why would a white man make an effort to protect a coloured man, even if that man did happen to be one of his employees? After all, there were many more like him. In fact, Masozi's position had been filled before he even died, while he still lay motionless in a coma, and work on the Vorster farm had continued without missing a beat.

So what was the point? Why had Andrew Vorster even bothered to get involved?

Chioma couldn't allow herself to believe it might be that Andrew had a kind heart, or that he cared about the life of someone of another race and therefore beneath his social class. Yet, no matter how hard she tried, she couldn't come up with any other explanation.

"Chioma?"

Chioma spun around, her heart racing at the unexpected sound of the soft, female voice behind her. Though she had often come into contact with Mrs. Vorster while working in the big house, Chioma was still uncomfortable in her presence—and even more so now, as she tried to look at her without directly doing so.

"Yes, madam...Mrs. Vorster. How...how can I help you?"

The middle-aged woman's features were as soft as her voice, and Chioma had often thought she was a direct contrast to her large, gruff husband. Chioma supposed the woman could even be considered pretty, in a pale sort of way.

Mrs. Vorster smiled—more with her eyes than her lips. "How are you, Chioma? Are you doing...better?"

Chioma paused. How was she to answer? She assumed the woman was referring to Masozi's death, but never having had a personal discussion with her before, Chioma was apprehensive about assuming.

"I'm...not sure what you mean, madam."

Mrs. Vorster's smile had faded, and in spite of herself, Chioma sneaked a peek at the woman's pale blue eyes, which reflected concern and sadness, confirming Chioma's assumption that the woman had been referring to Masozi's death.

"It's difficult to lose a loved one," Mrs. Vorster said, and Chioma thought she heard a slight catch in her voice. Chioma knew the Vorster family had lost a child some years back, but the subject was not openly discussed among the servants. Perhaps it was that memory that had evoked the emotion in Chioma's employer, rather than any sorrow or regret over the death of a young black servant.

It was obvious the woman expected some sort of response from Chioma, so she simply said, "Yes. Very difficult."

At that moment Chioma realized that Mrs. Vorster felt nearly as uncomfortable as she, and probably regretted having spoken to Chioma in the first place. But the woman had initiated the conversation, and it certainly wasn't Chioma's place to end it.

"I'm very sorry for your loss," Mrs. Vorster said then, her words causing a flash flood of emotion in Chioma that shocked her in its intensity.

Oh, no, she thought. *I don't want to cry! Not here and now...not in front of her!*

The eruption of tears in her own eyes brought a similar response from Mrs. Vorster, but before either could yield to the watery onslaught, Andrew stepped into the doorway, standing nearly a foot taller than his mother, his face flushed from the sun and grimy with sweat and dust. He had obviously been out working the farm, as he did nearly every day, but it seemed that neither Chioma nor Mrs. Vorster had heard him approaching.

He stood without moving, understandably puzzled to find his mother and Chioma in conversation, particularly one involving such a deep undercurrent of emotion. Before he could speak, his mother nodded to Chioma and said, "I shall let you get back to your work," and then excused herself and left the room.

When Andrew didn't immediately leave with her, Anana Vorster returned and gave him a look that spoke louder than any words ever could. Just before turning to follow her out of the room, Andrew's questioning eyes aligned with Chioma's, and she prayed he would leave quickly, before her legs gave out and she yielded to the spinning of the room.

When she was sure he was gone and relatively certain he wouldn't return, she did something she had never done before. She sat down on the edge of Andrew's bed, though she knew better. But she had no choice; her legs would hold her no longer.

Still shaking, she breathed deeply, trying to regain her composure. She hated that the young *baas* affected her as he did, and her resolve to leave this place, to escape the hold he had on her, grew with every throbbing, aching beat of her heart. It was obvious if she didn't get out of here quickly, away from the Vorster farm and all that went with it, she would end up in some sort of horrible trouble, worse than anything she had already experienced in her sixteen years of life. And there was little doubt in her mind that she wouldn't be able to endure anything of such magnitude.

❖❖❖

"You can't go, Chioma," Mandisa sobbed, as they huddled together on Chioma's bedroll. "Not with Themba! He's a dangerous man. I've heard of him attacking farms and outposts. He's rumored to...to leave no witnesses. Please, Chioma, don't leave me here!"

Chioma's heart ached as Mandisa clutched at her, begging her to stay. Mbhali had warned Chioma not to tell Mandisa of their plans, but Chioma couldn't simply disappear without explanation. How many times had Mandisa said that Chioma was like a sister to her, the only family she had left? Sweet, gentle Mandisa, so aptly named and far too tenderhearted to join Chioma and Mbhali as a freedom fighter for the cause that had fueled Chioma's passions since she was old enough to understand words. If only there were some way to make the younger girl understand, to reassure her that she would be all right here on the farm, alone.

"I have to go," Chioma explained, stroking Mandisa's hair as she held her close. "*We* have to go—Mbhali and I. We can't stay here and take a chance on letting the cause die with Mandela."

"Then take me with you," Mandisa pleaded, her head still buried in Chioma's neck and her tears wetting Chioma's shoulder.

"Oh, Mandisa, I wish we could," Chioma said, meaning every word. "But we can't. It would be no life for someone like you."

Mandisa pulled back and fixed her dark, wet eyes on Chioma. "But what will be left for me here, once you're gone? You know I'll be blamed for you leaving, for not telling them so they could try to stop you. What if...what if they turn me out and I have nowhere to go?"

She had a point, and Chioma had wondered about it herself. Would Mandisa be worse off if they took her along—or left her behind? The apparent kindness Chioma had noted—but tried to deny—in both Andrew and Mrs. Vorster gave her hope that Mandisa would be all right if she stayed. And yet...

Chioma's heart twisted with indecision. Mandisa truly was like a sister to her, unlike Mbhali, who was simply a strong personality who challenged Chioma to fulfill her destiny. And then, of course, there was Andrew...

No! She shook her head, forcing herself to block out the picture of the young *baas*, staring at her as they stood in his room or riding past on his horse and nodding at her in silent acknowledgment. More painful yet was the memory of Andrew's visit to her after the funeral service and his clumsy attempt to comfort her on the loss of her brother. And then there was the ever-present scenario of his futile attempt to rescue Masozi...

I can't think of it, she told herself. *I won't! I must think only of the cause—of my parents and Masozi...of Nelson Mandela, languishing in prison and now possibly dying from tuberculosis...of the thousands upon thousands of my ancestors who have died at the hands of the white devils... Once I'm gone from here, I'll no longer think of the white man who tugs at my heart and confuses my thoughts!*

She heard footsteps approaching, and she knew Mbhali would open the door at any moment. Darkness had fallen, and Chioma was torn as never before. What was she to do? She had made a pact with Mbhali, and she couldn't back down. Yet how was she to leave Mandisa behind? Did she dare hope that the soft-spoken Mrs. Vorster, who carefully carried her own sorrow just behind her blue eyes, would care for the gentle young girl, protect and provide for her when Chioma and Mbhali had gone? It was a thin sliver of hope indeed, but at the moment, it was all Chioma had.

❖❖❖

The light from the bedside lamp was just enough to read by, but Andrew couldn't concentrate. Several times he found himself having turned the page, only to realize he had no idea what he had read. He finally gave up and tossed his book to the floor.

Maybe he should have agreed to go out with his drinking buddies after all. They had tried to convince him to ride along with them into town, but ever since the tragedy at the roadside, Andrew had been reluctant to have anything to do with the men he had once considered his friends. He now knew better, of course, and wished he had trusted his instincts and severed their relationship long ago, but it was too late for wishing. The damage was done.

Resting on the pillows he had stacked behind him, he stared straight ahead, as visions rolled through his head, jumbling together in a kaleidoscope of beauty and horror. Chioma's round, dark eyes, one minute filled with anger, the next overwhelmed with fear and sadness. The shovelfuls of dirt, dropping onto the crude coffin. The crack of the boy's head against the tree...

Why couldn't he let it go, as his father had instructed and his mother had counseled? Chioma was, for all intents and purposes, forbidden territory. So why did his desire to go to her increase with every passing day? Why did he long to protect and care for her, to take away her pain and comfort her? Was it as simple as guilt, compounded with a desire to defy his father's apartheid beliefs? Or was there something more?

He closed his eyes, but the images danced on. *Why?* he cried silently. *God, if You're there, if You're listening, tell me why! Why did this have to happen? Why couldn't You have stopped it? And why do I have to care so much? Why can't I just put it behind me and move on, the way my father wants me to?*

No answer came. Not that he had really expected one, but he needed one—desperately. And if God didn't have an answer for him, then who did?

Maybe God doesn't talk to people with words, he thought. *Maybe just with signs, or through other people, or... with messages?*

His eyes snapped open, and he turned to fumble in the drawer beside his bed. His Bible, worn from years of carrying it to church services but seldom from personal use, sat tucked away in its usual corner. He pulled it out and stared at it. Was it possible? Could God really speak to him through the words on these pages—words written thousands of years ago by men long dead and gone?

The thought had always seemed absurd to him, but suddenly he saw it as his only hope. He opened the book to somewhere in the middle, but he had no idea where to begin reading. Then he remembered someone once telling him if he ever wanted to get to know Jesus more personally, he should start by reading the Gospel of John.

Andrew flipped to the contents, found what he was looking for, and thumbed his way to the proper page, starting at chapter 1, verse 1:

In the beginning was the Word, and the Word was with God, and the Word was God.

What was that supposed to mean? He had spent enough time in church to know that Jesus was often referred to as "the Word," so he decided that must be what the verse was referring to—that Jesus was eternal and had existed with God from before the beginning of time.

A good point, and not one Andrew would argue with, but how was that supposed to help him with his own situation?

He continued to read, stopping occasionally to meditate on a particular phrase or verse, particularly in chapter 3, which talked about God's love for the world and how He had given His Son to save whoever would believe in Him.

His eyes were growing heavy by the time he reached chapter 15 and began to read of Jesus' requirements for love. The last thing he read before his eyes closed were verses 12 and 13: "My command is this: Love each other as I have loved you. Greater love has no one than this, that he lay down his life for his friends."

With the words echoing in his heart and a picture of Jesus forming in his mind that somehow contradicted what he imagined as the teachings of his father and the apartheid system, Andrew Vorster drifted off to sleep, as the haunting images of pain-filled eyes and dirt-covered graves gave way to a sense of hope and promise.

❖❖❖

Chioma knew she probably shouldn't be outside, wandering around after dark, but she had lain in a pool of sweat as long as she could stand it, listening to Mbhali and Mandisa breathe and wishing she, too, could drop off to sleep. With every moment that passed, her restlessness increased, until she felt she would start screaming if she didn't get up and move about. Finally she opened the wooden door, hoping the creak wouldn't awaken her roommates, and tiptoed out into the sultry night.

Without planning to, she followed the pale shaft of moonlight and ended up by the creek that meandered through the Vorster property. She considered it one of the most peaceful places on earth, and she came here to this particular clearing whenever she could sneak away, just to sit on the same large, flat rock, dangle her feet in the cool water, and wonder what her life might have been like if she had been born in another place or another time—or in another color of skin.

Tonight was no different. The night air, though hot and still, was quiet except for the occasional call of a bush creature, but the moonlight sparkling on the creek and the steady trickle of water over her feet and ankles soothed and calmed her. Eyes closed, she let her mind wander, back to the time when she still had a family—a mother, a father, a brother. She remembered the shack where they all lived—poor but happy to be together, and always dreaming of a better life. She thought of the evenings beside the fire, listening to her father's stories of Mandela and the ANC, of Sharpeville, of the cause.

Chioma's mother had tried to stop her husband from talking to their children about the cause. "You'll turn them into rebels," she had warned. "They're too young to be soldiers — too young to die. Leave them alone, and let them be children for a while."

But her father would counter with, "If we leave them alone, they'll die anyway — without ever knowing their heritage or fighting for it. Then, whether they die old or young, it will be without honor. What's the point in that? What good is a long but wasted life? I'd rather they learn to be proud and to fight for what is theirs — even if it means they die young. At least they'll live and die with dignity."

And so it had been for her father. He had lived and died with dignity, refusing to renounce his beliefs or abandon the cause. Her mother had died, too, groveling at the feet of their captors and begging for her life and her husband's. As Chioma had watched their executions from her hiding place, her hand over Masozi's mouth so he wouldn't cry out, she had decided — if ever given the choice — that she would die with dignity, like her father.

Why did I have to be there to see it? First my parents' death, and then Masozi's. Wasn't it enough that I lost my entire family? Must I also live with the horror of those scenes emblazoned on my memory?

Shuddering, she pulled her thoughts back to the time before her parents were killed. She pictured her mother — her huge, dark eyes, small nose, creamy skin, even lighter than Chioma's... And then she remembered the time, just weeks before she and Masozi were orphaned, when she had asked her mother why her skin was so much lighter than Chioma's father's. Her mother had smiled down at her.

"Things happen," she said. "Things we don't always have control over. Life can change in a moment, and all we can do is accept it. There is white blood in my veins, Chioma... and in yours and Masozi's, though it's more obvious in you. But it doesn't change who you are inside." She laid her hand against Chioma's heart. "Your heart is pure, and that's all that matters. Do you understand, my daughter?"

Chioma had nodded, though she didn't understand at all. Thinking she would wait until she was older and ask her mother again one day, she didn't realize that death would soon steal that opportunity from her.

And now she would never know the story behind her mother's light skin—or hers. All she knew for sure was that she was coloured, not black. She could accept that so long as she thought of it in those terms. It was more difficult and painful to consider that she was part white. And she couldn't help but wonder if that fact had something to do with her attraction to the young *baas*—for that's what it was, and she could no longer deny it. It was the reason she had to get away from the Vorster farm as soon as possible. She must align herself with Themba and his freedom fighters, no matter how violent he might be, if ever she was to break the hold of the white blood that flowed within her.

"You shouldn't be here, you know."

The soft, deep voice, so close to the rock where she sat, ripped into her consciousness like a knife, searing and terrifying, yanking her back to the present. Her eyes snapped open, and she jerked her head to the left, toward the sound of the words that had shattered her solitude.

"Andrew," she said, realizing even as she spoke that it was the first time she had said his name aloud.

He didn't immediately answer, instead standing over her, looking tall and regal and—white, even in the semidarkness.

Her heart pounded against her rib cage, pumping her part-white blood through her veins, and she wondered if she should run, or try to explain herself, or just sit there and hope he really was as kind as he had appeared in the last few weeks. The only thing she knew for sure was that she shouldn't be looking into his eyes—and yet she couldn't look away.

Andrew examined the large rock where Chioma sat, then raised his eyes back to hers and asked, "May I sit down?"

Chioma swallowed and breathed deeply. Wisdom screamed to her to say no, to escape while she still had a chance, but she knew her legs would betray her if she tried. She also knew no words would come if she opened her mouth to speak, so she simply nodded her assent.

Once settled beside her, the scent of him—leather, soap, and a hint of sweat—made her light-headed. Why had she come here? Why couldn't she be more like Mbhali or Mandisa? Though the two girls were complete opposites of one another, at least they both had the good sense to be sleeping peacefully in their own beds, in the relative safety of their room.

For several minutes, neither of them spoke. And then Chioma caught her breath, terrified as Andrew began to untie and remove his shoes. What was he doing? What was he—?

When he dropped his bare feet into the water, his pale skin nearly shining in contrast to hers, she exhaled and felt her shoulders relax. What a strange man, this Andrew Vorster! Were all white men so unpredictable and odd?

Still they didn't speak. Chioma kept her eyes straight ahead as they sat in silence, occasionally feeling his gaze on her but refusing to return it. She had never felt so completely vulnerable and helpless in her entire life—not even when she had stood at the humble graveside of her murdered brother. How was it possible for anyone to have such power over another human being? How was it possible that his presence could call to her—draw her—without his even speaking a word? Could it be this white man truly was a devil after all?

"It's beautiful out here," Andrew said at last. He paused, and when she didn't answer, he said, "Like you, Chioma."

Chioma thought her heart would stop and she would die, right there on the rock next to the white man who had tried to save Masozi, the white man who smelled of leather and soap and sweat. Why would he say such a thing? Didn't he know they could never speak of such things—to each other or anyone else? Many people had died for much less—her people, at least, despite the fact that the Mixed Marriages Act had been repealed and, technically, people of different races could now marry, though they would have to renounce their citizenship and leave the country to find a safe place to coexist.

Oh, if only she had the strength to jump up from that rock and run away, as far and as fast as she could! But her heart, which had indeed started beating again and was now pumping at double-time, had betrayed her and refused to allow her to move. The realization that the reason she wasn't getting up to escape was because she wanted to stay, to be as close to the tall white man with the sky-blue eyes as possible, was more terrifying than anything she had ever experienced.

When Andrew took her hand in his, Chioma once again felt the hot tears rising up behind her eyes, and though she tried to blink them back, one by one they escaped and dripped down her cheeks and onto her lap. When one of them landed on their joined hands, Andrew used his other hand to turn her face toward his. With the glow of the moon and stars lightening the darkness around them, and the electrifying sensation of his fingers on her face, she gasped with surprise. Nothing could have prepared her for the shock of seeing that his eyes were also filled with tears.

"How long do we fight this, Chioma?" he asked, his voice husky and low, sending shivers down her back.

"As long as it takes," she answered, surprised that she was able to speak. "Forever—or they will kill us."

Andrew's eyebrows rose slightly. "They might not like it, but I doubt it would cause anything that drastic."

"That's because you're white," Chioma argued. "You haven't seen what I've seen. They'll kill us, I tell you—me, at least."

"She could be right, you know."

The deep male voice behind them froze Chioma's blood, as she and Andrew turned in unison, their hands still joined, only to find themselves face-to-face with the man who had slammed Masozi into a tree, ending his life before it had a chance to begin.

Chioma closed her eyes, remembering her parents and reminding herself that if tonight was her time to die, she wouldn't grovel or beg. She would die with dignity, like her father—though she regretted that she would do so without first accomplishing something for the cause.

Andrew had never really trusted Hendrie or any of the three, for that matter.

Chapter 5

ANDREW SENSED A FLASH OF FEAR SHOOT THROUGH him, but it was quickly lost in anger over his so-called friend's rude interruption. Hendrie du Preez had been a troublemaker for as long as Andrew had known him—and that was most of his twenty-one years. Hendrie and his younger brother, Johannes, lived with their family on the adjoining farm, and as a result, Andrew and the du Preez boys had practically grown up together. The other member of their foursome, Marius Davies, lived on another nearby farm, and he, too, was known for getting into trouble, especially when he'd had too much to drink, which was more and more often these days.

Andrew had never really trusted Hendrie—or any of the three, for that matter. But proximity and commonality had thrown them together from their youth. After the experience on the roadside that led to Masozi's death, however, Andrew had purposely distanced himself from his former companions, though they continued to try to convince him to rejoin them.

"What are you doing here?" Andrew demanded, dropping Chioma's hand and standing to his full height so he could look down at Hendrie, who was several inches shorter. "I thought you and Johannes and Marius were all going to town."

Hendrie smirked, apparently not cowed by Andrew's height. "I'm sure you did. And we were going to, but then we decided to come back and give you another chance to join us." He folded his arms across his chest. "I figured your parents wouldn't answer the door at this hour, so I went around back to your room and looked inside. When I didn't see you, I thought I might find you here. I know how much you like coming down here, especially at night." He grinned. "Now I know why. Guess I also know why you didn't want to head into town with me and the boys."

Andrew looked into the darkness behind Hendrie, but he saw no sign of Johannes or Marius. He had no problem taking on one or two of them, if it came to that, but he was not sure about all three, especially Marius, who was taller and more muscular even than Andrew. And if they had been drinking, which he was sure they had, there would be no reasoning with them.

"Don't worry," Hendrie said. "The boys are waiting in the truck, up by the house." He smirked again, and Andrew thought he saw Hendrie sway a bit, confirming Andrew's suspicions that the trio had already begun drinking. But if what Hendrie had said was true about Johannes and Marius, then at least the odds were stacked in Andrew's favor.

As if he could read Andrew's thoughts, Hendrie added, "But all it would take is one yell from me, and they'd be down here to join me." He raised his eyebrows questioningly. "But then, why would I want to yell and bring them running? Any reason you can think of, Vorster?"

Andrew glared, weighing his options. His primary concern was to diffuse the situation and get Chioma out of there—safely and quickly. Hendrie had proven himself to be the bully Andrew always suspected him to be when he killed Chioma's brother, even if the incident had been ruled an accident, and Andrew's heart told him the young hothead wouldn't hesitate to kill Chioma as well.

"What do you want, Hendrie?" he demanded, his voice steady, even as he eyed his friend-turned-foe, watching for the slightest movement. "You came here once and invited me to go with you, and I said no. I'm saying it again, so why don't you just go on back to your friends and head into town? There's nothing for you here."

Hendrie's eyes moved from Andrew's face to a place behind his back, where Andrew knew Chioma huddled, silent and no doubt terrified. Why had he come here and put her in danger? When he had awakened from his brief sleep, thinking of the words he had read from the Bible, why hadn't he just rolled over and gone back to sleep instead of walking out onto the veranda for a breath of fresh air? And when he had seen Chioma making her way toward the creek, why hadn't he just let her go? He'd had no business following her, putting her in a compromising and dangerous situation. If he had stayed at home where he belonged, he could have intercepted Hendrie and the others, and Chioma would be safe. And, of course, if he had heeded his parents' admonitions to maintain a strict separation of the races, none of this would even be an issue.

Greater love has no one than this...

The words he had read earlier that evening echoed in his heart, as if someone were speaking them, calling out to him—

The words from within were interrupted by Hendrie's voice. "I'm not so sure about that. I think maybe there is something here for me—maybe the truth of what has been going on right under our noses, the reason you got so upset about the death of one worthless coloured boy." His eyes squinted

65

and his chin came up, as his shoulders squared. "Now I think maybe you have something going on with the boy's sister. Maybe—"

Andrew's fist exploded from his side and caught Hendrie squarely in the middle of his face. The crack of cartilage and the eruption of blood told Andrew his former friend's nose was broken, but he didn't care.

"Run, Chioma!" he shouted, grabbing Hendrie and slamming him to the ground. "Get out of here before the others arrive!"

"No," she cried. "I won't leave you!"

Hendrie was clawing at Andrew's face, as he tried to throw the bigger man off him. "You have to!" Andrew yelled. "I can't protect you from all of them. Go!"

After only a moment's hesitation, he heard her fleeing through the veld toward the house, sobbing as she ran. *Oh, God,* he prayed silently, his hands pinning his captive's shoulders beneath him, *don't let the others see her!*

He flinched, crying out in pain as one of Hendrie's fingers gouged his eye, but he held on. He had to keep him there until Chioma had time to get away.

For God so loved…that He gave…

More snatches of verses spilled through Andrew's mind as he wrestled with his thrashing opponent. He sensed that what he heard without words was more than just flashes of memory from the Scriptures he had read; it was God, speaking to him, trying to make him understand something…

"Help!" Hendrie called, weakly at first, then louder. "Johannes! Marius! Help me!"

Andrew removed his right hand from Hendrie's shoulder and clamped it over the writhing man's mouth, praying the others hadn't heard, as Hendrie continued to struggle beneath him. And then Andrew felt the searing fire of Hendrie's teeth sink into the flesh of his palm, and he bellowed in agony, yanking his hand away and freeing Hendrie to start yelling once again.

He knew then there was little chance the others hadn't heard the commotion by now; he could only hope that his father and some of the other workers on the farm had heard it as well and would come to investigate. *Oh, God, whatever happens, let Chioma be safe, please!*

Forcing himself to ignore the pain, he pulled his right arm back to punch Hendrie once again, but he was too late. Before he could slam his fist into Hendrie's face and silence his screams, he felt someone grab his arm from behind. He was yanked to his feet and had just enough time to see Marius's hate-filled eyes in front of his own, and then the bigger man slammed him in the stomach, and Andrew felt the air explode out of his lungs.

Oh, God, where are You? Where is Chioma? Doubled over, grasping his stomach and gasping for air, he prayed she had escaped in time.

He who believes in the Son has eternal life… Do you believe, Andrew? Do you believe in My Son?

Andrew felt Marius grab him by the hair and yank his head back to look into his face. To the side he could see Hendrie pulling himself up from the ground. But where was Johannes?

His eyes darted around the clearing, as much as he was able without turning his head. And then he heard it—muffled sobs and shuffling feet, moving in his direction—and he knew Johannes had captured her.

Andrew renewed his struggle with his captor, raging against the iron grip that had now turned him to stare at Chioma and Johannes as they stumbled into his radius of vision. Marius had pulled Andrew against him, forcing him to face outward, while held in place by Marius's muscular right arm clamped across Andrew's neck and throat. Andrew's hand throbbed where Hendrie had bitten him, and his breath still came in short gasps. But none of that mattered when he saw the terrified look on Chioma's face—and the smirk on Johannes's as he clasped her to him in similar fashion to the way Marius held Andrew.

Hendrie, his nose still dripping blood, seemed to be recovering from Andrew's battering, as he rose to his feet, smirking at the scene in front of him. "So," he said, his eyes darting between Chioma and Andrew, "still want to play hero?" He laughed, flinching as he did so and putting his hand to his obviously painful nose.

For just as the Father raises the dead and gives them life, even so the Son gives life to whom he is pleased to give it...

There it was again, that sense that God was speaking directly to him, trying to get his attention. Well, it was working.

"I don't understand," Andrew answered, not realizing he had spoken the words out loud.

Marius tightened his grip against Andrew's neck, momentarily interrupting his air supply. As Andrew fought to maintain consciousness, Marius eased his grip and said, "What is there to understand, Vorster? You know the rules—and you know the consequences when you break them." He leaned in to Andrew's ear and whispered, "And not getting *pally-pally* with the blacks and coloureds is one of those rules you really don't want to break."

Andrew saw Chioma's dark eyes widen, and he knew she had heard every word. He struggled to pull away, but it was useless.

"What's the matter?" Marius asked, jerking Andrew into submission. "You want to get away, do you? Well, now, I think that could be arranged—under the right conditions."

Andrew felt himself grow cold, as the realization that Chioma's warning only a few moments earlier just might come true—at least for her, as she had said. He could, no doubt, save himself by denouncing any affection for her, and he might be able to pull that off, especially since he was still a bit unclear as to the true motives behind his feelings. But an ugly and horrifying thought that such a denouncement would not be enough to stop the escalating violence began to snake its way up his spine and around his throat, choking him more surely than Marius's arm.

"Let her go," he rasped, still struggling to breathe. "This isn't her fault. She's done nothing wrong. Let her go!"

Marius laughed, and Hendrie and Johannes quickly joined in, even as Johannes visibly tightened his grip on Chioma, provoking a yelp of pain from the helpless young woman.

"Sure, we'll let her go," Marius said, and then leaned in to Andrew's ear and added, "just as soon as we're through with her."

The rage exploded inside Andrew once again, and he fought with a strength he didn't know he had. But it wasn't enough—especially when he heard Chioma's cries and struggles rising above his own.

He stopped fighting and focused on Chioma, who now fought to stay on her feet between Hendrie and Johannes, each of whom firmly held one of her hands in his, pulling her arms straight out, as her body jerked from one side to the other while they yanked her back and forth.

"We can't decide which one of us gets her first," Hendrie laughed, "so we'll rip her right down the middle—like the Bible story about the two mothers who wanted the same baby. Just keep fighting, Andrew old boy, and we'll show you how hard we can really pull!"

Chioma appeared ready to faint at this pronouncement, and though Hendrie's words only served to reinforce Andrew's desire to get free and fight them all, he knew he could never win—not and save Chioma at the same time.

He felt the fight drain out of him then, and he relaxed, as he silently begged Chioma to understand that he was trying to save her. *Help will come soon*, he wanted to say. *Surely someone has heard us by now and will be here any minute to rescue us!* And though he wanted to believe that was true, he couldn't be sure.

There was always the possibility that everyone at the house might sleep right through the commotion.

Oh, God, help us, Andrew prayed silently. *I know I don't deserve Your help, but Chioma doesn't deserve to be treated this way, either. Please, God, I'm asking it in the name of Your Son, who died for me—and for Chioma. Help us, Lord! Save us! Please, God!*

"So," Marius said, his words jerking Andrew back to the desperate situation around him, "you've finally decided to quit fighting. Wise choice, Vorster." His grasp on Andrew loosened slightly, as he directed his words to Hendrie and Johannes. "Forget pulling her in half. Just do what you want with her . . . but save some for me, will you?"

Marius laughed as Chioma stiffened, then opened her mouth to scream. Horrified, Andrew watched as Hendrie clamped his hand over her mouth and, together with Johannes, pushed her to the ground.

It was more than Andrew could bear. With a roar, he burst free of Marius's hold and threw himself at the du Preez brothers, knocking Johannes aside with one quick blow and then grabbing Hendrie and pushing him off Chioma. He wrapped his hands around Hendrie's throat as together they rolled across the dirt.

"Run, Chioma!" he cried. "Get out of here!" But before he could utter another word or check to see if Chioma had responded, he was attacked from behind and nearly smothered in what felt like an army of bodies. He prayed that both Marius and Johannes had jumped him, leaving Chioma free to escape.

The last thing he remembered before the jagged pain that crashed down upon the top of his head was Marius's voice, yelling, "Get the girl, you idiot! Don't let her get away!"

The crashing footsteps behind her were drawing nearer, closing the gap, and her heart felt as if it would explode from her chest.

Chapter 6

CHIOMA'S FATHER HAD ALWAYS TOLD HER THAT SHE ran like the wind, but now it felt as if she were running against it. Torn between the need to escape and the pull to stay with Andrew, she pushed forward, telling herself she would get help at the big house and Andrew would be all right. But even then she sensed that wasn't true. When had it ever been that way for anyone she cared for? All were gone now, dead and buried, and she had little doubt that Andrew was about to join them.

The crashing footsteps behind her were drawing nearer, closing the gap, and her heart felt as if it would explode from her chest. "Mr. Vorster!" she screamed, coming into view of the farmhouse and praying her voice would be heard before her pursuer caught up with her. "Mr. Vorster, help, *baas*! Help!"

Just steps from the yard, she finally saw a light come on, and then another. As she reached the gate, the front door opened and Mr. Vorster stood framed in the doorway, shotgun in hand. The thought crossed her mind that the man could end her life in a split second, but she dismissed the possibility as quickly as it had come.

"Mr. Vorster," she gasped, "*baas*, please! Help Andrew! He's at the creek, and I'm afraid they're going to kill him if—"

Before she could say another word, the man was racing down the porch steps and the walkway, straight toward her, shotgun clutched in his right hand. Terrified, Chioma stepped back as the gate slammed open and he sped by in the direction of the creek. Chioma's employer hadn't even glanced at her as he charged by, so intent was he on his mission.

He's going to be all right, she told herself. *Andrew's going to be all right! The* baas *will save him!*

Gulping air and glancing around in search of her pursuer, she relaxed only slightly when she realized no one else was in sight. Mr. Vorster's appearance must have scared him off. Shaking, she turned in the direction of her one-room home, knowing Mandisa and Mbhali would have heard the commotion by now and realized she was gone.

The thought that the three attackers would likely be heading back toward their vehicle, which was parked in front of the farmhouse, spurred Chioma to action. Racing to her room, she thrust the door open and found her two roommates huddled together in the semidarkness, Mandisa crying and Mbhali cursing Chioma for being gone.

"Where have you been?" Mbahli demanded as soon as Chioma stepped inside and slammed the door behind her. "And what were you doing that caused so much trouble?"

Chioma was still struggling to catch her breath, but she shook her head and answered as best she could between gulps of air. "I was just...down at the creek...cooling off when..." She paused and swallowed. "When Andrew showed up and—"

"I knew it!" Mbhali's anger was evident as she interrupted Chioma midsentence. "You were with him! I knew it!" She peeled herself from Mandisa's grasp and stood up, stepping closer to Chioma. "What happened? What's going on out there, Chioma? And how is it going to affect us?"

Chioma breathed as deeply as she was able, trying to form her explanation, but the words wouldn't come. How could she explain what she didn't know? How could she tell Mbhali that Andrew Vorster could be dead, and trouble like they had never seen before could be about to break loose on her and anyone who happened to be associated with her? For ultimately, whatever the outcome of the confrontation at the creek, it would be blamed on her; of that she had no doubt.

Mbhali grabbed Chioma's arms and held them tight, her fingers pressing into her flesh. "Tell me!" she demanded. "Are we in danger, Chioma? Do we need to get out of here?"

Chioma opened her mouth. What was she to say? Mbhali was right. They needed to get away—all three of them—as quickly as possible.

She nodded. "Yes. We're in danger—all of us. We'd better go . . . as fast as we can."

Mandisa sobbed and Mbhali shot her a stern look, then turned back to Chioma. "You'll explain this to me later," she said, her voice hard and threatening. "But now, we go. I know where Themba might be hiding, and he'll help us."

"But I don't want to go," Mandisa cried. "Not now, not in the middle of the night. What will we do? What will happen to us out there?"

"I don't know," Mbhali said. "But I don't even want to think about what could happen if we stay here." She bent down and yanked Mandisa from the bed. "Now!" she commanded. "We go now. Get your shoes, and take only what you can carry."

Chioma was too stunned to move. How had it come to this? Less than an hour ago she was dangling her feet in the cool water, and now they were running away to join up with Mbhali's cousin, a known freedom fighter who lived where he could and whose life was always in danger.

Oh, Andrew, are you all right? Are you alive? Forgive me for leaving you!

❖❖❖

"Don't move, son. You'll be all right. Help is on the way."

Pieter Vorster's voice seemed to reach Andrew from another time and place, far away, garbled and indistinct. And yet he recognized it, and it comforted him somehow to know his father was near.

He thought he should speak to him, but he didn't have the strength. His eyes felt so heavy, the blackness so thick...

"Andrew, listen to me, boy." His father was speaking again. "Who did this to you? It was those du Preez boys, wasn't it? I saw the truck in front of the house. I always knew they were no good. Tell me, Andrew. Was it them?"

How was he to answer? How could he explain? It hurt to breathe, let alone talk. It would be so much easier to drift away, to let it all go...

Then he remembered Chioma, and he groaned. *Oh, God, where is she? Did she get away? Oh, God, hide her! Help her! If they find her, they'll kill her, and it'll be my fault!*

"Chioma..."

Had he spoken her name, or imagined it? Had any of this really happened, or was it just some awful nightmare?

He felt a hand on his face—his father's, no doubt.

"Andrew, what is it? What are you trying to tell me?"

So he had spoken. His father had heard him, even if he hadn't understood. Andrew had to try again, had to convince his father to help Chioma. He opened his mouth, but before he could breathe a word, his father stopped him.

"Don't talk, son. Save your strength. Your mother has called for help. They'll be here soon. Rest, my son. You're going to be all right. You can tell me about it later. I know who did this. I didn't get here in time to see their faces, but I heard them running away, and now they've taken off in their truck. They will not get away with this, son. I promise you that."

"But...Chioma..." It had drained him, but at least he had spoken her name loud enough for his father to hear. How would he get enough energy to tell him the rest, to beg him to protect Chioma, to help her?

"Chioma?" His father's voice had taken on a wary edge, and he removed his hand from Andrew's face. "What about her? Did she...? Was she responsible for this somehow? Because if she is, I—"

"No!" Oh, the effort and pain to shake his head and utter that word! But he had to make him understand. He couldn't let his father believe that any of this was Chioma's fault.

"Not...Chioma," he gasped, fighting to maintain consciousness. He couldn't let himself slip away, not yet—not until he had explained things.

"Stop, son. Enough. Save your strength. You can tell me later. It doesn't matter. Right now you need to rest."

But it did matter. Andrew knew that more surely than he knew anything. It mattered that his father understood. It mattered that Chioma was protected and safe. He wasn't even sure why he felt that way, but he knew her well-being was paramount. So where was she? Had she gotten away? Where would she go? How would she take care of herself?

"I'm here, *baas*."

The voice seemed to come from miles away, drifting, soothing... How could it be? Chioma had run away. She couldn't be here. He had sent her away. It couldn't be her voice. Surely he was imagining it!

But he wasn't. Chioma was speaking to Andrew's father, begging to be allowed to talk to Andrew. His father was telling her to go away, to leave them alone and he would deal with her later.

"Chioma!" Andrew spoke as forcefully as he was able, and his father and Chioma stopped talking. He felt Chioma drop at his side and take his hand in hers.

"Andrew."

Her voice seemed to flow over him like warm honey, and he smiled. So much he wanted to say to her...

"Get away from him!" His father's voice now, ordering Chioma away.

Andrew gripped her hand more firmly. "Stay," he breathed.

"I ran like you said," she whispered, her lips near his ear now. "But I couldn't leave you. I couldn't!"

Andrew smiled. Though he knew Chioma had put herself in danger by coming back, his heart rejoiced that she was beside him at that moment.

I tell you the truth, whoever hears my word and believes him who sent me has eternal life and will not be condemned; he has crossed over from death to life.

The voice was back, speaking words that seemed to echo hope and love, even as he felt himself slipping further away from the world he knew.

"Father?"

"I am here, son," Mr. Vorster said, his voice coming from somewhere behind Chioma.

Then Andrew heard the answer he was waiting for. *Yes, son. I am your Father.*

Andrew's heart broke. Had God always been so close, just a heartbeat away? Why hadn't Andrew called out to Him before? Why had he waited until now?

"Forgive me," Andrew whispered.

It is finished, said the voice.

"Andrew?" Chioma was calling him, even as he felt himself leaving her, going home to his Father...

"Hold on, son!" His earthly father now, calling him back... but Andrew knew it was too late. He could never return.

But what about Chioma? He had to tell her, had to let her know where he was going, that he was going to be all right, that she, too, could come one day...

"Jesus."

He spoke the word with his final breath, as the everlasting arms gathered him into an eternal embrace.

❖❖❖

"Andrew?" Chioma's heart raced. Why wasn't he responding? She had felt his hand go limp, as if his life had left his body...

She dropped her head. She had seen it too many times before, and there was no mistaking it now. Andrew was dead — like her mother and father, like Masozi. Dead. And this time it was her fault.

She felt someone grabbing her from behind, pulling her up and shoving her away. It was Andrew's father, trying to get close to his son. But it would do him no good. Chioma knew far too well that once someone you loved was gone, there was no bringing him back, no hope of seeing him ever again. Anything you once shared was now over, a memory to torment you for as long as you remained on this earth.

Chioma had no idea how long she stood there, pain swirling around and through her, but soon she heard it — that haunting, keening wail that could come only from a woman whose loved one has died. Anana Vorster had joined her husband and was mourning her son. It was time for Chioma to leave.

Blinking her eyes to clear her vision, she saw that a small crowd of servants had joined her *baas* and his wife around Andrew's lifeless body, and while they had the luxury to stay and mourn, Chioma didn't. And so, while the others cried, she slipped away into the darkness. If she hurried, she could catch up with Mbhali and Mandisa before they got to Themba.

Steeling her heart, she took a deep breath and left Andrew to his white family — and to his white God, who had so obviously failed him.

The hair on the back of her neck raised up, as she stood exposed in the moonlight.

Chapter 7

FINDING HER FRIENDS HAD NOT BEEN NEARLY AS difficult as Chioma had anticipated. To be more specific, it was they who found her. In a completely uncharacteristic gesture, Mandisa had courageously stood up to Mbhali and insisted they move slowly, even stopping occasionally to allow Chioma time to catch up. Though Mbhali had protested, she had grudgingly conceded, with the condition that if Chioma hadn't joined them within the hour, they would leave her behind and hurry on as quickly as possible.

The hour was nearly past when Chioma stumbled into a clearing and heard her name whispered from a stand of thorn trees to her right. The hair on the back of her neck raised up, as she stood exposed in the moonlight and told herself it had to be Mandisa or Mbhali who called to her.

Tense and motionless, she waited, until at last her friends crept into sight. Exhaling and allowing herself to relax, she fell gratefully into Mandisa's arms, wanting nothing more than to sob out her story on the girl's shoulder but knowing there was no time for such an act. Besides, she didn't dare express her sorrow over the death of a white man in Mbhali's hearing. Chioma would have to hold her grief inside. But she was experienced at such emotional restraint and would will herself to be so yet again.

"Where have you been?" Mandisa asked, her voice scarcely above a whisper, as she pushed back and held Chioma at arm's length so she could gaze into her face. "I was worried about you."

The moonlight illuminated enough of Mandisa's concerned expression that Chioma knew her own showed as well, so she doubled her efforts to hide her pain.

"I stopped to be sure the...white killers drove away in the direction of their home and not after us," she offered, hoping her friends would leave it at that. She wasn't sure how strong she could be if they began inquiring about Andrew's fate.

"Killers?" Mbhali stood beside Mandisa now, peering into Chioma's face. "Killers of Masozi...or the young *baas*?"

Chioma felt her jaw muscles clench, and she swallowed the burning lump in her throat before answering, doing her best to keep her voice strong and steady. "Both," she admitted, being careful not to utter Andrew's name. "The young *baas* is also dead."

Mandisa gasped, letting go of Chioma's arms and throwing her hands over her own mouth as if to stifle a scream, even as Mbhali raised her perfectly arched eyebrows questioningly.

"So," Mbhali said, "the white devil who attempted to beguile you is dead." She held Chioma's gaze for a moment, then turned and spat on the ground. "One less of them to worry about. It's not a loss worth mentioning." She shot her eyes to Mandisa and then back to Chioma. "It's even more important now that we find Themba—and that we do it quickly."

Without another word, Mbhali turned and strode purposefully in the direction where she and Mandisa had been hiding in the trees. At the edge of the clearing, she stopped, looked back, and frowned at Chioma and Mandisa, who still stood in the middle of the clearing, unresponsive and unmoving.

"Well? What are you waiting for?" Mbhali demanded. "Are you two coming with me, or must I leave you here and go find my cousin alone?"

Chioma blinked, pulling herself back from the tidal wave of emotion that called to her, demanding recognition. Instead, she set her eyes on Mbhali and determined to push on. After all, what choice did she have? And if she chose to follow after Mbhali, she knew Mandisa would do the same. Staying behind was not an option.

She took a step, determined not to let her mind drift backward. Mandisa quickly fell in behind her, establishing what would soon become their unspoken order of travel, with Mbhali always out in front by several strides. Chioma could only hope the determined leader of their trio knew where she was going.

❖❖❖

The moonlight was gone, and the faint rays of a rising sun would soon brighten the edges of the horizon. Chioma was sure she couldn't take another step, and she wondered how long Mbhali would continue her resolute march. Mandisa was already whimpering from exhaustion, and Chioma knew the girl who plodded faithfully behind her couldn't continue much longer. The way had already been long and hard, and more than once they had come across multiple lines of barbed-wire fence, necessitating added steps on their journey as they searched for open gates. But not even barbed wire or the unspoken prohibition of trespassing on private property, or the distinct possibility of running into one of many deadly night snakes had deterred Mbhali, as she pressed forward at a pace that left her companions nearly breathless. At last, as if she had read Chioma's thoughts, Mbhali stopped so suddenly that Chioma and Mandisa nearly piled into her.

"It's getting light," Mbhali observed, gazing off into the distance. "The jackals and owls will be silent soon, and even the frogs will stop their singing. We, too, must stop and get some rest before going any farther."

As they gathered around the base of an acacia tree, well hidden in the midst of a thick stand and shaded from the rising sun, Chioma sighed with relief as she sank down to the ground and pulled her knees up to her chin. She hoped she was tired enough to block out the painful memories that tormented her and fall asleep quickly, as she doubted Mbhali would wait long before ordering them back on their way.

She had scarcely closed her eyes when she felt Mandisa take her hand. Turning her head slightly toward her younger companion, Chioma came dangerously close to giving free rein to her emotions when she saw the compassion mirrored in Mandisa's eyes. Instead, she squeezed the girl's hand and then turned away, determined to maintain control.

With her eyes closed once again and her head leaning back against the tree trunk, Chioma counted slowly, forcing herself to breathe evenly and deeply, willing away the images that danced through her mind, stabbing her with fresh, searing pain and deep regret. If only she hadn't gone to the creek! If only she had run away when Andrew first approached. If only...

If only she had not convinced Masozi to stop beneath that other tree those few weeks ago—weeks that seemed like years. If only the truck hadn't stopped. If only her father and mother hadn't been killed, leaving her and Masozi to fend for themselves. If only she had been born with a different color skin...or somewhere other than South Africa...or Mandela hadn't been put into prison...or apartheid had never become a reality...

As the if-onlys finally drifted into the recesses of her mind, Chioma slept fitfully for what couldn't have been more than a couple of hours before she heard Mbhali calling to her.

"Wake up," she ordered, shaking Chioma's arm. "Both of you, get up! We must get moving before those white devils decide to come looking for us. We won't be safe until we find Themba. Come."

Chioma and Mandisa rose slowly, rubbing the sleep from their eyes even as Chioma wondered at the eerie sensation that surrounded them. And then she realized it was the absence of the *sonbesies* that made the daylight seem so foreign to her. For weeks now the armies of little beetles had filled the air from sunup to sundown with their monotonous buzzing, but this morning it was obvious that the time of the *sonbesies* had passed. Another cycle of the moon had come and gone, and it was time, as Mbhali had said, to move on with their lives and to find Themba.

But would finding him truly provide them with safety, Chioma wondered. Indeed, could anything or anyone provide them with safety in this life? Hadn't Andrew tried to protect both Masozi and then Chioma herself? And look how that had turned out!

Falling into place as the middle link of their little human chain, Chioma reminded herself to conserve her energy, even as the blazing sun, which would soon be directly overhead, sapped it with every step she took. Her lips and throat were dry and her tongue was beginning to feel thick, as she struggled to push on, knowing Mandisa and Mbhali felt the same and wondering how Mbhali managed to maintain her brisk pace without lagging or complaint.

Just when Chioma thought she could not possibly go on for another moment, she detected the sound of a running brook. Her companions quite obviously heard it, too, as they veered to the right in unison, picking up their pace as they neared the welcome respite. Before Chioma and Mandisa could break into a run, however, Mbhali held them back with an outstretched arm, as she checked the surrounding area with wary eyes and open ears. At last satisfied there was no immediate danger, she led them forward.

As the three girls dropped to their stomachs and plunged their cupped hands into the water, eagerly lifting the welcome liquid to their lips, Chioma wondered how much longer it would be before they located Themba—or if, indeed, they would find him at all. If they didn't, what would they do then?

The crack of a rifle so close behind them froze her in place, stopping even her heart, as her hand halted midway between the softly rippling creek and her open mouth. Chioma felt her eyes widen, and for a split second she questioned how many years they would spend in jail—or just how long and how severely they would suffer before they died.

❖❖❖

And then the strong, rough hands were around her waist, yanking her to her feet. The smell of sweat and earth was strong in her nostrils, as she heard Mandisa cry out. All three of them had been grabbed from behind and pulled up from the ground, and now stood face-to-face with their captors. With only a very brief sense of relief that the armed group of half a dozen men standing before them were black, Chioma also noticed that none of them looked at all friendly or welcoming. But at least they didn't appear to be Zulus, sworn enemies of all ANC followers, so there was yet a ray of hope that the three young women might survive this encounter.

She swallowed. Should she speak, ask questions, try to defend herself in some way? As outnumbered as they were, there seemed no point. Escape was out of the question, so she waited, silently, her heart having restarted and now pounding a rapid tattoo against her rib cage. No sound came from either Mbhali or Mandisa, so Chioma assumed they, too, had wisely opted for silence.

The deep-throated laugh that broke that silence startled Chioma more than anything that had happened in the last minute or so since she had gratefully lapped the cool water. She turned her attention to the tall, muscular man from whom the ongoing laughter emanated, and her breath caught in her throat. It had been months since she had seen him, but she would recognize him anywhere—Themba, Mbhali's fiercely handsome, almost terrifyingly strong warrior-cousin, with his battle scar descending down and across his chest like a military ribbon.

Chioma exhaled, a sense of relief washing over her as Mbhali's laughter joined Themba's, and she rushed to him and fell into his arms. Chioma took Mandisa's hand as they watched the joyful reunion.

"You came!" Themba's pleased exclamation rang out again and again, as he twirled Mbhali around several times before setting her down in front of him. "You finally came to join us!"

Mbhali nodded, her joy evident as her ear-to-ear grin reflected in her dancing eyes. "Yes! Yes, I have come, and I brought Chioma and Mandisa with me. We want to join you, cousin—all of us—to fight for the cause, for our people!"

Themba laughed again. "Is that so?" His almost almond-shaped eyes slid to Chioma and Mandisa, examining them as if they were slabs of meat—naked, helpless slabs of meat, Chioma thought—hanging on display in a window somewhere. She shuddered, at once terrified, repulsed, and yet strangely captivated, even as she fought to ignore her conflicting feelings and to avoid direct eye contact with this fearsome warrior. She couldn't even imagine what poor Mandisa must be thinking, her eyes downcast as the towering man studied them both with unabashed curiosity.

When Chioma realized Themba was no longer laughing, the butterflies already flitting around in her stomach began dancing in overtime. Why did Themba now appear so serious? What did that mean? What was going through his mind as he continued to assess the "baggage" his cousin had brought along with her? What would happen to them if he decided there was no room for baggage in the life of his rebel band? Equally disconcerting was the question of what would happen to them if he decided to let them stay.

She shook her head and opted to stand her ground. She had never gotten anywhere before by letting her fear show. Lifting her chin, she forced herself to return Themba's gaze until the light rekindled in his eyes and he once again showed signs of breaking into a smile.

"So," he said, nodding and speaking to Mbhali but still eyeing Chioma, "what do you and your companions have to offer us? You are my cousin—my family, my blood. But what of them? Why should I let them stay? Why, for that matter, should I even let them live?"

Chioma sensed Mandisa stiffen beside her, and they tightened their grip on one another, as they awaited Mbhali's answer. What could she say to convince Themba to spare their lives and possibly even allow them to live among them? As he had said, why should he? What could they possibly do for him and his valiant freedom fighters?

Chioma suppressed another shudder, refusing to allow her mind to wander in the direction of a likely answer to that question. Perhaps a quick death might be preferable to living with these wild, bloodthirsty fugitives, however righteous the cause they represented.

And then Mbhali spoke, and Chioma felt her heart beating in her throat as she listened, knowing her fate and Mandisa's hung in the balance of Themba's reaction to his cousin's words.

"Because they have nothing left," Mbhali said, her voice matter-of-fact. "I have you. They have nothing—or no one. All are dead. They have nothing left to lose."

Themba's eyes moved away from Chioma and Mandisa and rested on Mbhali, as if considering her logic. As the three young women waited, the fate of at least two of them about to be decided by the leader of this fearsome group, Chioma realized how strong a leader Themba must be. For it was not just she and her two companions who hung on his every word, but the men who followed him as well. From the moment the girls had been captured as they lay beside the water, the other men had looked to Themba for direction, following his lead in everything, speaking and acting only at his command. Though still fearful of this intimidating cousin of Mbhali's, Chioma could not quell the rising respect she felt for him in her heart.

At last Themba nodded. "That's good," he said, glancing again at Mandisa and Chioma before returning his gaze to his cousin. "If they have nothing to lose, then they won't expect anything in return." He grunted and slung his battered assault rifle over his shoulder. "I grant them their lives, and my protection so long as they are with us and cause no trouble. But they must earn their keep and work for the cause. I tolerate no laziness. Is that clear?" Before any of them could answer, he added, "And if anyone betrays us or the cause, they will be dead before they take another breath." Then he turned back to Chioma and Mandisa, his eyes narrowing and his veins popping out on his neck as he demanded, "Is that clear?"

Chioma's determination not to show fear forgotten, she nodded quickly, not trusting herself to speak. Mandisa whimpered but said nothing as she, too, nodded. The deal had been made. They were under Themba's protection—and at his mercy.

Then, as quickly as they had seemingly come from nowhere, Themba and his men began to move away from the women at a rapid pace. Just before they were out of sight, Mbhali grabbed Chioma's arm.

"Come," she ordered. "Both of you. We must follow them. Hurry!"

And once again, in their previously ordered human chain of Mbhali in the front and Mandisa in the rear, Chioma plowed ahead between the two, their pace increased dramatically from what it had been before meeting up with the men.

Where was this seemingly violent band taking them? What would they expect from them in return for their protection and as a result of their silent pledge to unquestioning loyalty?

And yet, in the midst of the many questions and uncertainties that danced through Chioma's mind, she couldn't help but remember Themba's admonition that they must "work for the cause." Isn't that what she had always wanted, what she had dreamed of since she was a little girl, sitting beside the fire and listening to her father's many stories?

Her father's stories! Nearly stumbling at the thought, Chioma reached into her apron pocket, anxious to feel the worn cover of the journal that had been her one remnant from her past life . . . but it wasn't there. Her pocket was empty, and she knew with certainty that the journal had dropped out during the scuffle that eventually took Andrew's life.

Suddenly the emotions she had held in check throughout the long hours of the night surfaced with a power she hadn't known possible. Unable to restrain them any longer, she allowed the tears to flow freely as she walked, silently grieving the loss of the beloved words, the scratchy scrawl, the familiar penmanship that had been her father's written history of the South Africa he loved, and eventually died trying to change. Of all Chioma had lost, the journal seemed the most painful— and final. It was at that moment that she knew it no longer mattered what the future held or what was required of her to survive it. She would do whatever was necessary, so long as it included revenge against those who had used their power to take everything from her, and from her people.

All that was left now was the cause, and through her tears she vowed to give herself to it without reservation.

She caught her breath, the impact of
the repeated words nearly knocking her
from her chair.

Chapter 8

ANANA VORSTER SAT SILENT AND STILL IN THE wicker chair on the wide, open veranda in front of her home, outside alone where Pieter had told her never to go in the middle of the night. But she didn't care. Why should she? She had buried the second of her two children, as well as what was left of her heart. What purpose was there to continue living? What did she have left? She almost wished she could give in to the need for revenge, to pursue her son's killers and make sure they paid, though she knew there was little chance of that happening under the circumstances. Andrew was not there to defend himself, and Chioma had disappeared into the night and wouldn't be considered a reliable witness anyway. From the look of things, the three troublemakers would go unpunished yet again, despite Pieter Vorster's vow to make sure that didn't happen.

Guilt sliced her conscience as she thought of her dear husband, sleeping now though unaware he did so alone. He, too, was grieving, and Anana knew that even if justice wasn't served in Andrew's death, she had to live for Pieter, to help him through from one day to the next...but for what? To oversee the running of the farm? To be sure the crops were tended and the cows milked? Was there nothing else, nothing of lasting value or limitless worth, nothing that truly mattered?

I am.

The eternal whisper came from somewhere within her, and yet from outside her as well. She knew the Source, and she didn't doubt the Truth of what she heard. And yet...she felt so disconnected, so unrelated, though she was well aware the words had come from her Father.

"Why can't I feel You?" she whispered. "Why do You seem so far away?"

I am always with you, daughter. I never leave you. The words were like wind, soft and gentle, fading even as they lingered in her heart.

Anana felt the tears rising up from the seemingly endless cistern within her, as they had day and night since Andrew left them. Would the pain of missing him ever end? A picture of Gertie flashed through her mind, and she had her answer.

"How will I bear it, Lord?" she cried. "How will I go on? And why should I?"

I am.

She caught her breath, the impact of the repeated words nearly knocking her from her chair. *The promises within those words should be enough for me. And ultimately they will be. But right now...*

Reaching into her pocket for a handkerchief, Anana touched the rough binding of the journal she had carried with her since Andrew's death. She drew it out and held it gently in her hands, gazing down at it though it was too dark to read the words that had become so familiar to her since she found the worn book beside her son's broken body that fateful night.

"You meant for me to find this, didn't You, Lord?" She was whispering again. "It was no accident that Chioma left it behind. There are things in here I need to understand. But I...I confess I don't truly understand them, Father. Not really, not completely...though I'm willing."

She dabbed at her eyes with her handkerchief, as the book lay unopened in her lap. "What do You want me to learn from it, Lord? Show me, Father. Teach me. Help me to understand..."

The light from inside the house blinked on even as she heard Pieter's voice.

"Anana? Are you out here?"

"Coming, Pieter," she called, jumping up from her seat, which now sat exposed in the stream of light emanating from the screen door.

The door squeaked open and Pieter peeked out. "Anana? What are you doing out here? I've told you, you shouldn't be out here alone, not at night."

"I know, Pieter," she said, quickly tucking the journal back into her pocket before going inside to join her husband. "And I'm sorry if I worried you, my dear. But I'm fine. Truly I am."

❖❖❖

The compound was more dirt than anything else, but it served as a gathering place and was easily evacuated if necessary. In the three days Chioma and her companions had been there, they had learned little except that temporary was a way of life, and nothing was permanent or certain. That the group had occupied this particular compound for nearly a month was a record.

"We stay ready to move at a moment's notice," Themba had informed them. "There is a bounty on our heads, and if we're caught, there will be no trial."

Chioma knew that included her, simply because she was there. It wouldn't matter that she hadn't participated in any of the crimes or terrorism for which the group was wanted. She was coloured, and she was guilty by association. She had therefore decided she would become guilty by commission when necessary, which she imagined wouldn't be long. To be truthful, a part of her looked forward to that moment with longing, for with every drop of blood that had been spilled of someone close to her, Chioma's need for revenge had grown.

Still, she knew she could not push. Mbhali had been more readily accepted into the group because of her blood relationship to Themba. Chioma and Mandisa, however, would have to prove themselves before they would be viewed with anything but wary tolerance.

Of course, they were not the only women in the compound, though they did appear to be the youngest. Of the handful of women who lived with the group, all appeared to be in their mid- to late twenties or early thirties. One of the youngest, Ebele, was pregnant and looked to be near her delivery date. When Chioma inquired as to the whereabouts of the baby's father, she was met with knowing smiles or vague responses, which served only to confirm her existing concerns that she and Mandisa might be expected to contribute to the group in ways she didn't even want to consider.

Chioma watched Ebele as the days progressed, marveling at the young woman's ability to maintain her share of work. Apparently Themba's admonition that everyone do their part extended even to those about to give birth.

As Chioma tended the small fire one morning, making coffee and warming the hard bread that served as their first meal of the day, her mind drifted to the many times she had cooked at the Vorster farm. They, too, had coffee in the morning, called *boerekoffie*, though it was mostly made of hot milk, in which they would dip their rusks, the hard bread that was a staple for many in South Africa. But some white farmers also indulged in occasional delicacies that few blacks or coloureds had ever tasted.

As Chioma's thoughts began to settle on her memories of Andrew, she was interrupted by Mandisa's soft voice. Startled, she turned to her friend, who stood beside her, sleepy-eyed.

"Sure could use some of that coffee," she mumbled.

Chioma smiled. Mandisa had always had a hard time waking up, and for the first hour or so after she got out of bed, she reminded Chioma of a little girl, in need of a mother's lap. *But then, aren't we all?* she wondered.

"Just about ready," she assured her friend.

Ebele joined them then, her stomach seeming to show up quite a bit ahead of the rest of her. Chioma marveled at the tautness of the young woman's skin, stretched beyond reasonable limits over a baby that rolled and kicked and elbowed its mother unmercifully. From the first time Chioma laid eyes on Ebele's bare stomach—which she refused to cover, saying the baby needed air—Chioma was stunned that the woman could even walk, let alone do anything else. Chioma wished the pregnant woman would wear something to cover the constant reminder of her condition, as the very sight made Chioma uneasy. Perhaps it was the thought of bringing yet another life into a world that would be less than kind to it. Whatever the reason, it was enough to make Chioma swear off of ever having children.

"How are you this morning, Ebele?" Mandisa asked, her eyes soft as they always were when she gazed at the pregnant woman's protruding belly. Chioma shook her head. How could Mandisa be so captivated by a sight that repulsed Chioma? For a brief moment she allowed herself to think of Masozi and wonder how things might have been had he lived long enough to become a man and take Mandisa for his bride. Would she have walked around with equal pride and excitement over a pending new life, created by the love she shared with her husband? When that thought led Chioma to a glimpse of Andrew's eyes, looking down at her in the moonlight that last night at the farm, she quickly shook it off.

The coffee was ready and the bread warm, but before Chioma could fill their cups, Themba strode up to them, followed by two companions, whom Chioma assumed were his bodyguards. The men were ready to eat; the rest of them would have to wait.

She quickly filled three cups and handed them to the men, who seemed not to notice her except to thanklessly accept her offering. But as his companions grabbed chunks of bread and walked away, Themba remained for a moment, his eyes fixed on Chioma, causing her to drop her gaze in embarrassment.

"You are well?" he asked.

Chioma swallowed. It was the first time he had spoken to her in a personal way since their arrival at the camp, and his seeming concern confused her. What did it mean? Why would he ask her and not the others? She sneaked a glance at his eyes in an attempt to read his thoughts, but the two dark orbs were as impenetrable as flints, unblinking and focused. Why did Chioma feel naked when the man looked at her? Surely he wasn't interested in her as a woman, and she certainly wasn't interested in him—or any other man, for that matter, she reminded herself quickly. Still, it would be easier if he weren't constantly walking around without a shirt, wearing his scar with obvious pride and allowing his muscles to ripple with his every move.

Settling her gaze above his scarred chest but below his eyes, while blocking out the image of Andrew that always danced at the edges of her memory, she forced herself to speak. "I'm...well. Thank you."

Unmoving for several heartbeats, Themba finally nodded and turned away, leaving Chioma weakened. From fear? She wasn't sure. What else could it be?

When the men were out of earshot, Ebele whispered, "Our leader has eyes for you. Interesting. I haven't seen that from him before—at least not to such an extent." Chioma noticed a flash of something—pain, confusion, anger—in Ebele's eyes before the girl continued. "He takes what he wants, yes, but never does he show that level of interest. You must have made quite an impression for him to want you so."

Chioma inhaled sharply, ready to counter the woman's words, but Ebele shook her head. "Don't deny it," she cautioned. "Themba is a brave warrior. He takes care of us, and he fights valiantly for the cause and for our people. But when he says he's in charge, he means it. If Themba wants you, he'll have you. It's simply the way of things out here—the only way any of us can survive."

Out here. What was that supposed to mean? In her heart she knew, and Chioma swallowed again, her hands going damp at the implications of Ebele's declaration. *If he wants me, he'll have me. What if I don't want him? What if I want to be left alone?*

Her eyes darted then to Ebele's stomach, and she suppressed a gasp. Had the pregnant woman been trying to tell her something? Is that what had happened to her? Is that why she seemed to have no husband, no man to care for her or the child she was about to bring into the world? Was it possible Themba was the baby's father?

Ebele's stomach rolled then, from one side to the other, and Chioma recoiled, even as Mandisa squealed with delight and placed her hand on the undulating belly. It was obvious the three young women were not cut from the same cloth, and Chioma knew she was the mismatch in the group. It was little comfort when she thought of Themba's dark eyes holding hers like magnets, and the words of Ebele: "If Themba wants you, he'll have you."

She realized then that as badly as she wanted to fight for the cause, she would also leave this place if she just had somewhere else to go. But she didn't, and so she would stay. But she would do so with a wary eye, even when she slept.

❖❖❖

Emma Rhoades parked her five-year-old Ford LTD station wagon in the garage and made her way to the door that led inside to the kitchen. It had been a long day, but an exciting one. The arrangements were made, and soon she would be on a plane headed for Johannesburg and her beloved South Africa. Though she hadn't lived there in nearly twenty-five years, since meeting and marrying John, an American businessman, and relocating to the United States, a large part of her heart had never left her homeland. Now that she was a new widow and the insurance claim would be settled soon, there was no reason she shouldn't fly home for a visit.

Home. The word brought tears to her blue eyes, eyes that John had repeatedly told her were so like her younger sister's. Poor, dear Anana! It was tragic enough to lose one child, but to lose them both, first a daughter and then a son, was beyond imagining. Though John's passing had left a sizeable hole in Emma's heart, she still had her daughter and son-in-law, as well as a soon-to-be-born grandchild, to comfort her. Anana and Pieter would never know the joy of holding a grandchild on their lap or watching them grow, and instead would bear the pain of missing their only children until they joined them in heaven.

Emma sighed as she pulled some nondescript leftovers from the refrigerator and dumped them into a pan. Adjusting the flame under the pot, she dropped the lid in place and then put some water on to boil for tea. She wished her reason for going on this trip was a bit more positive. She hadn't spent much time with her only nephew over the years, or any of her sister's family for that matter, simply because they were separated by so many miles. But she smiled as she remembered how Pieter and Anana had made that one trip to Southern California to visit Emma and her family, bringing along their two adorable children, Gertrude, named after Anana and Emma's mother, and Andrew, named after Pieter's father. Emma and John's daughter, Mariana, only a few months older than Andrew, had taken great delight in showing her cousins everything American—including Disneyland.

Emma closed her eyes, remembering the picture-perfect day they had all spent at the "happiest place on earth," and how the children had laughed and squealed with delight when they had their pictures taken with Mickey Mouse. Emma and Anana had stood hand in hand, watching their offspring at play and marveling at the overflowing joy and blessings in all of their lives.

Then Pieter and Anana had taken their children and flown back across the ocean to their faraway plot of land in South Africa, only to lose their precious daughter in a tragic accident just two months later. Though Anana had clung to her faith and persevered, Emma knew she had never again been as happy as she had been that day when they all stood in line, eating popcorn and waiting to swoop down the Matterhorn.

Emma lifted the lid and stirred her unappetizing meal, trying to blink away the stinging tears that seemed to have resurfaced since Andrew's death. She had wanted to go to her sister right away, but John was too sick, too near his own death. Now that he was gone...

A tear spilled over onto her cheek, and she swiped at it with her sleeve. No wonder she had done so much crying lately! Was there no end to the tragedies their family must endure? Both of her parents gone now, as well as her husband and her niece and nephew, not to mention Pieter's parents... Wasn't that enough?

"I'm sorry, God," she whispered. "I know it's not my place to question Your timing or Your ways. But I must admit, there are times I wonder..."

She shook her head, reminding herself that she wasn't going home to bring her sister more grief. Despite their many losses and the fact that they would undoubtedly shed some tears together, they could also enjoy their long-overdue visit. In addition, Emma was especially pleased that while she was there she would be able to include a visit to a young missionary couple, sponsored by Emma's church, and friends of Mariana. Emma would be delivering a much-needed box of Bibles and study materials to the couple, and she looked forward to that almost as much as to her time with Anana and Pieter.

Emma smiled, scooping her now hot food onto a plate. Yes, it would be a good visit, despite their personal losses and the turmoil in South Africa. What a blessing that God had provided everything she needed to make such a timely trip! Emma couldn't help but believe good things would come from it.

Anana had suffered so much loss in her forty-two years of life that it seemed a miracle she could smile at anything.

Chapter 9

E MMA IS COMING! OH, PIETER, MY SISTER IS COMING to visit!"

Pieter Vorster watched his wife nearly twirl around the sitting room in anticipation of once again seeing her only sibling. With thousands of miles of ocean separating them for nearly a quarter of a century now, it was not a visit they enjoyed often. Pieter and Anana and the children had flown to America to see Emma and her family only once, while Emma's little clan had managed to cross the waters to South Africa three times—in part, Pieter imagined, to quell Emma's ever-present longing for her beloved homeland.

Pieter smiled, hoping his sadness didn't show through. It seemed it had been so long since either he or Anana had smiled at anything, and if Emma's visit was what it took to coax Anana's mouth to curve upward again, then Pieter would also rejoice at the news, despite the underlying sorrows that might have precipitated the reunion.

"That is wonderful, my dear," Pieter said, his voice soft as he leaned to plant a kiss on his wife's cheek. The almost forgotten glow in her pale blue eyes made any effort on his part worthwhile. Anana had suffered so much loss in her forty-two years of life that it seemed a miracle she could smile at anything.

Of course, Pieter was no stranger to grief himself. In addition to sharing with Anana the death of their only children, he had also lost his parents in an automobile accident when he was scarcely out of his teens. Marrying Anana when he was twenty-three and she nineteen had been the point of rescue and hope he had so desperately needed to keep him believing in life. Never had he dreamed on their glorious wedding day that he would have to witness his gentle bride endure such harsh realities.

"She'll be here in a couple of weeks," Anana announced as if for the first time, though she had already informed him of this fact several times. "I must get the guest room ready. She's allergic to feathers, you know, so the feather bed must be replaced with blankets, and the pillows with foam."

Pieter's heart warmed to hear his wife's familiar chatter, something their home had sadly lacked since Andrew's death. *Death. Why can't I call it what it really was? It was murder, plain and simple. Had it been a black or coloured who struck the fatal blow, rather than one of those spoiled whites who called himself Andrew's friend, it would have been murder for sure. Or if Andrew had been defending the honor of a white woman...* Instead, it appeared those three hooligans would get off with a slap on the wrist. Where was the justice in that?

He shut down his thoughts. Nothing constructive could come of allowing them to drift in such an impossible direction. The situation was what it was, and the legal system—including apartheid—was not going to change because the Vorsters' personal circumstances were adversely affected by it. Still, Pieter had always rationalized and even justified the special treatment inherent in apartheid—before. Now that this special treatment had reared its head in his own home, nothing seemed as certain as it once had.

"Pieter? Are you listening?"

He pulled himself back to the present, forcing a smile as he realized Anana was speaking to him. "I'm sorry, my dear. I was daydreaming. What were you saying?"

The hint of understanding that invaded her eyes threatened to extinguish the light that still flickered there, but before it could, Pieter took her in his arms and pulled her to himself. "I love you," he whispered. "Don't let me—or anything—interfere with your joy at seeing your sister again." He kissed the top of her head, marveling at the sweet, clean smell of her blond hair, neatly clasped at the back of her neck. "It will be a wonderful visit, and I'll help you prepare for it any way I can."

Anana's arms tightened around his waist as she pressed against him. Regardless of all else that came into their lives, he was thankful beyond words for the strength he drew from the woman God had given him to be his partner. Though her presence didn't take away the pain of losing their children, her sharing of that loss made it bearable. He only hoped the anticipated visit with Emma would prove to be the positive experience Anana so obviously needed.

❖❖❖

The airport was crowded, and Emma was grateful that Mariana had been able to accompany her into the city to see her off. Even after more than twenty years of living in the ever-expanding Los Angeles area, Emma wasn't comfortable driving beyond the beach town of Santa Monica, and especially now that John was no longer there to chauffeur her around. Though the residents of Santa Monica and other small Southern California towns had seen their share of growth in the past few decades, the streets were still relatively quiet and crime-free. The stop-and-go traffic she and Mariana had run into on their way to LAX that morning had only reinforced Emma's appreciation for her own family-oriented neighborhood, as well as the Vorster farm that represented all she held dear about her native land.

Sunny South Africa, my beloved homeland! At last I will see you again—walk upon your earth, smell the flowers and the foods that are so unique to our people, and yes, even hear the cries of conflict that are also such a part of who we are.

She sighed, wishing Mariana weren't so far along in her pregnancy and could accompany her on this month-long trek, but Emma understood why her son-in-law, Eric, wouldn't want his wife taking such a chance, particularly in a country going through so much upheaval. Both Eric and Mariana had tried to dissuade Emma from making the trip herself, without her husband at her side, warning that danger was a very real concern. But Emma knew they felt as they did because they had never lived in South Africa and therefore had no passion for the country. Their loyalty was with America, as well it should be. She, too, was an American citizen now, and yet...

A smile played on her lips, as she closed her eyes and remembered the years when she and Anana had grown up on their Afrikaner parents' farm, blissfully unaware that across the land trouble brewed and tempers flared. The way of life the young girls knew was peaceful and happy because their mother and father made it so; there was no room for alarm or concern for their two daughters. Emma had enjoyed free run of the farm, with her four-years-younger sister, Anana, tagging along behind. The farm's many servants doted on the two towheaded charmers, and often covered for them when they got into something they shouldn't. Never had either of the girls experienced a fearful or negative event due to their Afrikaner beliefs or their carefully maintained but separate coexistence with those who didn't share those beliefs—or their skin color. It had been as close to idyllic as any life could be, and though Emma knew she could never recapture those carefree days, she did look forward to reminiscing about them with Anana.

"Mom?"

Emma started. She hadn't realized how far away she had drifted until Mariana interrupted her daydreaming. Emma opened her eyes and turned to her daughter, who sat beside her in the waiting area, her rounded stomach nearly bursting at the seams of her cotton smock. Nearly all the seats in front of the gate were filled. Soon they would begin boarding, and Emma would be alone among strangers.

"Forgive me," Emma said. "My mind was wandering."

Mariana smiled, and Emma's heart constricted as she once again saw her husband's kindness and warmth reflected in their daughter's brown eyes. Though Mariana had inherited the blonde hair of their Dutch ancestry, she had the doe-like brown eyes of her fun-loving, Italian father. *John, how I miss you! This is the first time I've ever flown anywhere without you beside me!*

Mariana patted her mother's hand. "Nothing wrong with that, Mom." Her smile faded then, and her eyes took on the serious look that had also been such a part of John's personality. "I know you miss Daddy." Her voice cracked. "So do I. But you're going to have a good time visiting Auntie Anana and Uncle Pieter. It will be good for you, though I hate to think of you going alone. If things were different with me, I—"

Emma raised her hand and shook her head. "Don't be silly, sweetheart. You're expecting a baby! I certainly don't expect you to leave your husband behind and fly halfway around the world with me—though I'll admit, I'd certainly love it if you could." She smiled. "But don't worry. I'll be back before that little one makes an appearance. And maybe next time I go, you and Eric can both come, and bring your baby for your auntie and uncle to see."

Mariana returned her smile and nodded. "Yes. Next time, Mom." The concerned look returned, as she added, "But, please, be careful. You know how much turmoil is going on in South Africa right now. We read of kidnappings and murders all the time, and—"

This time Emma interrupted her daughter by placing a finger against her lips. "Don't worry about me. We've prayed, and we'll trust God to take care of me—of all of us. He'll bring me home safely to you, I promise."

With only a brief hesitation, Mariana nodded again. "Of course He will. And I'll pray for you every day while you're gone."

Emma smiled. "I know you will, my dear, as I will for you."

Mariana leaned across the plastic divider of their chairs and kissed Emma's cheek. "I'll miss you," she whispered.

Emma felt the all-too-familiar sting of tears against the back of her eyelids. "I know," she said, not trusting herself to say more but grateful that God had blessed her with such a loving and caring daughter. Of course He would bring her back safely, she reassured herself. Why on earth would He choose to do anything else?

❖❖❖

The moonlight was gentle as it spilled through the trees onto the small, secluded spot just outside the camp where Chioma sat, remembering the moonlight that had shone overhead just one thirty-day cycle earlier. The creek running over their feet, Andrew's eyes as he looked at her, his words as he spoke of his feelings for her...and then the terror—

She closed her eyes. No matter how hard she tried to block out the memories, it seemed they were always there, lurking just beneath the surface, waiting to pounce the moment she allowed herself even a brief respite from the exhausting routine that had become her life since joining the group. If she had thought she was busy when she lived and worked on the Vorster farm, it had been nothing compared to the pace she kept at the compound. Now, of course, she had a purpose. She was working for the cause, at last. Whether loading bullets or cooking meager rations over an open fire, there was no time for regret or recriminations during the day. But when the sun went down and everyone else curled up in a blanket to rejuvenate for the coming day, Chioma wandered away to a private place to think and clear her mind before trying to sleep.

In the beginning she thought the nonstop labor of the long days would enable her to sleep the moment she closed her eyes. Such was not the case. The loneliness and haunting memories had become her constant companions, and whether alone or sleeping side-by-side in a tiny lean-to with Mandisa and Mbhali, her pain was palpable. And so she chose to give vent to it as best she could, away from prying eyes and listening ears.

But even in the relative privacy of her little spot among the trees, she was careful not to allow herself to weep aloud. When tears seeped out of her eyes and drifted down her cheeks, she made no sounds that would alert others to her grief. If the gods truly existed and were listening, they knew, and that was enough.

She had been in the compound sufficient time now to recognize which sounds, muted or otherwise, were a normal part of the communal lifestyle or the surrounding wildlife, and which were warnings of possible danger. The snap of a twig to her left was too near to be someone walking in the camp, and she felt the hair rise on her arms and the back of her neck as she realized she was no longer alone.

Lifting her head toward the sound that had caught her attention, she felt her heart skip at the sight of the tall figure standing over her. His head was bent, looking down at her, and there was just enough moonlight to see that familiar look of hunger in his eyes. She recoiled, partially from fear of what lay behind that look, but also because she sensed yet again that inexplicable drawing toward him, that feeling of compulsion to go to him, regardless of the outcome.

She clenched her jaw and lifted her chin, determined not to show her feelings, yet sensing he already knew what they were. What was it about this man that she could find him both terrifying and attractive at the same time?

"You're quite a loner, I see," Themba announced, deftly lowering himself to a sitting position beside her. "I think maybe you need some company."

Chioma's heart raced, and she forced herself to breathe slowly and evenly as she turned her gaze from him to look straight ahead. "I may be a loner, but I'm not lonely, and I don't need or want company."

After a moment of stunned silence, Themba's familiar laugh erupted, brief and staccato-like, into the night sky, startling more than a few sleeping pigeons from a nearby tree. If anyone from the camp heard it, they undoubtedly recognized its source and ignored it.

In spite of herself, she turned back to look at him. He never ceased to amaze her, this man who struck terror into the hearts of nearly everyone who met him and yet seemed to have such a caring and even humorous side. Chioma couldn't help but wonder if he was unique in his dual personality, or if everyone had such a perplexing mix of personality traits buried deep within.

"So," he said, his smile still in place, "you're not in need of company." He paused, watching her as she tried not to squirm under his gaze. "But perhaps I am. Perhaps I desire your company this fine evening. What would you say to that?"

Chioma swallowed, wondering if she might faint from fear, certain she would if he made even one move toward her. What was he trying to say? Surely he didn't mean . . .

She tried to suppress a shudder, but she was certain he had seen it. No matter. Though she had been telling herself ever since arriving in the compound that she would pay any price to be accepted into the group and allowed to participate in whatever possible acts of revenge against their common enemies, she knew in her heart this was one thing she couldn't do—not willingly, at least. If he decided to force himself, he might win, but he wouldn't do so unscathed.

"I'd say you'd better find your company somewhere else," she said, her voice no longer calm or steady, but at least the words were clear and understandable. She squared her shoulders, realizing the effect was greatly diminished by the fact that she was now trembling uncontrollably. "I'm sure there are many women who'd find spending time with you . . . attractive. I'm not one of them."

There. She had said it. If she must die, here at the hands of Mbhali's rebel cousin, so be it. But she would die with dignity, as her father had done. She wouldn't grovel or beg, and she hoped she wouldn't cry.

The flash of anger in Themba's eyes was brief, but enough to send an arrow of terror through Chioma's heart. Then his eyes softened, and she saw his jaw twitch before he spoke. "You are a brave woman, Chioma—brave and beautiful. I've decided to let you live, though you defy me as no one has ever done before . . . and survived."

He reached out then, caressing her cheek with his large, rough hand and amazing her at the gentleness in his touch. Mesmerized, she waited, afraid to breathe. He had said he would let her live. What did that mean? What else might he do to her, even at the cost of sparing her life?

"Listen to my words, brave and beautiful woman," Themba crooned, sending a shiver up Chioma's spine. "I spare you for a reason. I have long wanted a wife to fight at my side and to one day bear my children, should we live that long. But never before have I found anyone worthy to take that place." He nodded, moving his hand to cup her chin and tilt her face to his. "Now I've found you, and though I'll be patient for a time, you'll soon become the wife I've searched for." His eyes narrowed and his grip on her chin tightened slightly. "I won't wait long. Do you understand me, Chioma?"

Before she realized what she was doing, Chioma found herself nodding in agreement. What was she thinking? Surely he understood she had acquiesced from fear, not from desire. Whatever the reason, he was now smiling, as his dark eyes danced with delight.

"Good," he said, releasing her chin. "Then it's settled. You'll be my wife—soon. Until then, you're under my personal protection. No one will bother you. They'll know you're my woman."

Chioma felt her eyes widen. His woman? His wife? How had it come to this? Just a month earlier she had sat next to Andrew, trying to resist the forbidden love of an Afrikaner farmer's son, and now she was pledged to marry a black rebel who struck terror into her heart—and for good reason. His reputation as a ruthless killer and a violent warrior was not unwarranted. How could she ever share her life—and her heart—with such a man, despite the seemingly tender side she had glimpsed in him? Was there no other choice for her, no hope of deliverance or escape?

The lingering smile on his lips as he rose to leave left little doubt that indeed there was none.

And where else was she to go? Her fate
was sealed, and she knew she couldn't prolong
the inevitable for long...

Chapter 10

SO, NOW WE ARE TRULY SISTERS."

Mbhali's matter-of-fact statement confirmed Chioma's suspicion that Themba had already announced the news of their "relationship," as Chioma's standing in the community had suddenly gained a higher level of respect. Those who used to eye her with suspicion now nodded in deference when she passed by. Mbhali, however, had been the first to verbalize it.

Chioma sighed. There was no sense denying what she couldn't avoid or change, but she wouldn't admit to anything that had yet to transpire. "If you mean because you and Themba are cousins, then you and I are related," Chioma said, "that's not the case—not yet anyway. I'm not his wife."

Mbhali raised her eyebrows. "But you will be. And you're already his woman. He said so, and that makes it so for all of us—including you."

Once again, as she had many times over the last few days, Chioma wondered at how her situation had changed so quickly.

Did she no longer have any say in her own future? She sighed again. Apparently not—at least not so long as she lived with this rebel band. And where else was she to go? Her fate was sealed, and she knew she couldn't prolong the inevitable for long—unless, of course, something happened to Themba before...

She shook her head. She mustn't think that way. It was far too dangerous. Better to accept what must be and make the best of it—even while hoping for some sort of miraculous reprieve or change of heart on Themba's behalf.

Lifting her head, she locked eyes with Mbhali. "What you say is true, though it's not by my choice."

Mbhali's dark eyes flashed, and she leaned toward her friend, grabbing her arm as she hissed, "Sometimes we don't get to choose how we live, Chioma—or with whom. So never speak those words again. Do you hear me?"

Chioma's arm hurt where Mbhali's nails dug into her flesh. Why was she being so dramatic? Of course Chioma knew about choices—or lack of them. If she had been able to make her own choices all along, she certainly wouldn't be living in a dirty compound while her loved ones lay dead and buried under the South African dirt.

Chioma shook her arm free. "I know that," she said, doing her best to sound confident. "But I thought I could speak my feelings to you, of all people. Who knows better how things are with me—with all our people? We do what we must to survive. I'm only too aware of that fact."

Mbhali's face remained close to Chioma as she warned, "Then keep your feelings to yourself. It's safer that way—for everyone concerned."

Chioma paused, wondering if she was reading too much into Mbhali's warning. At last she nodded in affirmation, and the subject was closed, at least for the time being. Chioma's heart, however, was anything but comforted, and the fear that had been gnawing at her gut continued to grow more pronounced.

❖❖❖

It had been a long flight, and Emma was exhausted, but the closer they got to their destination, the more energized she became.

Home. At last she would see her beautiful homeland once again! She had come to love America, but it would never take the place of the beloved country where she had grown up in a close-knit family and enjoyed a relatively carefree life. Though Anana had been four years younger than Emma, the two had been inseparable. When Emma met and fell in love with John, she had been faced with the most difficult decision of her entire life—let him fly to America without her, or leave her parents and little sister, as well as her home and everything familiar to her, behind. She had quite obviously chosen the latter, and she didn't regret it one bit, and yet . . .

Blinking back tears, Emma determined not to dwell on the negative; they had all experienced far too much of that already. There would be time for tears when she and Anana were alone. For now, she would think only of the joy of setting foot on South African soil, and of sharing precious days and weeks with her only sibling.

If only John could be here to share it with her, as he had been on her previous visits. And if only Andrew would be among Emma's welcoming clan when she stepped off the plane . . .

She shook her head, peering out the window into the early morning darkness, which was just beginning to be dispelled as they flew toward the sunlight. In a matter of only a few hours now, she would watch the achingly familiar outline of Johannesburg rise up to greet them, and her heart reached out in longing.

❖❖❖

Anna could scarcely contain her excitement, and it amazed her that she could once again experience such a positive emotion. It nearly immersed her in guilt to think she could rejoice over anything while still in the midst of grieving the loss of her only son. And yet she knew Andrew would want her to rejoice and to look forward to her visit with his Auntie Emma with great anticipation.

She needed this, she thought. They all did. The heavy pall that had settled over the Vorster home after Andrew's death had nearly suffocated the life out of Anana, and she had come close to giving up altogether. Then she had received the phone call. When she heard Emma's voice on the other end of the line, her heart had seemingly jumped into her throat. Receiving phone calls from halfway around the world was not an everyday occurrence, and they were never made frivolously. Emma's last call had been to inform them of John's death, made not long after Anana's call to Emma to convey their loss of Andrew. How thrilled Anana was when Emma delivered the good news that she was coming for a visit! It had been the lifeline Anana needed.

She and Pieter would leave for the airport soon. Anana made one more trip into the guest room, smoothing the soft blankets that had replaced the feather bed, and fluffing the foam pillows one last time. The scent of candles freshened the room, and Kagiso, one of the new servants they hired when Chioma and the others left, had dusted the dark mahogany furniture to a sparkling sheen. All was ready.

Anana took a deep breath and went to find Pieter. It was time to leave, and she didn't want to take any chances on being late.

❖❖❖

The midmorning sun was already beating down on Chioma's head, as she went about cleaning up the camp before beginning her bullet-loading and knife-sharpening duties. Her so-called betrothal to Themba had apparently not lessened her obligations to the group.

The buzz of an annoying fly was interrupted by the faint sound of a plane overhead, and Chioma stilled the sweep of her nearly threadbare broom long enough to gaze up into the azure sky. She had never been near enough to an airplane to know what one actually looked like close up, but she never ceased to marvel when one flew above her, never failed to wonder who the giant silver bird was carrying to or from her home in South Africa, or how many of the huge flying machines might even now be soaring through the sky. She never wondered about them long, however, as she knew she would never ride on one herself. Her destiny was here, in her homeland, to live and die for the cause.

At the thought, she shivered, even under the sun's warm rays, when her mind wandered, as it often did these days, to the handsome but terrifying leader of their group, Themba, to whom she was now pledged for life. *My fate is in his hands. If only I knew what that would bring...*

The plane was gone from sight now, and she turned back to her work, but before she could stir up another swirl of dust with her battered broom, Mbhali joined her. "Have you seen him?" she whispered, leaning close.

Chioma frowned. "Seen who? What are you talking about?"

Mbhali cut her eyes to the small cluster of men across the yard. "There. The new one, to the right."

Chioma followed her friend's gaze, her eyes landing on a broad-shouldered, bare-chested man with almost ebony skin and muscles that looked as if they could snap a man in two as easily as a twig.

"Who is he?" she asked. "I haven't seen him before."

"That's because he just arrived," Mbhali explained, keeping her voice low. "His name is Abrafo—'troublemaker' or 'executioner.' From what I hear, both names are appropriate. His own band of followers was killed in a raid last week. Somehow he managed to escape, and now he's come to join us."

When she stopped speaking, Chioma turned her gaze from the newcomer to her friend, whose eyes had narrowed with intensity, though she continued to inspect the object of their conversation. "It doesn't bode well for us," Mbhali continued. "There's bad blood between Abrafo and Themba. Though they fight for the same cause, they've never been brothers. I don't like it. There's trouble in the wind."

Though this was the first Chioma had heard of any of it, she realized she didn't like it, either. She looked back in the direction of Abrafo just as he turned his head and caught her gazing at him. She felt her eyes widen as he fixed his stare on her, and a cold fear crept up her spine. The half smile he soon cast her way was more of a sneer, and the evil behind it was undeniable.

Quickly she looked away. "Why is he looking at me like that?" she whispered.

Mbhali hesitated before answering. "I don't know," she said at last, and in a rare occurrence, Chioma heard fear in her friend's voice. "But if it's what I think it is, it can only add to the trouble that already exists between him and my cousin."

Emma reached across the table and placed her hand on her sister's.

Chapter 11

THOUGH EACH VISIT BETWEEN ANANA AND HER sister had been memorable, none had been more needed than this one. Thank goodness the plane had arrived on time, and they were now home with their precious cargo.

Anana puttered around the kitchen, smiling at the memory of their reunion. Even Pieter had joined in the hugging and welcoming ritual, but then had fallen silent as he drove back to the farm, chauffeur-style and alone in the front seat, allowing the sisters to sit together in back and chatter the entire way. Anana resolved to make a point to thank her husband for his quiet thoughtfulness.

Now, with Emma settling into the guest room, Anana was determined to make *boerekoffie* the way her sister liked and complained she was never able to get in America. Anana wasn't about to trust Kagiso or any of the other servants to make this special Afrikaner coffee; it must be exactly as only Anana could make it.

Anana was also planning a special meal for Emma that evening, and though she wouldn't do the cooking herself, she would be careful to oversee every aspect of the preparation. She wanted this first day back in South Africa to be especially perfect for her sister.

Deep down Anana harbored the wish that Emma would move back to her homeland now that John was gone, but she also knew how unlikely that was, since Emma would never be willing to leave Mariana or her family behind in America. But how lovely it would be for Anana to have her only sibling nearby, where they could visit daily and share their everyday events—and their pain.

The reminder of Andrew's death, as well as John's, stabbed at Anana's heart, disturbing the unabashed joy she had felt since first laying eyes on her sister. Admittedly she had been shocked at the white hair that now highlighted Emma's temples, though the woman was still four years shy of fifty. And yet, Pieter's hair was already showing signs of gray, and he and Emma were the same age. Why should Anana be surprised that Emma would reflect those same changes?

Because I don't see her every day, Anana told herself. *With Pieter, it's such a gradual change that I don't notice; with Emma…*

She shook her head. Though Emma would always be her "big sister," it was difficult to accept that she was no longer the young and vibrant mentor who had held Anana's admiration for decades.

But then, I'm not so young and vibrant anymore, either. I might have thought I was, before Andrew died, but now I know better.

She sighed, measuring just the right amount of milk into the pot. *So many things I thought were true before Andrew died—*

Anana started at the sound of Emma's voice behind her, nearly dropping the pot of milk as she spun around to see her sister's surprised expression.

"Are you all right?" Emma asked. "I'm sorry if I startled you."

Anana smiled, her heart rate quickly returning to normal. "I'm fine," she assured her, turning back to place the pot on the stove before giving her attention to Emma. "I was just...daydreaming, I suppose." She smiled, hoping to reassure her sister.

Emma returned the smile, and the softness in her blue eyes, so much like Anana's, telegraphed her empathy. "I understand. My mind drifts more than ever these days...to happier times."

Anana nodded, wiping her hands on her apron as the two of them seated themselves around the small wooden table. "Happier times. It's difficult not to daydream when those happier times are all in the past."

Emma reached across the table and placed her hand on her sister's. "Don't allow yourself to think that way, dear one. It's true we've lost loved ones and our hearts are heavy, but it's not true that we can never be happy again. We must be willing to allow God to bring what He wills into our lives—including happiness."

Anana locked her eyes with Emma's, willing her big sister to convince her of the words she had spoken. She wanted to believe them—needed to if she was to find any meaning or purpose in getting out of bed each day. But did Emma truly believe them, or was she simply trying to cheer up her little sister, as she had done so many times over the years?

"I'd better check the milk," Anana said at last, pulling her hand away and rising from her chair. She was sure it wasn't ready, but she hadn't been able to wait any longer for an answer she wasn't sure she was ready to hear. If Emma, of all people, couldn't convince her there were better times ahead, what was the point of continuing on? Gertie was gone, and now Andrew. Once Emma returned to America, Anana's only reason for breathing would be to keep Pieter going. Though he came across as a bit of a gruff but strong farmer, Anana knew his heart was ragged with pain. Life had dealt them both some heavy blows, but at least they still had one another. *If anything ever happened to Pieter—*

She stopped before her thoughts could take her any further. Emma was here, recovering from the loss of her own dear husband, and it was time to experience the gift of companionship God had given them, even if only for a brief time. They would start by enjoying a perfect cup of *boerekoffie*.

❖❖❖

Pieter sat atop the bay mare that had been Andrew's mount for several years. Pieter had never particularly cared for the horse—or for any horse, which was a strange thing for a farmer. But riding the animal that had been so much a part of Andrew's life somehow helped Pieter stay connected to the son he so desperately missed.

As he slowly rode the fence line that Andrew had inspected from this same vantage point so many times, Pieter's heart pounded painfully with each clop of the mare's hooves. It was masochistic, he knew, but he just couldn't seem to break away from the animal that had carried the one who would always be so beloved to Pieter.

Father. Pieter would never forget that one of Andrew's last words was *father*. Looking back, he now suspected his son was speaking to God and not to him. He was glad Andrew's last thoughts on this earth were of his heavenly Father, whom he was about to meet face-to-face, but Pieter couldn't help but wish his son had spoken to him one more time before he breathed his last.

His heart squeezed with the agony of missing his boy, the young man in whom Pieter had placed all his hopes and dreams, the one who was to carry on the Vorster name and the Afrikaner ways. Why, he asked himself for what seemed the thousandth time, had Andrew chosen to get involved with that coloured girl? Why couldn't he have left her alone, and then he, not Pieter, would be riding the mare and checking the fence line, and his parents would not be suffering nearly unfathomable grief?

Pieter shook his head, determined to clear his mind of such macabre thoughts. He knew they did no good, accomplished nothing positive, but how was he to be free of them? How could he move past the pain and get on with his life—or help his dear Anana do the same?

Briefly he comforted himself with the thought that at least for now—for a few days and weeks—Anana would have Emma to help cheer her. Pieter knew it wasn't enough, but it was more than he could give her, and for that he was grateful.

❖❖❖

Mandisa had been watching Chioma, and she knew her friend was in trouble. It was obvious it was only a matter of time until her situation with Themba—and now Abrafo—came to a head. What would Chioma do? Themba was frightening, yes, but even in his otherwise boorish ways, he was a gentleman compared to Abrafo. And Mandisa couldn't help but believe that their fearless leader truly cared for Chioma.

Mandisa had watched the interloper's arrival, having been on sentry duty the day he showed up. Her skin had crawled as the newcomer stared her down, and she had been thankful for the other guard who had escorted the terrifying man to Themba. She had no desire to be alone with Abrafo and always kept as wide a space between them as possible.

Chioma was not so fortunate. Though Abrafo had quickly been set straight about the relationship between Themba and Chioma and therefore kept his distance when Themba was present, he still cast leering glances her way. And when Themba was gone, Abrafo made every effort to get close to her, though his unwelcome advances were always met by a fleeing Chioma before he got near enough to verbalize his interest.

Mandisa watched him carefully this day, wondering when he would make his move now that Themba had left the camp, announcing before he did that he wouldn't return for several hours. Mandisa had seen the look of alarm in Chioma's eyes when she heard Themba's words, and it was obvious Chioma was terrified of Abrafo.

True to expectations, Abrafo rose from the circle where he sat with his growing number of admirers, a handful of men Mandisa was sure Abrafo was trying to win over from Themba. Without hesitation, Abrafo went straight to the fire, where Chioma tended the large pot of *pap*, the daily staple that served as the late afternoon meal for everyone in the camp. Mandisa wished she had the courage to warn her friend or to at least go and stand beside her, but she felt frozen in place as she watched the scene play out.

Abrafo was only steps from the fire when Chioma lifted her head and spotted him, her eyes widening at the sight.

❖❖❖

From the moment Chioma sensed the approaching evil, she knew it was Abrafo. She had anticipated it from the moment she heard Themba's announcement of his departure. Chioma had considered running off into the trees to hide until Themba returned, but she knew she would pay a hefty price for abandoning her duties. Torn, she had stayed beside the fire, reassuring herself that even Abrafo wouldn't try anything under the watchful eyes of those remaining in the compound.

But now he stood just inches from her, his rock-hard chest rising and falling as he glared down at her, his dark eyes firing darts of contempt in her direction. Chioma's heart raced, and it took every bit of self-control she had to stand her ground. But she raised her chin in defiance, even as she avoided his eyes and determined not to speak to the arrogant man who stood belligerently in front of her, wordlessly daring her to try to escape.

At last he spoke, and his words were as intimidating as his size and the malevolence of his expression. "Where's your hero now?" he asked, keeping his voice low. "You no longer have a protector in the camp. Where will you fly to escape me, little bird?" When she didn't answer, he raised his clenched fist in front of her. "You know I could catch you and crush you before you made it outside the camp, don't you?"

Chioma felt her head begin to swim, and she was having trouble breathing. Forgetting her decision not to speak, she raised her eyes to meet his and opened her mouth, but no words came out.

The sneer that spread across Abrafo's lips as she stood there, quivering and speechless, was followed by words so evil Chioma thought she would rather die at that very moment than continue to live in such terror.

"So you think you belong to Themba?" Abrafo hissed. "You're wrong, little bird. You belong to me. And once I've rid this place of your so-called brave leader, I'll have you to myself—until you displease me. Then I'll find another little bird to take your place. And you? I'll pluck your feathers and wring your neck like a chicken that's outlived its usefulness." He paused, leaning in toward Chioma's face. The smell of sweat and dirt nearly knocked her from her feet. "The secret is not to displease me," he said, as she squeezed her eyes shut in an attempt to block out the vision of his malevolent grin.

When he laughed, she couldn't help but compare the promise of trouble she heard in the sound with the deep, joy-filled laughter of Themba. Their leader might be frightening and demanding, but at the moment there was nothing Chioma wanted more than to hear his voice nearby.

As if in answer to an unspoken prayer, Themba's words interrupted Abrafo's laugh, and Chioma's eyes snapped open. Themba and his companions had returned. Nearly forgetting to breathe, Chioma watched as Abrafo moved from her side and back toward the circle of men he had been sitting with moments earlier. If Themba noticed any of this action, there was no acknowledgment of it on his part, as he gathered additional weapons and once again prepared to leave. As if it were an afterthought, he stopped at the edge of the compound and turned back toward the small circle of men where Abrafo now sat.

"You," he said, nodding at Abrafo, "come with us. We need another warrior on this raid."

The battle of wills that played out between the locked eyes of the two men was short-lived, and soon Abrafo was gone, along with Themba and the others. Had Themba come back for the express purpose of checking on Abrafo? Was Themba aware of this new threat to his leadership in the camp, as well as to his relationship with his future wife?

Chioma couldn't be sure, but she found herself exhaling in relief that Themba had returned when he did. Though she didn't eagerly anticipate a future with Themba, at least he had talked about one day having children with her, which meant he would give himself to protecting her and preserving her life. Abrafo, on the other hand, had promised only to use her until she displeased him—and then to wring her neck like a worthless chicken.

Why had she ever believed that running away from the farm with Mbhali and Mandisa and joining Themba's band of freedom fighters would afford her some sort of safety? For only a brief moment, she wondered if she might have been safer staying behind at the Vorster farm, even after Andrew's death...

The need to belong. That's what she heard in the cry.

Chapter 12

THE CRY WAS SO FAINT SHE WASN'T EVEN SURE SHE heard it. She was, after all, dreaming. Somehow she sensed that. And yet...

There it was again, louder this time, though still no one else seemed to notice.

Anana looked around her, unfamiliar with her surroundings or the people she saw there, and yet certain she was exactly where she was supposed to be. The cry was somehow a sign that God had heard the cry of her own heart, that lonesome, aching wail that is born out of fear and abandonment—and aching, aching loneliness.

The need to belong. That's what she heard in the cry. And somehow she knew it was up to her to convey that belonging.

Running now, as if through quicksand, Anana struggled to move forward, to reach the crying child, opening her mouth to call for help—but no sound came forth. The only audible component of her struggle was the continuing cry of the baby, a newborn, she was sure.

Mine? No, I'm too old. A grandchild, perhaps? No. Even that's impossible now. Then whose baby? And why me? What purpose do I have in all this?

Sipho...

The strange but vaguely familiar word echoed in her mind. What did it mean? And what did it have to do with her struggle to reach the crying infant?

Sipho. Sipho. Sipho...

Anana bolted upright to a sitting position, clutching her feather bed covering to her chest as Pieter sat up beside her and pulled her to himself.

"What is it, my dear?" he whispered. "Did you have a dream, a nightmare?"

Anana waited while her heart slowed and her mind cleared. Yes, she'd had a dream. But a nightmare? No. Though it was confusing, she didn't sense the darkness that came with nightmares.

She leaned against her husband, grateful for his arms that held her. "No. Not a nightmare. Just a dream about...a baby. Crying."

Pieter hesitated. "A baby? What baby? One of...ours?"

Anana knew what he was thinking, that she had dreamed of Gertie or Andrew.

"No. Not Gertie or Andrew. But–" It was her turn to hesitate. In some strange way the baby really had seemed like hers, but that made no sense. And if she couldn't understand it, there was no reason to think she could explain it to Pieter.

"But what?" Pieter asked.

"Nothing. It was just a dream. You know how confusing dreams can be."

As they lay back against the pillows, Anana settled into the crook of Pieter's arm and rested her head on his shoulder. She sighed, grateful for the sense of security she always found in the familiarity of her husband's nearness. Perhaps, if she lay very still, she would fall back to sleep and make it through the rest of the night without any more disturbing dreams.

"Who is Sipho?" Pieter asked.

Startled, Anana bolted upright once again. "Sipho?" she gasped, looking down at Pieter in the semidarkness. "What do you mean? Why do you ask?"

"Because you spoke the name before you woke up." He reached up and pulled her back to him. "I believe it means 'gift' and is common among the Xhosa. But why would you say it?"

Shrugging, she tried to make light of it. "I heard it in my dream, but I didn't realize I said it. I must have heard one of the servants using it at one time or another. It's . . . not important." She kissed his cheek. "Go back to sleep, my love. Morning will come far too quickly."

❖❖❖

Morning did indeed break quickly over the Vorster farm — and beautifully. After a slight predawn rain that left the air smelling fresh and fragrant, Pieter was up and off to oversee the never-ending work that kept his mind occupied and his heart on hold throughout the day. Anana and Emma, on the other hand, settled into the wicker chairs on the veranda, sipping *boerekoffie* and reveling in one another's company as they listened to the distant chirping of the small weaver birds near the creek that ran through the Vorster property.

"Did you sleep well?" Anana asked, her gaze lingering over the expanse of veld that spread out from the front of her home.

Emma smiled, her hands clasped around the large, steaming cup. "I did. Your guest room is as comfortable as I remember.

And the bed—" She choked on the word, pausing before continuing, and Anana knew Emma was remembering her previous visits, when she had slept in that same bed with John. "The bed is very comfortable," Emma added, her smile taking on a forced strain.

"You miss him very much, don't you?" Anana asked, her voice soft as she, too, hugged her cup with her hands.

Emma's eyes dropped before she nodded. "It's as if half of me has been ripped away. I knew it was coming, of course—he was sick for so long. And I'm truly glad he's no longer suffering. But..."

Anana sighed. Her sister's trail of tears had been different from her own, but no less painful. The thought of losing Pieter, of not having him there beside her when she awoke from a dream or faced yet another loss...

"I'm sorry," Anana said. "It was foolish of me to ask. Of course you miss him. You were married for nearly twenty-five years."

Emma looked up, her pale blue eyes glistening. "Don't apologize, dear sister. You were just making an observation, not prying. And there are no secrets between us." She smiled. "Not even when we were children."

Anana returned her smile. "That's true. Though I'm afraid we kept them from Ma and Pa on occasion."

Emma laughed, and Anana felt a tingle of excitement at the familiar sound. On previous visits they had laughed nearly all the time; she realized that morning, however, that though they had chattered a lot since Emma's arrival, they hadn't laughed until now. Perhaps they had been too focused on not crying.

"Yes," Emma agreed. "We did keep a few secrets to ourselves, didn't we? Including that abandoned kitten we found behind the barn that time, remember? Oh, how we wanted a cat! Pa was allergic, and we knew we weren't allowed. But finding one that needed a home...well, we couldn't possibly leave him there to die."

Anana laughed, too. "I'd forgotten about that. What was that pitiful cat's name? It was orange and white, wasn't it?"

Emma nodded. "Yes. I believe we called it Pretty, or something equally unoriginal. And we got away with it for almost a week, if I remember correctly."

"Even when Pa's sneezing got out of hand and Ma commented on how much worse it got each time he came into our room to kiss us good night, but still they didn't catch us."

Emma laughed again. "Do you remember how nervous we were, each time anyone came into our room—not just Pa? We were so worried that Pretty would meow at the wrong time. I think she must have known she'd lose her home if she did, though, because she always seemed to sleep quietly in her box under the bed whenever anyone was there."

"Until Ma ordered the servants to begin the spring house-cleaning. Then, as they say in your country, the jig was up!" Anana laughed. "I'll never forget Ma's face when the servant came walking from our room, carrying the box with Pretty still sleeping in it. I guess we never realized they'd clean under the bed."

The memory of her ma, eyes wide and a storm cloud gathering around her head at the sight of the culprit that had been causing her husband's allergy attacks, swam in Anana's mind, bringing a warmth of nostalgia to her heart. "Ma wasn't happy, but once she settled down, she did agree to let us keep her in the barn, remember?"

Emma nodded. "Yes. Ma blustered a lot, but underneath she was as soft as that kitten's fur." Smiling, she added, "We had a good life growing up, didn't we?"

"We certainly did. But oh, how I miss Ma and Pa!"

Anana had scarcely completed voicing her thought when she paused, frowning. "Do you hear that?"

It was Emma's turn to frown, as she answered with a question of her own. "Hear what?"

Anana spoke without thinking. "That baby. It's crying—somewhere..." Her voice trailed off and she looked at Emma, realizing how strange she must sound, particularly since it seemed Emma didn't hear anything. Come to think of it, Anana no longer heard it either. What was wrong with her? Had she imagined it? Of course she had. But it had seemed so real...like the baby from her dream last night, calling to her...

"Are you all right?" Emma asked.

Anana blinked. Perhaps she hadn't been getting enough sleep lately. Or maybe it was a reaction to losing yet another child...

"I'm fine. It must have been...the wind, or...or one of the servants." She shook her head. "It's nothing. Really. Just my imagination getting the better of me." She smiled. "Can I get you another cup?"

Emma nodded. "I'd like that."

❖❖❖

By the time Pieter returned to the house, it was late afternoon, and Anana was in the kitchen, supervising the making of dinner while Emma read in the sitting room. When Emma looked up from her book and saw Pieter walk by, heading in the direction of the master bedroom, she called his name, then smiled in welcome when he returned to stand in the doorway.

"Hello, Pieter. How was your day?"

"Good. And yours?"

"Anana and I have scarcely stopped talking for a moment. We have so much to catch up on."

Pieter nodded, smiling, though Emma sensed his heart wasn't in it. "That's good," he said. "I'm glad you're here. Anana needs this visit."

"As do I. And you? How are you doing, Pieter?"

The tall, lean man, dusty from many hours of work, shifted from one foot to the other. "Fine. Good."

Emma could almost feel Pieter's unease, and she understood it well, as John, too, had been uncomfortable discussing his feelings. She had better turn the conversation to something more comfortable.

"Your house is as lovely as ever. I always sleep well in your guest room. Anana thinks of every possible comfort and convenience."

Pieter smiled again. "Yes. She's very thoughtful."

Emma eyed her brother-in-law, recognizing his pride in Anana but sensing something else as well. "Is everything...all right? With Anana, I mean."

Pieter frowned, taking a step into the room before stopping again. "I... As well as can be expected, I suppose. But..." He swallowed, and Emma watched his Adam's apple bob up and then down again before he continued. "She had a dream last night. I could tell it bothered her more than she'd admit."

Emma raised her eyebrows. "What sort of dream? Did she tell you?"

"A little...but not all of it, I'm sure. She said it was about a...a baby. That she heard it crying."

Emma nearly dropped her book to the floor, as she felt her eyes widen and her heart rate increase. "A baby? Crying?"

Pieter frowned. "Yes. Why? Is there something strange about that? Something I should know about?"

Emma shrugged and shook her head. "I...don't know, Pieter, but..." She took a deep breath, wondering why she was even mentioning it, since there was obviously no connection. And yet...

"She...said she heard a baby this morning—crying—while we were sitting out on the veranda. But I...heard nothing. When I asked her about it, she shook it off, said it had probably just been the wind or one of the servants—or her imagination, which no doubt is the case. But...like the dream, I think it bothered her more than she let on."

Pieter's eyes narrowed and his frown deepened. "Emma," he said, stepping closer to her and lowering his voice, "do you think Anana is all right? She's been through so much..."

Emma nodded, wanting to reassure Pieter but unsure even as she spoke the words. "Of course, she is. But you're right. She's been through a lot, and this may just be part of how she's grieving." She paused, locking eyes with Pieter in hopes of receiving some sort of reassurance that her words were true.

"Don't you agree? Don't you imagine that's all it is?"

Pieter returned her stare, but his words of assurance seemed shaky at best. "Yes. I'm sure that's it. What else could it be?"

"Nothing," she answered quickly. "I...shouldn't even have brought it up. She'll be fine in time, I'm sure."

Pieter continued to hold her gaze for a moment, then nodded. "I must go wash up for dinner," he said, turning to leave the room.

Emma watched him go, then leaned back and picked up her book, breathing a silent prayer for her younger sister who had begun to hear a baby crying...somewhere.

❖❖❖

The contractions were coming quicker now, and Chioma knew it was up to her and Mandisa to deliver Ebele's baby. How could that be? Neither of them had ever even been pregnant, let alone helped to deliver a child! If only they had taken more interest when one of the servants on the Vorster farm had given birth in the presence of a midwife, but it was too late now for wishing or regret. All the others in the camp had gone on a raid, and now Ebele was screaming with pain, though both Chioma and Mandisa urged her to remember Themba's admonition to remain as quiet as possible within the camp. But even the rag Ebele twisted and bit down on didn't drown out her agony.

"Do you think she'll be all right?" Mandisa whispered, her eyes wide with fright as she and Chioma knelt on either side of the writhing, moaning Ebele.

"How would I know?" Chioma shot back, irritated that Mandisa would expect her to be more experienced in this sort of thing simply because she was slightly older. Chioma had seen a few animals born on the farm, but that was the extent of her personal experience. Oh, if only Mbhali or one of the other women had stayed behind! But Themba had insisted he needed all available comrades at his side. Only Chioma and Mandisa were left behind with Ebele, who had already been complaining of not feeling well.

"What should we do?" Mandisa asked, persisting in her apparent delusion that Chioma had an answer for her.

"Why do you ask me?" Chioma spat. "Do I look like someone who's done this sort of thing before?"

Ebele yanked the rag from her mouth and reached out to grab Chioma's arm, nearly squeezing a scream of terror from the hapless young woman. "Help me," Ebele begged. "Can't you see that I'm in trouble, that the baby is distressed? Something isn't right. You must fix it—quickly."

Chioma's eyes widened, as she sucked in a deep breath. "What do you mean? How do you know something's wrong? And how can I possibly fix it?"

Ebele shook her sweat-drenched head. "The baby—it needs to be turned. Surely you know how to do that."

Chioma looked at Mandisa, who appeared more distraught than ever. It was obvious neither had any idea what to do, though Chioma did remember once seeing one of the men servants on the farm reach inside a cow and turn the calf so it could be born. But she had been so far away, watching from a distance—and it had been an animal, not a human!

Terrified, Chioma answered, "I'll go for help. I'm sure I can find Themba and the others. They can't be too far away. Mandisa will stay here with you until I return..."

Chioma heard Mandisa squeal in protest, even as Ebele dug her fingernails into Chioma's flesh. "You...will... not...leave...me," she demanded, her jaws clenched as she issued her order one definitive word at a time. "Turn...my... baby...now!"

Chioma tried to break free, pulling her arm in an attempt to jump up and run away, but Ebele would have none of it. Her grip on Chioma only tightened as another contraction sent her screaming for relief. "Help me or I'll die!" she screeched. "And my baby, too! Help us, Chioma, please!"

Why me? thought Chioma. *Why do I have to do this?* She looked at Mandisa, but the poor girl was trembling, her eyes wide with terror. Quite obviously, if anyone was going to do anything—right or wrong—it would have to be Chioma. She only hoped her efforts would be successful.

When Ebele's contraction eased, Chioma took a deep breath and said, "All right. Tell me what to do."

It was apparent Ebele's strength was ebbing and there was not much time, so with the pain-wracked woman directing the process, Chioma obeyed, praying silently to whatever unknown gods might be listening that she would be used to save a life—preferably two—before this horrifying event was over.

In less than an hour, Chioma found herself holding a wet newborn in her hands, a tiny boy that lay lifeless as Mandisa wailed beside them. When Chioma raised her eyes to look at Ebele, whose name meant "mercy," she knew her prayers had not been answered, nor had Ebele's name done her any good. Despite their best efforts, they had lost her too. The last push to expel her baby into the world had finished the young mother's life on earth.

As Chioma stared at the dead woman, she decided it was best the infant had died as well. How would they care for a newborn orphan? It was as it should be. Maybe they had received mercy, after all.

And then the baby stirred—just a kick, but Chioma was so shocked she nearly dropped him. Jerking her head down to look at the now squirming child, she opened her mouth in amazement—even as the child opened his mouth and uttered his first cry.

"Sipho," Mandisa muttered, and Chioma turned to look at her friend.

"Sipho," Mandisa repeated, her eyes shining as she looked from the screaming baby to Chioma, then back again. "We should call him Sipho. I had a cousin by that name. It means 'gift.'"

As Mandisa gazed in wonder at the little one who intermittently shoved a fist in his mouth to suck on it and then removed it to wave it in the air and cry again, Chioma nodded. Sipho it would be...though she could think of no reason to be grateful for such an unwanted or untimely gift.

She noticed for the first time the small bag
he held in his left hand.

Chapter 13

B Y THE TIME THEMBA AND THE OTHERS RETURNED, Mandisa was holding a quiet Sipho, exhausted from screaming for nourishment. Chioma was nearly frantic with worry about how they would feed the helpless infant, not to mention what Themba would say when he discovered what had happened in his absence.

She didn't have long to wait.

"So, Chioma," Themba barked, fixing his dark eyes on hers, while seemingly ignoring Mandisa who stood beside her, "I leave for a few hours and come back to find a dead woman in my camp. What am I to think?"

Chioma swallowed. She had no answer for him, as she had no idea what to think herself. "I...don't know, Themba. It just...happened..."

The tall warrior, with his ever-present chest scar and what appeared to be fresh blood on the front of his faded khaki pants, continued to stare down at her. Chioma noticed the flash of light in his eyes just before he broke into laughter. "Yes. That sort of thing does just happen, doesn't it? One life ends..." He paused and, still smiling, turned his eyes to the silent bundle in Mandisa's arms before looking back to Chioma. "...and another begins."

Chioma recognized the meaning in Themba's comment but chose to ignore it. What would happen now? Would she and Mandisa be punished for Ebele's death? Would the baby be allowed to live? If so, how would they care for it?

Themba broke eye contact with Chioma and quickly searched the compound. Apparently spotting the object of his search, he called to one of the men, who hurried to Themba's side.

"Find a milk goat," Themba ordered, "and bring it here. Quickly."

Without question, the man turned and hurried from the camp, as Themba turned back to the two waiting women. He raised his eyebrows. "Babies need milk, don't they?"

Mandisa was the first to respond. Nodding rapidly, she said, "Yes, Themba. And thank you very much for your kindness and wisdom! I knew you'd take care of things when you returned."

Chioma gave her friend a quick, surprised glance. It was the first time she had heard words of praise for their leader coming from the young woman. Maybe it would have been better if Themba had set his sights on Mandisa...

But, of course, he hadn't. Chioma was his woman and would soon be his wife—at least, according to Themba. Chioma knew that in her mind, but the rest of her had yet to accept it. And yet, this surprisingly tender side of him, showing through in the way he dealt with little Sipho, tugged at her heart in a way that surprised her.

Allowing her eyes to sweep from Themba's face down to his feet and up again, she noticed for the first time the small bag he held in his left hand. She studied it for a moment, then raised her eyes to his face, only to find him gazing at her, grinning. Had he mistaken her glance of curiosity for one of desire? She felt her face grow hot and dropped her eyes. Even then, she could feel him watching her.

At last she knew he had turned his attention back to Mandisa, as Chioma heard him say, "Is it a man-child?"

Without hesitation, though with trembling in her voice, Mandisa answered, "His name is Sipho."

Chioma dared to lift her head and look at Themba, whose surprised but amused expression was still aimed at Mandisa. Finally he said, "*Sipho*. Gift." He nodded. "So it shall be. And you shall be mother to this little gift. Take care, Mandisa, that he thrives and grows up brave and strong. We need to raise comrades for the cause."

Chioma darted her eyes toward Mandisa just in time to see her friend's shocked reaction. It was almost as if she had received a physical blow, as she stumbled backward, almost falling in the process. "Me?" she squeaked at last. "I am to be Sipho's mother? But...why me?"

Chioma wondered at her friend's extreme response. Didn't Mandisa realize she was the obvious choice to mother the little orphan? Or was it simply that she imagined someone else in their community more qualified?

Once again Chioma saw Themba raise his eyebrows, his amused smile gone. "Because I said so. Isn't that enough?"

Chioma held her breath, waiting for her friend's response. When it came, she breathed a sigh of relief.

"Yes," Mandisa said, a glow coming over her face as she spoke. "It's enough, Themba. And I thank you for the honor. I'll raise him well."

Themba nodded. "Good. Before the milk goat arrives, find a way to feed your little comrade."

Turning his attention back to Chioma then, he dropped the bag at her feet. "This is for you," he said. With that he turned and strode to his lean-to without another glance at Mandisa and the baby...or Chioma.

❖❖❖

The evening was quiet, the farm peaceful as Anana and Emma sat, once again, in the wicker chairs on the veranda. Dinner was over, the servants had cleaned up and retired to their rooms for the night, and Pieter was in his study, going over the books. It was the quality "sister time" Anana had so loved and missed over the years.

"It's beautiful out here," Emma observed, her face alight in the glow from the open door. "Just as I remembered it."

Anana nodded. "Yes. I have often thought how very much you must have loved John to give all this up and move so far away."

Emma turned toward her, a wistful smile teasing her lips. "I did. I do. I have loved him almost from the day we met, and I shall always love him."

Anana nodded again. She understood exactly. Her passion for Pieter, though tempered and matured over the years, was no less now than on the day she had become his bride. How fortunate she and Emma were to have married men they loved so dearly—and who loved them in return. It seemed a rare commodity these days.

"I always wanted that same type of enduring love for my children," Anana said, and then stopped. Why had she brought that up? Gertie had been dead for years, and now Andrew, too, was gone. There would be no loving relationships or marriage or children for either of them, and that was a grief that nearly exceeded Anana's own loss.

Emma reached over and laid her hand on her sister's. "Now it's my turn to understand. And I do. I, too, wished—indeed, prayed—for that sort of love for Mariana." Emma paused before continuing, and Anana knew it was out of consideration for her loss. "I know how blessed I am to have seen those prayers answered. Eric and Mariana have such a wonderful marriage, and I am so looking forward to becoming a grandmother."

Anana smiled. Despite the stark difference in their lives, she truly was happy for her sister. Emma might have lost John, but she still had Mariana and her family to help keep his memory alive.

Anana's heart constricted yet again at the thought of what it would be like if she lost Pieter. He was all she had left—no children or grandchildren to give her life meaning or to fill her house with joy and laughter. Unbidden, the memory of Andrew's last night on earth flashed through her mind—the sight of him, lying motionless on the ground near the river, Pieter kneeling beside him...and yes, the young woman, Chioma, standing in the distance, looking on.

Was it possible Andrew and Chioma could ever have experienced the type of love Anana and Pieter shared? The very thought was so foreign it seemed unfathomable. And yet, if Andrew had lived and apartheid had died, was it possible...?

Emma squeezed her hand, bringing her back to the present. "You're daydreaming again."

Anana smiled sheepishly and nodded. "About Andrew...and the night he died." Her voice cracked, as she dared to speak to Emma about something she had held inside since Andrew's death. "And about...Chioma."

Emma's eyebrows raised. "Chioma? Wasn't she one of your maids?"

Anana nodded again. "Yes. She came to us with her younger brother, Masozi, some years ago. Though I never learned all the details, I'm sure their parents were dead. We took them in, gave them work..." She stopped, wondering if she could go on but knowing she must.

"And then..." She paused. "Just a few months ago...Masozi died."

Emma squeezed her hand again. "That must have been very hard on Chioma. What happened?"

"He was..." Anana had not said the word before, not even to Pieter. She took a deep breath. "He was...murdered."

She heard the sharp intake of Emma's breath, saw the shaken look on her face. "How?"

Anana had known the question was coming, but still she wasn't prepared. "By the same ones who...murdered Andrew." She could scarcely believe she had said the words, but there they were, almost visibly hanging in the air between them. For a moment, neither of them spoke. At last Emma opened her mouth and broke the silence.

"I...thought Andrew's death was an accident."

The tears came then, and Anana knew there was no point in trying to hold them back. Giving them free rein, she clung to Emma's hand as the story poured out, everything from Masozi's death to Andrew's, and all that had transpired in between—at least as much as Anana knew, and some she only suspected. By the time she finished, she was exhausted but felt hopeful for the first time in many weeks. At last she could talk with someone about all the awful things that had happened— someone besides Pieter, who preferred to deal with his pain by not discussing it any more than necessary.

"Oh, Anana," Emma whispered, "I'm so sorry! However have you been able to bear it—all this pain, all this deception and cover-up? Is no one to be punished for these awful crimes?"

"Apparently not," Anana answered, surprised at the note of bitterness in her voice. She understood the way things were in South Africa and the complications of how the murders took place, particularly Andrew's involvement with Chioma and the fact that much in both cases would have rested on her word against the word of white Afrikaners. And yet...

For a few moments, neither of them spoke, taking solace in their clasped hands and united hearts. Then, quietly, Emma said, "Tell me about apartheid. I know. I've lived here. I was raised in it. I should understand. But I've been away a long time, and...there's much that doesn't make sense to me." She paused. "I think maybe you feel the same way. Am I right, dear sister?"

With fresh tears pooling in her eyes, Anana nodded. Oh, yes! There was so much that didn't make sense about their way of life, so much she didn't understand and wanted to cry out against. Was it safe at last to speak of these things, to pour out her heart to perhaps the only one who would receive her words and lock them away in a safe place? How long had she yearned for this opportunity without being aware of it?

At that moment she thought of something, and she knew she had to share it with Emma. "Wait here," she said, rising from her chair as a puzzled Emma gazed up at her. "There's something I must show you."

Anana went into the house and crept past Pieter's study and into their room, where she pulled something from the drawer beside her bed. When she returned to the veranda and to her sister, who still sat where Anana had left her, she held a small black journal in her hand. Perhaps it would be easier to read the entries together...

❖❖❖

Chioma sat silently in the darkness, hunkered down in the quiet spot that had become her refuge. The camp was sleeping at last, including Mandisa and little Sipho, who had slurped his meal through a makeshift bottle consisting of twisted rags soaked in goat's milk and then, content and full, drifted off for a few hours' sleep.

Once she was certain her friend and the newest addition to their compound were out for a while, Chioma slipped away, carrying with her the contents of the bag Themba had given her. She was puzzled. Though she remembered an instance when Themba overheard and commented on a conversation between Chioma and Mandisa, during which Chioma mentioned that her father had taught her to read and write and how she regretted leaving his journal behind, she never expected their gruff leader to respond by bringing her a gift. She imagined that Themba considered the books to be the traditional gift from a man to his new bride, but she was uncomfortable with the thought. And yet, what other explanation was there for Themba bringing back such an offering from his most recent raid and presenting it to her? Two of the books in the bag hadn't interested her, but the third…

She pulled it out now, laying aside the bag with the other two books as she held the third book in her lap and caressed it. There was no moonlight tonight and it was impossible to read it, but there was something about it that spoke to her, called to her, as if it were alive.

Holy Bible. That is what the words in gold on the front of the book said. Immediately upon seeing them, Chioma had thought of Andrew. She knew he believed in the God spoken of in this book, though she herself did not. She had heard about Him many times from Andrew's father, the *dominee* who led the mandatory services for all the servants on his farm, but she had seen no reason to believe in the white man's God, since He apparently condoned the oppression of one race by another. But there was something about this book—a connection to Andrew perhaps—that overrode the hypocrisy she had seen in the lives of the so-called white Christians she had known over the years. Might she better understand them—Andrew most of all—if she read this book?

Determined to find the time and opportunity to do so, she marveled that it was Themba who had brought it to her.

Daily, it seemed, she was amazed at the slivers of kindness that peeked through his battle-worn exterior. But what would he think if he knew the thoughts it provoked as she touched it? Would he take it from her? Deciding that was a definite possibility, she tucked it back into the bag and then rose to return to the camp.

"I thought I'd find you here."

The hard voice of Abrafo nearly knocked her back to the ground, as she realized he was standing just inches from her. Had he been watching her? Why hadn't she heard him approach? What did he want from her? What would he do? Should she cry out for Themba? She was, after all, Themba's woman, and he was sworn to protect her.

As if reading her mind, Abrafo leaned close, his hot breath against her face. "If you're considering calling out to your intended, don't bother. I have no intention of taking you—not here and not now. If things were different, I would have made my intentions clear, publicly, from the beginning. But remember, you can't get away from me, little bird. I know where you are at all times, and sooner or later, I'll find you when even Themba himself is not around to interfere." He paused. "One day I'll find Themba alone as well, and when I finish with him, I'll come for you." He grabbed her arm and yanked her even closer, until their foreheads touched. "Do you understand me, little bird?"

Chioma was too terrified even to answer. She wished only that she truly was a little bird and could fly away from this evil creature...but, of course, she couldn't. And so she stood, eyes wide and mouth clamped shut, as she clutched her bag and waited.

After what seemed an eternity, Abrafo shook her loose. "Go back to the camp," he growled. "But remember, I'm watching, restraining myself because of the way things are at the moment. But one day soon, those things will change, and I'll do a lot more than watch."

A tiny cry escaped Chioma's lips then, and she broke into a run, more frightened even than on the night she had run from the scene where Andrew was killed. Must she forever run for her life, chased by demons and devils alike? Was there no peace or safety for her anywhere?

Back in her lean-to between Mbhali and Mandisa, who slept with Sipho in the crook of her arm, Chioma bit her lip so she wouldn't awaken them with sobs. If only she knew what to do! Should she tell Themba? Would he believe her? And what if Themba went after Abrafo, only to be killed himself, leaving the rest of them at the mercy of a man who had none?

Hugging the bag of books to her chest, much the way Mandisa hugged her new little charge, Chioma lay in the darkness for a very long time before she finally drifted off into a restless sleep.

I will devot my life to freeing my people.
And if I die I die.

Chapter 14

THE HAUNTING STATEMENT WITH MISSPELLED words was the opening sentence in the worn journal.

I have come to the sad conclushen that sometimes vilence is warented.

The words tore at Anana's heart—and, she could tell, at Emma's as well. Was it true? Was violence indeed warranted? And exactly what circumstances qualified it to be so?

On a more personal level, what had driven the author of the statement to believe the words he wrote? Anana, of course, had read the journal entries—many times now—and had been able to discern that the author was Chioma's father. She had also been able to string together at least part of what had transpired in the man's life, both before and after putting his pen to this painful revelation nearly thirty years earlier. But she still had many questions. Maybe reading the journal with Emma would help her understand.

She listened as Emma's voice spoke the words that followed the opening statement.

It greaves me to beleeve this and yet what choise do I have? We gather for a politicle discushen, and they kill us men, women, and childern. After Sharpeville nothing can ever be the same...

Emma laid the book in her lap and looked at her sister. "I remember hearing about Sharpeville," she said, her voice soft. "The first time was when I was in high school. But I must admit, I was too busy with my studies and social life to be concerned with what happened there."

Anana nodded. "As was I. When I heard that sixty-nine blacks and coloureds were killed in the Sharpeville township, I remember asking Pa why. He said the police had been defending themselves, quelling a violent riot, protecting our way of life and stopping the spread of communism." She dropped her eyes for a moment before lifting them again. "I accepted his explanation and scarcely gave it another thought after that."

"How different it must have been for the families of those sixty-nine who died," Emma mused. "And for other blacks and coloureds as well. I've heard several times since that those people were shot in the back. How is that possible if the police were simply defending themselves?"

Anana had no answer for her. She, too, had wondered at that very inconsistency. Quite obviously one of the two accounts was incorrect. Or was it possible the truth lay somewhere between the two versions of the story? And why had she never carried her questioning any further? Why had it taken so much personal tragedy for her to care enough to seek the actual truth? For since beginning to read the journal, that is exactly what she had wanted to find.

Emma returned to her reading.

One thing is sure. I will never mary. How can I bring childern into a world where I am not alowed to protect them? I will devot my life to freing my people. And if I die I die. At least I wont take a famly to the grave with me...

Emma's voice trailed off, and Anana saw a tear trickle down her sister's cheek, speaking more eloquently than either of them could do with words. Quite obviously circumstances had changed in the author's life, to the point that he had chosen to take the risk to marry and have children. Anana reasoned that Chioma's mother must have been a very special lady to have overcome this man's concerns about taking on the responsibilities of providing and caring for a family. But then, Anana mused, truly great love had a way of overcoming nearly anything.

Silently and together, the two sisters considered what this man had penned nearly three decades earlier...and wondered how it would affect their own lives in the future.

❖❖❖

Chioma knew she didn't have much time before someone noticed she wasn't at her post, but she desperately wanted to sneak a look at the book Themba had brought her. She had transferred it from the bag to her apron pocket, where she once carried her father's beloved journal. Carefully, hiding behind a tree and taking one last look to verify that no one was near, she opened the book to the first page of what appeared to be the first chapter.

In the beginning God created the heaven and the earth.

So, it was a history book of the world. She didn't remember *Dominee* Vorster reading this part of the book during any of the services on the farm. Or perhaps he had and she had just not paid attention. At any rate, she was curious to see what else this book had to say about the past.

And the earth was without form, and void; and darkness was upon the face of the deep. And the Spirit of God moved upon the face of the waters.

She paused in her reading. *If I'm to believe this, then the earth was once dark and wet. And this God of the whites is a Spirit who moves through the air. What good is a God like that to me? How is He any different from the spirit gods of my ancestors?*

Closing the book and placing it back in her pocket, she promised herself she would read from a different section when she had more time. She remember the *dominee* speaking of the white man's God as if he were a man—Jesus, who walked the earth a couple of thousand years ago, healing people and playing with children. Though it was hard to imagine such a personal God, perhaps He was a God she could relate to, even if the pictures she had seen of this Jesus showed that He was the wrong color. She decided she would consider it while she served her shift as sentry.

Taking up her position at the top of a rise, she nodded at the two men she replaced, watching them walk back to the camp and wondering who would come to stand with her. She shivered, suppressing the fear that it might be Abrafo.

No. Themba oversees the choosing of the sentries, and he would never allow Abrafo to be alone with me.

And then she spotted the approaching figure, and her heart leapt. He was tall and broad-shouldered, and he walked like... But why would Themba stoop to perform a duty more easily covered by someone of lesser stature in the camp?

Before she could find a plausible answer to her question, Themba was nearly in front of her, his AK-47 slung over his shoulder as a grin spread across his face. "So, my brave and beautiful woman is on guard duty today. How appropriate."

Chioma moved her gaze up from the scar on his chest but not as far as his eyes, to settle somewhere around his chin. It seemed the safest place, though even then the sight of his grin unnerved her. Why would he say it was appropriate for her to be on guard duty today? Was there some special reason that made this day different from any other?

Once again, seemingly tracking with her thoughts, Themba's mouth opened and he said, "You're very beautiful. You know that, don't you?"

Chioma felt her heart skip, and against her will her eyes moved up to lock with his. What was this power he seemed to have over her? Was it just that he was their leader, that they all followed and obeyed him? Or was it something else, something much more personal?

Though she knew it was wrong, she tried to pull up the memory of Andrew, the forbidden white man who had also drawn her to himself and had even given his life for her. She had always known their relationship could only lead to disaster, as well it had, but now she relied on it to help her keep the wall up between herself and Themba. Frighteningly, Andrew's visage remained faint, while Themba's shone in the sunlight, not two feet from her.

"Are you unable to speak today, Chioma?" Themba asked, the smile fading from his lips but still dancing in his dark eyes. "Is something wrong?"

She knew he was toying with her, but there was nothing she could do about it. She was, after all, his "woman," giving him certain rights. Her stomach churned at the thought.

"I... Of course I can speak. I just don't have anything to say."

Themba's now-familiar laugh burst from his mouth, and Chioma flinched. Swallowing, she squared her shoulders and determined not to show any more fear.

And then the man with the muscles of steel reached toward her and took her arms in his hands, pulling her to himself before she realized what had happened. Suddenly her cheek was pressed against his chest, and she could feel his scar touching her face. Terrified, she wondered if he could feel her heart pounding against her ribs, ready to burst out and fly away. What was he doing? What was he planning to do? And what would he do if she fought him and wrestled herself from his grasp?

All these thoughts and more raced through her mind, and yet she stood, unmoving, skin against skin, heartbeat against heartbeat, waiting and wondering if this would be the day she finally joined her ancestors—and Andrew—in the next life, if indeed there was one.

"I told you before," he said at last, "you're my woman. It's appropriate that you stand guard as my woman today, for tonight you will become my wife. I've already instructed Mbhali to move your things from your lean-to into mine. We'll have the ceremony after the evening meal. As for the bride-price, since you don't have a living relative, I'll pay it directly to the community, as we're your family now."

Chioma felt the air being sucked from her lungs, as blackness invaded the edges of her sight. She was going to faint, and there was nothing she could do except trust the man who was about to become her husband to catch her before she fell.

❖❖❖

When she awoke, she was lying on the ground, her head in Themba's lap. Lifting her eyes, she saw that her intended sat in the dirt, leaning against a tree trunk as he gazed into the distance, alert for any intruders who dared to approach the encampment. Afraid to move, she lay perfectly still, studying him.

Within seconds, Themba grinned, though his eyes remained on the horizon. "You're watching me when you should be watching for our enemies. You're on guard duty, remember?" He glanced down and caught her eyes. "Don't think, beautiful woman, that as my wife you can shirk your duties. Everyone must work here. No exceptions."

She swallowed and nodded. He returned the gesture and then lifted his head to resume his watch. "So, why do you remain on the ground now that you're awake? I share your sentry duty today, but I don't carry it for you." He smiled and caressed her cheek, though he didn't look down at her. "Perhaps you haven't moved because you like being close to me. That's good, beautiful Chioma. Tonight you'll be especially close, and every night after that. But during the day, we're still two comrades who must do our duty. Understood?"

Chioma understood. Shoving her thoughts of what would take place tonight from her mind, she stood to her feet to resume her duties.

❖❖❖

By the time they returned to the camp, it was obvious that word had spread about the evening's festivities. The women smiled at Chioma as she passed by, and the men shot knowing grins toward their leader. Chioma realized the group was restraining themselves from what would otherwise be loud, boisterous, and even lewd remarks and gestures about the coming event, simply because their leader had instructed them to keep down the noise level within the camp at all times. Yet Chioma felt she was the butt of a giant joke, and she was the only one not laughing. But sometime during the hours of sentry duty, having completely forgotten she had planned to devote that time to considering what she had read in the book about the white man's God, Chioma had instead accepted her fate and resigned herself to go to Themba's lean-to without a fight.

"So, cousin," Mbhali said, smiling as she came up beside her, "at last the ceremony will take place and we will officially be family."

Chioma nodded but said nothing, not trusting her voice or the tears that felt dammed up behind her eyelids. She had always thought her wedding day would be a joyous one, filled with laughter and excitement and dreams of the future, with at least her brother in attendance. Instead, she felt only fear and dread, and a sad sense of loneliness and resignation—though she had to admit that as she stood pressed up against her betrothed, she had also experienced the stirrings of anticipation, wondering what it would be like to be married, to share her life so intimately with another. If only it could have happened in a different way...

Smiling bravely throughout the day, she made it nearly to the evening meal before tragedy struck. It was the noise that first caught her attention. To hear such shouting just beyond the camp's clearing where the meals were prepared was unnerving. Even more unnerving was the fact that her name seemed to be the primary word uttered in the midst of the shouting.

Hurrying toward the sound, along with everyone else from the compound, Chioma was horrified to break out of a stand of trees into a small clearing near the creek and see Themba and Abrafo glaring at one another, knives in hand. Already blood dripped from Themba's cheek and gushed from Abrafo's leg. What were they fighting about? Could it be her? If so, what would happen if Abrafo won?

Nearly dizzy with fear, Chioma found herself on the sidelines with the others, screaming Themba's name. Why didn't the men who were devoted to Themba rush in to help him, particularly his bodyguards? And then she realized there were others, traitors cultivated by Abrafo, who cheered their champion on instead. If Themba's supporters joined the fight, so would Abrafo's, and there would be mass carnage.

And so, as if by unspoken agreement, everyone stood back and let the two warriors circle and slice at one another. "Themba, be careful!" Chioma screamed, wondering if her desire was to preserve Themba's life or simply to end Abrafo's. Either way, there was no question in her mind how she wanted this confrontation to end.

She screamed again, as Abrafo lunged, tearing at Themba's chest and re-opening the old wound that had caught Chioma's eye each time she looked at the man who called her "beautiful woman." Was he going to die now, leaving them all in the hands of the madman Abrafo? Would she, the little bird, be the next to die at this interloper's hand?

But just when it looked as if Themba might be finished, he came roaring back, knocking Abrafo to the ground and quickly pounding his sharpened dagger into the man's throat. As blood spurted from Abrafo's neck, the crowd quieted, until all Chioma could hear was Themba's heavy breathing and a gurgling sound coming from Abrafo.

At last the gurgling stopped, but just as Chioma thought to race to Themba's side, he collapsed beside his defeated foe, face up and chest heaving, as blood continued to pour from his wound.

Chioma and Mbhali reached Themba at the same time, as Mbhali ripped at her skirt to form makeshift bandages while Chioma sobbed and clutched Themba's hand to her breast. "Don't die! Please, Themba, don't leave me! I can't bear it if you die, too!"

"Be quiet," Mbhali ordered. "If you're not going to help me stop his bleeding, then get out of the way and let someone else help. There's no time for your tears."

Chioma looked across the body of the man she was to have married that night and exchanged glances with Mbhali. Her friend was right, of course. Right now they must do whatever was necessary to save Themba's life. Her tears would come later if the two women failed in their efforts.

In the rush to save their leader, no one gave a thought to checking on Abrafo, who now lay lifeless on the ground just feet from Themba, or to the handful of men who only moments ago were chanting Abrafo's name in loyalty and now slunk off into the bush without a word.

They had continued to read the journal and to discuss its entries.

Chapter 15

THE SECLUDED VELD AMIDST THE STAND OF ACACIAS had long been Anana's favorite spot. It was one of the few places in the area where she could enjoy the brilliant splashes of color provided by South Africa's national flower, the King Protea, which favored this tiny location on their farm with its wild but protected presence. To sit there on a blanket under the warm midmorning sun with Emma and enjoy the peaceful surroundings as they snacked on a late but simple breakfast of *rusks* and fruit was about as close to perfect as Anana could imagine.

Her heart squeezed for a moment, as she realized how imperfect things really were, with John and Andrew gone, as well as Gertie. And yet, there was still much to be thankful for, much to appreciate. It was always a joy for Anana to watch her sister bask in the beauty of South Africa after having been away for such a long time.

Personally Anana could not visualize herself ever leaving her homeland. South Africa was such a part of her—and of Pieter as well. Of course, that was the difference. Anana had fallen in love with another Afrikaner, a son of the same beloved homeland as she, while Emma had chosen to share her life with an American. And so, the older sister had gone off to start a new life in a new land, with new customs and a new culture...

No. Though Anana could understand Emma's desire to follow her heart and her man to a faraway land, she could not understand ever transferring her loyalty from South Africa to another country or continent. South Africa defined Anana in so many ways. Who would she be if she no longer had this land, this spot of earth, to call her own?

The two women had discussed this very subject at length over the last few days, but not only as it related to them. They had continued to read the journal and to discuss its entries, and as a result they found themselves beginning to view their lives, as well as the lives of all other South Africans, in a very different light.

"Is it possible," Anana ventured now, her voice soft and trembling a bit, "that I—we Afrikaners—have been presumptuous in our sense of...ownership of South Africa?" Just saying the words caused her heart to race, and she watched her sister with great anticipation, waiting for her answer.

Emma, who had been gazing out over the land, "drinking it in," as she so often said, turned to face her. The blue of her eyes glistened in the muted sunlight that filtered through the trees. "Yes," she said, her voice firm. "I believe we have."

Anana raised her eyebrows, surprised less at Emma's frankness than at her self-inclusion in the statement. A sizeable portion of Emma's heart was obviously still connected to her original homeland, regardless of the ties she now had with America. Anana was pleased at the thought but disturbed by her sister's quick and clear-cut admission of guilt on the part of Afrikaners.

She glanced down at the journal that lay on the blanket be-tween them. Why did it seem to have such power over her, almost as if it had a life of its own? When she tried to ignore it, it called to her, begging her to read with her heart and not just her eyes...

Looking back at Emma, she knew her sister heard the same call. Wherever they went these days or whatever they did to pass the time, when they were alone they invariably returned to the journal. But it was the entry regarding the incident at Sharpeville — referred to by the journal's author as a "massacre" — that had disturbed the two women so deeply they hadn't been able to read on. Today, however, Anana knew they would, and her heart beat with anticipation and dread.

❖❖❖

Chioma's primary task now was to tend to her husband and help him heal from his wound, which thankfully had proved less serious than she had first imagined. Once again, Mbhali had assured her, the gods had spared Themba to fight on for the cause. All that remained was for Chioma to nurse him back to health and enable him to regain the strength he needed to resume his leadership position.

"He'll heal quickly," Mbhali had told her. "True leaders have little patience for ill health and weakness — and we certainly can't call for a doctor or healer." She grinned. "But I think my cousin will enjoy the personal attentions of his new wife."

Chioma felt the heat rise to her cheeks, as she remembered the informal ceremony that, even in his wounded state, Themba had insisted be performed. Now she would spend her wedding night tending to her husband. That tending included washing him—from head to foot—to minimize any chance of infection. Chioma had been horrified when Mbhali had instructed her to do it, once Themba had been moved to the relative privacy of his—now their—lean-to. Chioma had begged Mbhali to do it instead, but Mbhali had firmly refused, saying that Themba's care was now the concern of his wife.

As Chioma turned toward the lean-to where she would follow her friend's instructions, Mbhali grabbed her arm and turned her back to face her. "See that you perform your duties well. Our survival may depend on Themba's."

With shaking hands, Chioma had then spent the remainder of the evening carrying out Mbhali's instructions, sleeping fitfully beside her husband when she could. If he stirred or even moaned in his sleep, she was alert to his care and scurried to meet his needs. By the third morning Themba was showing the positive effects of her continual ministrations, as he slept quietly and without a fever.

"You have cared for me well," Themba said, the suddenness of his proclamation startling Chioma from her half-sleep. Her eyes snapped open in the first light of day, as she pulled herself back to the present. Had Themba spoken, or had she dreamt it?

Pushing herself up and leaning on one arm, she looked down at the man she had bathed and fed and watched over for the last three days, praying she would be successful in her efforts and trying not to think of what it would mean to her if she were not. She was surprised to find him staring up at her, a slight grin on his face.

"So, now you are more than my woman; you are my wife." He nodded. "As it should be. As I said it would be."

She swallowed. Though they had yet to consummate their union, Chioma now belonged to him, and there was nothing she could do about it. Surprisingly, she was not as repulsed by that fact as she might have been just days earlier, though she was unsure what had made the difference. But when she had seen Themba lying on the ground, bleeding and, for all she knew, dying, she had known she couldn't bear to lose one more human being who claimed to care for her.

With Abrafo it had been different. The beast had never even hinted that he cared about her, only that he wanted to use her—and then wring her neck like a chicken when he was through with her. Themba, on the other hand, had treated her with respect—though as leader he could have done otherwise—and promised to care for and protect her. To see even that taken from her had overwhelmed her, and she had lost all inhibitions at crying out to the unknown gods to spare Themba's life. Since then, many in the camp, including Mbhali and Mandisa, had commented on her obvious love for their leader.

Love. Chioma wondered if she had any idea what the word meant. She had loved her parents, but they were dead. She had loved Masozi, but he, too, was dead—as was Andrew. Had she loved him? She wasn't sure, nor was she sure he had loved her. They had never really had time to find out. But he had given his life for her. She would never forget that.

"What are you thinking, beautiful woman?" Themba asked, interrupting her reverie, his voice only slightly less booming than usual. "About me, I assume?"

He was grinning again, and Chioma tried not to squirm under his gaze. She was still uncomfortable with anyone looking directly into her eyes. And yet Themba was her husband now; she would have to get used to that idea quickly—especially once he regained his strength.

She felt her cheeks flame again at the thought, but cleared her throat and forced herself to speak. "How are you this morning, Themba? If there's anything you need or desire, I'll gladly get it for you."

Themba responded by reaching up to take her arm, surprising her by the strength that flowed from his grip. "The only thing I need or desire is you, my dear wife. And I shall have you as soon as I regain my strength. Then you'll know what it means to belong to a true leader."

She tried to suppress the sharp intake of her breath, but she was certain he heard it, as he smiled once again and pulled her close, so close she could feel his breath against her neck, even as she did her best to keep her gaze averted, fixed on the wall behind Themba's head.

"I can't promise you wealth or long life," Themba said, "but I promise you my protection. I'll defend you with my life. Do you understand that, Chioma?"

Chioma knew he was looking at her, but she couldn't bring herself to return his gaze. Instead she swallowed and nodded. "I understand."

He released her. "Good. So long as you also understand that I require complete loyalty in return—and to hear you call me 'husband' on occasion."

She nodded again. "Yes…husband," she managed to say. Chioma understood Themba's words—as well as all that was implied in them. She belonged to him now—body and soul. She was his wife, and only he could change that. If she was to believe his word, then so long as he lived and she did not betray him, all would be well.

❖❖❖

Though he couldn't put his finger on it, Pieter knew something was different with Anana—and possibly with Emma, too, but he didn't know his sister-in-law well enough to be certain.

As he rode the bay mare across the land he had loved for as long as he could remember, Pieter imagined the change must have something to do with the fact that the two sisters were discussing their losses. Commiserating and weeping together was something that seemed to help women heal—or so he had been told. There were times he wished it were as easy for men.

Spurring his horse on—the horse that had belonged to Andrew before Pieter's world was turned upside down, leaving him wounded and confused—Pieter wondered why his faith didn't give him more peace. Shouldn't the knowledge that his father's God existed somewhere "out there," caring for and watching over Pieter's every move, be a source of comfort for him? If not, what good was the religion that had been passed on to him by his parents, ingrained in him from childhood? Pieter had spent every Sunday in church since he was born into this world. He had been baptized and raised on the teachings of the church, one of which was the need for separation of the races. He had been the faithful *dominee* of the servants who had worked on his farm over the years, including the young woman who caused all the trouble that eventually took Andrew's life. Pieter had tried to teach them, tried to instill the Christian faith in them and set them free from their pagan ways, but what good had it done? Andrew was dead, the girl's brother was dead, and she was gone—who knew where? She had even taken two of the other servants with her, causing Pieter financial loss on top of everything else. Is that what he got for his obedient observance of religion? Couldn't he at least expect some comfort or reward from the God he so faithfully served?

His thoughts returned to Anana and Emma, and to the way they sometimes referred to God as if He were right there next to them, rather than inhabiting some faraway place called heaven where they all hoped to go one day. Was that the change Pieter was seeing in his wife and sister-in-law? Was their grief driving them to fanaticism—or were they simply working through their pain in one another's company?

Deciding it was the latter, Pieter Vorster once again spurred on his mount, determined to put away pointless musings and get back to work. There was a lot to do on a farm that size, and it was not about to run itself.

How is it possible that a man who might be considered our enemy suddenly seems so human?

Chapter 16

EMMA WAS STUNNED BY THE MOST RECENT journal entry, and it was obvious that Anana, though having read it several times already, felt the same.

I once considerd becomeing a Christian, but that was before Sharpeville. Now I am called by many a Comunist becaus I folow Mandela insted of the white man's god. I have herd that to be a Comunist is a bad thing. I dont no if that is true. Perhaps it is so only if it is a step down. For me it is a step up. And so I take that step for I see no other choise.

Each time Emma considered the often misspelled but always powerful and poignant words written by the now-deceased author, it was as if an electric shock had stung her heart. What had this man looked like? Who was he? Though she and Anana had searched the pages from start to finish, they found no mention of his name. They knew only from the final inscription that the author had met with a violent death, as had his wife, and that he had been the father of a boy named Masozi and a girl named Chioma, the one who had made that final journal entry about the death of her parents and who, according to Anana, had recently worked for the Vorster family and had been at least somewhat involved with Andrew and his death.

"How is it possible," Anana mused aloud, staring through the sitting room window into the darkness outside, "that a man who might be considered our enemy suddenly seems so human when we read these words from his heart?"

Dinner had long been served and eaten, and the servants had cleaned up and gone to their quarters. Pieter was in his office, finishing up some work on his books, while the sisters sat together, contemplating the contents of the little journal Chioma had left behind. Emma was becoming more and more convinced that God Himself had orchestrated the placement of that journal in their hands, though she was still a bit unclear on His purpose. Having lived in the States for many years now and grown away from her family's apartheid beliefs to settle with her husband and family in a more evangelical, racially mixed church setting, she couldn't help but wonder if at least part of God's reason was to help Anana see the error of the apartheid belief system as well. But was there more, something Emma also needed to see or learn?

"Quite possibly," Emma ventured, "it's because God is using the man's words to open our eyes to the truth that's been right in front of us all these years—not that the Bible or the Christian faith is wrong, for we know it isn't, but that we've not always interpreted it correctly or lived it as we should."

She waited then, watching Anana for a reaction. After a moment, her younger sister turned toward her, questions and tears intermingled in her blue eyes. "That's exactly what I'm afraid of," she said, her voice hushed. "It's something I've thought about for many years, something Andrew questioned as well, and now, suddenly, I can no longer avoid it." She paused, reaching out her hand to span the distance between their chairs. Her hand was light and trembling as she laid it on Emma's. "What do I do if I find that my questioning requires actions that might cause...trouble between me and Pieter?"

Emma swallowed. How was she to answer such a question? She knew how very close Anana and Pieter were, and she couldn't imagine anything coming between them. And yet...

"It's not for me to say," Emma answered at last, "for I really don't know. But I do know that God requires us to do what's right, even as He requires us to submit to our husbands. I'll pray for you, Anana—for wisdom and strength and courage. That's all I know to do."

Anana dropped her eyes, then looked up again and nodded slowly as she spoke. "It's exactly what you should do...and I as well. And I believe God will answer us both."

❖❖❖

Now that she was officially known as Themba's wife and the threats she had endured from Abrafo had been eliminated, Chioma felt even more compelled to read the little Bible she now kept in the pocket that once housed her father's journal. Though she would always miss being able to read the journal's precious words that held such bittersweet memories, nothing could ever steal her remembrances of the man who had been her hero from the time she was old enough to toddle after him and listen to his powerful stories.

Now she had another book, and she read at least something out of it each day. Today, as she sat in the relative privacy of the lean-to she shared with Themba, waiting for him to awaken so she could bring him his midmorning meal, she cautiously pulled the book from her pocket and found the place where she had left off reading the day before.

For he himself is our peace, who has made the two one and has destroyed the barrier, the dividing wall of hostility...

So many times as Chioma read this book, she felt a tugging at her heart—to continue reading and to really listen, as she had never bothered to do before. Despite having heard many of the verses read by *Dominee* Vorster, there were still so many words and phrases in this book that didn't make sense to her. This time, however, Chioma felt an immediate connection when she read the words "the barrier, the dividing wall," for she couldn't remember a time when there hadn't been a wall separating her people from the whites of South Africa. It was simply the way things were, and though she had dreamed for years of fighting for the cause, she had never even imagined that wall of separation between blacks and whites being broken down—until Andrew. Suddenly that wall had loomed larger than she had ever realized, even as a part of her dared to dream of what it would be like to scale it...

She shook her head. No. There were some walls that weren't meant to be scaled. Look what had happened to Andrew! Better to fight for the cause, while leaving the breaking down of walls to someone else.

"What are you reading, beautiful woman?"

Themba's words interrupted her thoughts, and she started, feeling guilty over her musings about Andrew and dropping the book to the floor beside her. Before she could retrieve it, Themba snatched it up and held it in front of his eyes. "Ah, the holy book. I wondered which you would choose of the three I brought you. I should have known."

He handed the book back to her, and she took it with trembling hands. Would he be angry that she was reading what many considered a white man's book? But why then would he have brought it to her? Surely he wouldn't object. She held her breath, waiting.

Themba smiled. "Few of our comrades can read, as I can. Fewer yet have wives who can. I'm honored to be one of them."

Chioma exhaled, a flood of relief shooting down from the top of her head to warm and relax her. He wasn't angry! She could read her book without hiding now. For reasons she couldn't clarify, even in her own mind, she was pleased. Themba could be terrifying at times, but he also treated her with kindness, though his position as her husband and as leader of their group didn't require him to do so.

Themba pulled himself to a sitting position, and Chioma could tell he did so with less effort than since before the fight with Abrafo. "Serve me my food. I'll eat it outside with the others so they'll see that I'm well enough to resume my position."

Instinctively Chioma reached out to lay her hand on his arm, alarmed at the thought that he would return to danger so soon after his injury. "Are you certain, Themba? Has your strength returned sufficiently to do so?"

Themba's dark eyes dropped to the place where her hand touched his arm. When he lifted his head to look into her face, all traces of good humor were gone. "Don't ever question my strength or my authority. You're my wife. Your job is to serve and obey me. Is that clear?"

Chioma snatched her hand away as if it had been burned. What had made her think this brute cared anything for her or would treat her any differently from any other man—than Abrafo, for that matter? Yet she knew she had crossed a line by questioning her husband's decision. She wouldn't be so foolish again.

She dropped her eyes. "Forgive me, my husband. I'll be more mindful of my place in the future."

Chioma heard his grunt of approval as he rose to his feet. He had stepped out into the sunlight before he turned back to her.

"Must I serve myself?" he demanded, his words nearly catapulting her from her sitting position to his side. She then hurried to the cooking pot, where many in the compound had already gathered. Murmurs of welcome and approval greeted

183

Themba as he stepped up beside her and took the plate she offered him.

With her eyes still downcast, she waited for Themba to dismiss her to eat with the women, while he joined the men who already awaited him. But Themba didn't move, and Chioma sensed his gaze nearly burning a hole in the top of her head. Slowly she looked up into his face and was surprised to see that it was not disdain or anger that greeted her, but rather open, blatant lust.

"Tonight, my wife, we will finish what we started."

❖❖❖

Though Chioma had slept in Themba's lean-to since the night of the fight that ended Abrafo's life, she had done so fully clothed and with nearly a foot of distance between herself and her husband. When she awoke the morning after Themba's declaration that they would finish what they had started, she was lying with her head on his broad shoulder. Though it had been more than four years since her parents were murdered, Chioma knew her mother would have told her she was a woman now, a wife in every sense of the term. How she wished her mother were still here to discuss all that had happened, particularly during the long night when she had made the passage from young girl to woman. But her mother was dead, and there was no one else. Chioma was not close to any of the women in the group, other than Mbhali and Mandisa. Chioma was certain Mbhali had already made the journey into womanhood, though she had no husband, but Chioma had no desire to discuss the most personal aspects of her life with her husband's cousin. And Mandisa? Though acting mother to little Sipho, the girl knew nothing about being a wife.

Chioma sighed, blinking back the tears that misted her sight. She had expected it to be much worse, and she realized it could have been had Themba treated her as some men might have done. For whatever reasons, her husband had shown her gentleness and consideration, and she would respond accordingly. After all, if she forgot her place again, she didn't doubt that Themba had another side to him that she would rather not experience on a personal level.

When she felt him stirring beneath her, she sat up, thinking to dress and then hurry to the cooking pot to bring him some nourishment. She reached for her clothes, but he was already pulling her back down to his chest. "No clothes," he said. "No breakfast. Today we stay here, together. Tomorrow I return as leader. In time, I may even take you with me so you can stand beside me as we fight for our people."

Chioma nearly gasped at the realization that soon she would have the opportunity she had dreamed of, to accompany Themba and the others as they raided the enemy, disrupted the government, and fought for the cause. At last, she would have the chance to avenge her ancestors... and yes, even Andrew.

She smiled. Not only was she a wife now, but she would soon be a true comrade as well.

Danger was an everyday reality.

Chapter 17

I T WAS THE FIRST DAY THEMBA HAD GONE WITH THE others, leaving Chioma nearly alone in the camp, with one guard on duty and only Mandisa and little Sipho for company. The baby slept peacefully, nestled against Mandisa's chest in a sling that hung from her neck. It was obvious the young woman had taken to motherhood, naturally and wholeheartedly, as she and Sipho had become inseparable.

Chioma smiled as she watched them, Mandisa tending the small garden she had convinced Themba to allow her to plant. Chioma knew they would not stay at their location long enough to reap any benefits from Mandisa's work, but it was obvious the young mother was in her element, nurturing both infant and newly planted seeds.

A pigeon cooed in a nearby tree, and Mandisa turned from her labor, flashing a smile when she spotted Chioma watching her. The two were as close as any sisters could ever be, Chioma thought, grateful for the young woman's companionship—

grateful, too, that Mandisa hadn't been left behind at the Vorster farm as Chioma and Mbhali had first considered doing. It almost seemed as if Mandisa had come to the camp just to raise Ebele's son, and though Chioma knew someone else would have taken the baby if Mandisa hadn't been around, it was obvious she was perfect for the job.

Such a short time since we were on the farm, Chioma mused, *working for the white man and...* An image of Andrew floated through her mind, and she shook her head. She belonged to Themba now; she had no right to think of another man. So much had happened since the three women had joined this rebel band. Mandisa had become a mother, Mbhali a proven comrade, and she—Chioma—was now a wife.

Her heart tugged at the thought. Though none of it had happened as she would have expected or desired, she already felt a fierce loyalty to Themba, and when he was away—as he was this day, for the first time since the fight—she worried about him. He was her protector, her provider and defender, the one sworn to care for her. What would happen to her if...?

Once again she shook her head. There was no time for such foolish speculation. Theirs was not a normal existence. Danger was an everyday reality. They all knew their lives could be taken from them at any moment. They had many enemies—those of their own kind who, like Abrafo, fought them for supremacy within the cause; those of Zulu heritage who, though they shared their skin color, didn't share their political views or ideals; and, of course, the white government, which would like nothing better than to kill them and save themselves the cost of throwing them into prison.

No, it was no easy life Chioma had chosen, but then her parents hadn't had an easy life either—or an easy death, for that matter. For a brief moment, Chioma allowed herself to close her eyes and think of the journal, of how she wished she had brought it with her and what a comfort it would have been to read the familiar words penned by her beloved father. But the journal was gone, and with it the thoughts of a great man.

All the more reason she, too, must be allowed to accompany Themba and the others as they went out during the day to fight for their cause and their people. Chioma opened her eyes and looked toward the lean-to she shared with her husband. Did she dare ask him to take her with him at the next sunrise? Her heart raced at the thought. He had been good to her, and she knew she could do much worse than to be his wife. But she also knew there were certain lines she dared not cross, at least not yet—

She lifted her head, every sense alert. Had she heard something, a noise that didn't belong to the usual *bushveld* chatter, a warning of some sort? Straining her ears, she glanced at Mandisa, who continued her work undisturbed. Surely if there were some sort of danger, Mandisa would also be aware of it, as would the guard stationed outside the camp.

When Chioma heard nothing more and all seemed at peace around her, she shrugged and turned her attention to the empty cooking pot. Themba and the rest would be back soon, and they would not be pleased if they returned and found no food awaiting them. She had better get busy if she wanted to be sure everything was ready on time.

But even as she began her preparations, the vague sense that something wasn't quite right gnawed at her gut and flitted around the edges of her thoughts.

❖❖❖

"When do you plan to make your trip to visit your missionary friends?" Anana asked, as the two sisters strolled the expansive veld in front of the Vorster home. The morning sun was still a welcome warmth, though they planned to complete their walk and return to the veranda for cool drinks before the golden orb made its way much farther into the sky overhead.

"I'd like to go soon," Emma answered. "Friday, perhaps. I want to spend a few days with them, but I also want to return in time for us to have another week together before I go home."

Anana fell silent, her head bowed and her eyes focused on her feet as she walked. She didn't want to think about her sister returning to the States, though she knew she had to do so. After all, Emma's life was in America now. But it would be so difficult when she left! If only she didn't have to take time from the precious days that remained to deliver the Bibles.

"Can you...have someone else deliver the Bibles to the missionaries?" she asked, sneaking a peek at Emma to see her reaction. "We could have one of our people take them..."

Emma stopped. Anana did the same, and they faced one another. "In many ways I wish I could," Emma said, her voice soft. "I don't want to miss any of our time together any more than you do, but..." She paused, smiling before she continued. "But I promised—Jeannie that I would come for a visit, Mariana that I would bring back pictures, and Jeannie's mother that I would check to be sure they're well. I must keep my promises."

Anana dropped her eyes, feeling the tears come. "I know." She took Emma's hands in her own. "It's one of the reasons I love you so dearly. I just...wish I could go with you."

Emma squeezed her hands before loosing them. "You know Pieter would never allow it. He's very protective of you—as he should be. If he feels there's any danger at all, he'd never let you go."

Anana knew Emma was right, but her heart squeezed with fear, and she felt her brow draw together in a frown. "Then you mustn't go, either. Emma, how could I bear it if anything happened to you?"

Emma smiled again. "The danger is too small for concern. I only mention it because I know how Pieter feels. My goodness,

Anana, all I'll be doing is riding out there in the company of one of your drivers, where I'll deliver a box of Bibles and visit with friends for a few days before returning when your driver comes to pick me up. What could possibly happen in such a simple arrangement?"

Anana did her best to return Emma's smile, but for a moment she felt a bit like Pieter, insisting that a loved one not be allowed to expose herself to any danger at all, regardless of how slim the possibility. Then she reminded herself that God could protect Emma, regardless of where she went or what she was doing—and particularly when it involved delivering Bibles to missionaries who worked with little children.

With that thought in mind, Anana turned to resume her walk, determined to leave her sister and her trip to deliver Bibles in the capable hands of a loving God.

Emma quickly fell in step beside her, as the two sisters crossed the veld toward the house.

❖❖❖

By the time Themba and the others returned, Chioma had their meal ready and waiting for them. When she heard them coming, she was surprised to realize how relieved she was that her husband had returned safely. But when she saw his face, she knew he hadn't survived the day without paying a price.

Sweat beaded his forehead, and though he walked tall and straight, she sensed there was pain in each step. When their eyes met, her instinct was to run to him and help him to the lean-to, where she would feed him and wipe him down with a cool cloth. But she had learned her lesson, and instead dropped her eyes and immediately scooped his meal into a bowl, holding it out to him as he stepped up beside her. He took it with a grunt, and then turned toward the lean-to. Without hesitation, Chioma followed him, concerned that he had not stopped to eat with the other men.

Silently she joined him on the mat that covered the dirt floor of what served as their home. When he finished eating, he handed her the bowl and said, "I'm tired. Get me some water, and then come and lie beside me so I can rest."

Obediently Chioma retrieved the water, and by the time she returned to the lean-to, Themba was lying on his back. When he saw her, he lifted his head just enough for her to hold the cup to his lips so he could drink.

"Would you like more?"

"No," he said, once again resting his head on the mat. "Just you. Here, beside me."

She set the cup down and stretched out next to him, careful to avoid his still-healing injury as she laid her head on his chest and he pulled her close. His heart sounded strong and regular, and she relaxed a little, but his breathing was labored, and she knew he had pushed himself throughout the long day.

"Do you need anything else, my husband?" she ventured, wanting to check his wound but knowing she couldn't unless he first asked her to do so.

"Just quiet."

She pressed her lips together and lay very still. Though she hadn't yet had time to eat her own meal, she would skip it tonight and think only of her husband's welfare. It was the least she could do as wife of the group's leader. She only wished she had been able to tell him of the noise she thought she heard, and of the strange feeling that followed—a feeling that someone was watching her, and the entire compound...someone who did not wish them well. But her husband had requested quiet, and she would grant it.

Her nerves and senses on high alert, she listened, even as she silently melted back into the trees, hiding herself from view.

Chapter 18

PAUL AND JEANNIE MCDERMOTT WERE MARRIED IN December of 1988, and by January of 1989 they had come to South Africa and set up housekeeping in the two-room block building that would be their home for the next year. Even as Jeannie had unpacked their few belongings and rejoiced that God had at last given her the desire of her heart to serve on the mission field, she also looked forward to the visit they would have from Emma Rhoades, Jeannie's longtime Sunday school teacher and her best friend's mother.

Now, settled into her new life in this strange but beautiful foreign country, she smiled at the realization that Emma would be coming in a few days to deliver the box of Bibles that had been too cumbersome for the young newlyweds to include in their own luggage. How lovely it would be to spend time with Mariana's mother in this breathtakingly lovely land of South Africa!

Jeannie hummed as she swept the floor and prepared to teach her morning class of twelve children, all under the age of ten. She so enjoyed having the little ones here, interacting with them and watching the light shine in their eyes when they correctly answered a question or did well on a quiz. Their sweetness and naïveté, combined with their eagerness to learn, had quickly endeared them to her heart. It was as if they were her own children, and she cheered each one accordingly.

She was sad, though, that she and Paul had only been given clearance to teach those under ten. She couldn't imagine that children so young were ready to trade in the furthering of their educations in favor of becoming breadwinners for their struggling families. And yet, she knew, the children who came to their missionary school were the fortunate ones, as there were so many others who didn't have such an opportunity, even in their earliest years.

Jeannie laid her hand on her stomach. There was no bulge and she hadn't yet seen a doctor to confirm her suspicions, but the child was there; she was sure of it. Her baby, and Paul's, conceived in love, was growing inside her. Tears stung her eyelids as she thought of the joy this child would bring, even as she considered the concern it would evoke from her own mother to think that her first grandchild would be born so far from home. Jeannie smiled then, as she realized that as soon as the news was formally announced, her mother would immediately begin making plans to travel to South Africa to be with her daughter when the baby was born.

Oh, Paul, please be happy about it, she prayed silently, knowing her husband would also be concerned when he realized they would be having a baby so far from home. But babies had been born far away from home for years, Jeannie reasoned. Even Jesus had made His entrance into this world in a town far from the village of Nazareth where Joseph and Mary lived, so the little one whose life Jeannie was certain had already begun inside her would be in very good company, indeed.

With that assurance, she went back to work, singing a song of praise from her heart.

❖❖❖

Pieter awoke in the dark, long before he needed to arise but as he often did in the early morning hours—especially since Andrew died.

He had done the same thing for months after Gertie died as well. Unlike Anana, who seemed unable to fall asleep quickly, he often dropped right off, only to awaken during the night and then lie there, staring at the ceiling and wondering how the God of his fathers had so failed them.

This early morning, however, easily more than an hour before the sun would begin to peek over the horizon, Pieter listened to his wife's steady breathing and thanked God she was sleeping peacefully. Though he still wrestled with so many questions and doubts regarding his faith and the religion he had been raised on, he did find himself appreciating the little things, now that he had lost so many of the more important ones.

First Gertie, now Andrew. How is it possible? And yet my dear wife continues to sleep beside me. For that I'm grateful, though I worry about her more than she can imagine. Another loss could finish her. If only I could find a way to convince Emma not to go on that trek to deliver the Bibles, to stay here with Anana instead. I've heard rumors of attacks, even on missionary compounds. If anything were to happen while Emma was there...

Anana stirred beside him, interrupting his fears, and despite his resolve to let her sleep, he moved toward her and gathered her into his arms. Murmuring his name, she snuggled close, laying her head on his chest as the scent of her hair brought tears to his eyes. Did this woman have any idea how very much he cherished her, how much he wanted to protect her and keep her from harm and pain? He had wanted to do that for her since the day she agreed to become his wife, but he had failed miserably. Though he had given her two children, he hadn't been able to keep either of them alive. Now all the grieving parents had left was one another.

Dear God, please don't take her from me, as You've done with our children. Please, if You can hear me, I beg You, don't take her from me...or me from her.

❖❖❖

Themba looked better this morning—stronger and healthier. The sleep had done him good, and Chioma noted that he sat with the other men and ate his morning meal without hesitation—another good sign.

Alert to his every movement, Chioma watched...and waited. Would he suggest she accompany them this day, or would she once again be left behind to tend the camp with Mandisa and Sipho?

Themba, standing now and surrounded by a group of men, turned to her and jerked his head toward the lean-to. She knew what he meant, and quickly retrieved his assault rifle and brought it to him, her heart racing with anticipation.

Before either of them had spoken to one another, Themba was gone. Without a word of explanation or good-bye, he had snatched the weapon from her outstretched hand, slung it over his shoulder, and grunted an order. The next thing Chioma knew, with the exception of the one sentry she knew Themba had left on guard, she and Mandisa and the baby were alone in the camp once again, staring at the place where the others had disappeared into the bush. Though Mandisa immediately began to hum as she prepared to tackle her day's duties, Chioma felt her heavy heart collapse at her feet. Would she ever be included with the others, or was she destined to remain in camp to cook and clean...and wait? Didn't Themba realize how much she longed to join them? Or perhaps he did realize, but he simply didn't care.

Dejected, she sighed and turned to join her friend in the many tasks that lay before them. It would be a long day, and a disappointing one—though in the back of her mind was the thought that perhaps her husband had left her behind because he truly did care and wanted to protect her.

❖❖❖

The midafternoon sun burned hot overhead, as Chioma took a rare respite from her work. Mandisa was at the creek, cooling Sipho with the refreshing water, while Chioma opted for the semi-privacy of the small clearing in the trees just outside the camp, where she still liked to steal away to be alone with her holy book.

Checking first for stickers and thorns, Chioma leaned her back against a tree and relaxed in the coolness of its shade. Dappled light shone through the leaves overhead onto the book that now lay open in her lap. She had given up reading where she had started, as she found it too confusing. Now she turned randomly to a page that read at the top "1 John." Scanning the page she saw the word *love* repeated often, and she wondered that a holy book would speak so much about such a human emotion. One verse in particular caught her eye: *If anyone acknowledges that Jesus is the Son of God, God lives in him and he in God.*

Jesus. She had heard the name often during *Dominee* Vorster's sermons, and she knew the whites believed this Jesus was God's Son. But how was that so? If Jesus was God's Son, who then, was His mother? Chioma had also heard of a woman named Mary, who was referred to as the mother of Jesus, but how could that be possible, since this Mary was supposed to be a virgin? Chioma might be only sixteen, but she was a woman now, and a wife besides. She knew enough to understand that a virgin could certainly not be a mother—unless, of course, she was a mother like Mandisa to Sipho. Yes, she supposed that could be the case with this Jesus and the woman named Mary.

She looked again at the curious verse. How could this holy book say that the white man's God lived inside people who believed that Jesus was God's Son? If the white man believed in only one God, He would have to be a very large God. How then could He fit inside a person, and how could He do so inside many people all at one time?

Chioma sighed and laid the book in her lap. If only this holy book wouldn't call to her, she would throw it into the creek and never worry about it again. After all, it made no sense, and it certainly didn't teach her anything that applied to her life. So why bother?

She had asked herself that question many times, but each time she came back to the conclusion that it truly must be a holy book or it wouldn't have the power to communicate with her heart. For that reason alone, she would restrain herself from throwing the book into the water—that and the fact that Themba had given it to her and might not take kindly to her tossing it away.

Tucking it back into her pocket, Chioma pulled herself to her feet, thinking she would walk to the creek to check on Mandisa and the baby. Before she could take a step, she felt it—that same sensation she had experienced the day before, that knowing that something wasn't right, that evil had invaded their territory.

Her nerves and senses on high alert, she listened, even as she silently melted back into the trees, hiding herself from view.

What was it? *Who* was it? What did they want? And where was the lone sentry Themba had left to guard the camp?

Then Mandisa screamed, and Chioma knew at least *where* the problem was, even if she didn't know who or what it might be. Realizing she couldn't count on any help from the guard, who undoubtedly had already met with his demise, Chioma made her decision. As she moved stealthily toward the lean-to, she made a quick visual sweep of the camp before stepping into view long enough to sneak into the lean-to and grab the rifle Themba always kept loaded and ready at his bedside. Chioma hadn't fired a gun in several years, not since her father had taught her when she was still quite young, but she was confident she could aim and fire at any danger that confronted her — or Mandisa and the baby.

Ignoring the shaking inside her, Chioma moved quickly but carefully through the shadows at the outskirts of the camp, avoiding the open areas but hurrying as quickly as possible toward the sound of Mandisa's cries, which had now been joined by the baby's, who no doubt sensed his mother's distress.

Reaching the edge of the tree line just before it broke into the open bank beside the creek, Chioma halted, her weapon held tightly in her right hand. There were three of them, their broad backs to her, facing Mandisa, who clutched the baby to her chest. It was obvious they had come upon her as she was not only bathing Sipho, but herself as well. The mother and child's nakedness only added to their vulnerability, as the men taunted Mandisa, casting lewd suggestions and even vicious threats her way.

As Chioma watched and Mandisa pleaded for her life and the child's, the men began to close in, laughing at their prey's fear. Chioma noted that only one appeared to be carrying an assault rifle, though she imagined the others also had weapons of some sort. She could easily shoot one and possibly two of these vultures before they reached her friend, but certainly not all three. For the first time, though it would have been unfamiliar and cumbersome, she wished Themba had left an automatic weapon instead of this older firearm. But at least she was somewhat familiar with the type of weapon she held in her hand, so maybe it was for the best after all. She would just have to go for the one with the AK-47 first, and then take her chances with the other two.

Stepping forward even as she cocked the rifle, she took aim before the men could respond to the sound and turn on her. Remembering her father's caution to prepare for the rifle's kick, she stood her ground, and her shot was straight and true. The man with the firearm dropped to the ground, even as the other two looked on in obvious astonishment. The element of surprise had served her well, but she would have to move quickly if she was going to take out the other two before they gathered their senses and ganged up on her.

Ignoring the ringing in her ears from the first shot, she now had the second man in her sights when she recognized him and realized who they were. These men had lived in the camp with them, fought at Themba's side, eaten from their communal cooking pot—and then sided with Abrafo when he fought their leader. They were three of the men who had disappeared when Themba killed Abrafo, and now they had come back.

A cold snake of fear slithered up Chioma's spine as she realized there were more than these three. By her count, seven men had sneaked away that night. Where were the other four?

The brief hesitation had cost her, and the two men were now focused on bringing her down before she dealt with them as she had with their companion. Bellowing with rage, they ran toward her, as Chioma pulled the trigger just in time to topple the man closest to her. He dropped, but she doubted he would stay down, as her aim had been shaky, and she could tell he was still moving.

She couldn't waste time worrying about him, though, as the other man was now on top of her. Before Chioma could even think about using her rifle, he had knocked it from her hands and put his own hands around her throat, as they toppled together to the ground. Kicking and writhing beneath him, Chioma fought for her life, and for Mandisa and Sipho's as well, for she knew this man would kill them, too, when he finished with her. But his strength was too great. The harder she fought, the tighter his grip grew around her throat. Her vision was beginning to go black when suddenly the man jerked and his hands loosened their grasp. Chioma gasped, catching the oxygen she needed to regain her sight, just as the man rolled off her and Chioma spotted Mandisa, still naked but standing over them, with Themba's rifle clutched in her hands like a club. Her eyes were wide with fright and her lips pressed together in a thin but determined line. It was obvious she had pushed past her fear and used the dropped weapon to deal Chioma's attacker a brutal blow.

Grateful but still unable to speak, Chioma sat up, rubbing her burning throat. Sipho wailed then, as he thrashed on the ground where Mandisa had placed him near the water, and the sound brought his adoptive mother racing back to his side. Chioma reached for the rifle Mandisa had dropped in her hurry to get to the baby, but before she could get her hand on it, the second man she had shot also made a move for it. Launching herself toward the gun, Chioma reached it just ahead of him and snatched it out of his grasp, though the look in his eyes told her he was not going to quit without a fight.

Chioma jumped to her feet and stepped back, as the man on the ground snatched a knife from his boot and aimed it in her direction. There was no time to think or consider. Chioma pulled the trigger. This time she knew she had finished him, as the bullet had penetrated his forehead and the man now lay facedown, unmoving, his knife still clutched in his hand.

Turning her attention to the third man, the one who had tried to strangle her and who had been stopped by Mandisa's powerful blow to his head with the rifle butt, Chioma saw that he wasn't moving either. Was he dead? Did she dare take a chance?

Her father's words echoed in her ears, as she remembered the first day he had taught her how to hold and fire a gun. "Never assume your prey can't turn on you and finish you off. Finish him first. Take no chances, my daughter."

Glancing quickly at Mandisa, who had slipped her clothes back on and was tending to the squalling baby, Chioma thought of the other four men who had also stolen away from the camp after Themba killed Abrafo. If she was going to have to take them on as well, she certainly didn't want this one coming back to fight her at the same time.

She took aim and fired, watching the body jerk and then settle back into quiet stillness. Her bullet had found its mark, and for now they were safe.

There had been too many rumors lately of uprisings and raids, of kidnappings and rapes and murders.

Chapter 19

EMMA HAD STRUGGLED WITH SAYING GOOD-BYE TO Anana, even for a few days, but she also looked forward to her visit with her daughter's friend and her new husband. Emma had attended Paul and Jeannie's wedding before they left for their one-year term in South Africa, and she had promised Jeannie's mother to send pictures. With her camera safely packed away in the one suitcase she had brought with her from Pieter and Anana's, along with the box of Bibles and study materials she was scheduled to deliver, she was on her way at last.

As the car proceeded toward its destination, Emma noticed the roads had become almost corrugated, more often made of sand than tar. She smiled, proud of the dedication of the newly married couple who had come to serve in this lovely area of the world, despite its turmoil and unrest—or perhaps because of it. She wondered if she would have had the same courage or dedication to make such a commitment when she was young and newly married. Many had commented on her courage to leave her homeland behind and move to America with her new husband, but that was entirely different. Yes, she'd had to deal with cultural changes, but she had been comfortable and, for the most part, safe. Besides, the move had been necessary in order to be with the man she loved. Jeannie and her husband had made this commitment out of love for God and for those who needed to learn about His great love for them. It was a noble sacrifice, indeed.

The driver slowed, and Emma was certain she heard him utter a curse under his breath before getting out of the car to move yet another rock from the roadway. This trip certainly wasn't anything like driving the crowded freeways of Southern California, but it seemed they were making nearly the same amount of progress as during rush hour in Los Angeles.

Rush hour. She smiled again. Nothing much rushed in LA during those heaviest of traffic times, except perhaps one's thoughts while sitting in a barely moving car. And yet, in its own way, Southern California—and America in general—had become dear to her after so many years. After all, she had raised her daughter there. She had friends there, and her church, and...

Her eyes teared, as she thought of the cemetery where John was buried and where she often went to pour out her lonely and aching heart. How she wished he were here with her now, to experience what would surely be a blessed visit with this young couple whose life together had just begun and who had such a promising future ahead of them!

She retrieved a tissue from her purse and dabbed at her eyes as the driver resumed his position in the front seat. Emma sighed. She would simply have to learn how to live on this earth without her beloved partner until she could join him in eternity. There were times she wished it wouldn't be long.

❖❖❖

Pieter was anxious, knowing how much work he wasn't getting done but determined to spend the day with Anana, helping her not dwell on Emma's temporary departure. He knew how concerned Anana was for Emma's safety, and though he had repeated his assurances that Emma would be fine, he himself had doubts. There had been too many rumors lately of uprisings and raids, of kidnappings and rapes and murders, extending on occasion even into their own relatively safe and quiet area. Going farther into the bush, as Emma was doing, only compounded her exposure to danger.

Pieter knew Anana was praying for her sister; the two women had, in fact, prayed together before Emma left. Pieter often wished his own faith were as strong and personal as Anana's and Emma's. He was a *dominee* who preached the gospel, yet he often questioned the very words he spoke. He knew Andrew had questioned those words as well, but he had seemed at peace as he lay dying on the ground near the creek on the family farm. Had his son discovered something in his last days or hours of life that Pieter had never experienced, some personal assurance or peace that Pieter longed for but despaired of finding?

He hoped so. Pieter thought losing a child would almost be bearable if he knew they would one day meet again, that their final farewell on earth was not so final. He knew what the Bible said, of course, but how could he be certain it was true?

He sighed. Maybe a walk across the veld and a picnic beneath the trees would be good for both Anana and himself. He went to the kitchen to instruct the maid to pack a lunch.

❖❖❖

By the time Themba and the others returned to camp, Chioma had the evening meal waiting for them, and she was relieved they didn't appear to have noticed the absence of the guard, whose body now lay in a heap with the three men she had killed. Then Themba went inside his lean-to and, when he came out, headed straight for Chioma, who stood at the cooking fire, pretending she didn't know that he approached.

"My gun has been fired," he announced. "And the sentry was not at his post."

She swallowed, wincing at the searing pain in her throat as she tried to calm her breathing and wondered how her husband would react when she told him of all that had transpired in his absence. Surely he wouldn't be angry with her! She had only defended herself and Mandisa and the baby. She had done what she had to do...hadn't she? But if she had done nothing wrong, why was she shaking so inside?

"I...had to shoot the men who came," she managed to say, though her voice was raspy from her near-strangling, and she still refused to raise her eyes to his. "Down by the water."

For a moment Themba didn't react. Then, turning on his heel, he ordered, "Follow me," and strode purposefully toward the creek. When she caught up with him, he was stopped at the edge of the trees, gazing down wide-eyed and slack-jawed at the four lifeless bodies stacked beside one another just inches from where he stood.

Chioma wanted to explain, but sensed it would be best to wait until he asked. At last he did.

"You did this? Alone?"

Chioma nodded, then realized he was still staring at the bodies and couldn't see her. She also noticed for the first time that she and Mandisa had placed the bodies next to a clump of wild King Proteas. The thought struck her that they were a protected flower, and she wondered why that would occur to her at that particular moment.

"Yes," she answered, her voice strained as she struggled to explain her actions. "I killed them, but Mandisa helped. She knocked one unconscious and then aided me in dragging the bodies into this one spot so they wouldn't be so noticeable."

For another moment Themba stood, silent and unmoving, and then he turned to her. "Look at me," he commanded.

Reluctantly she raised her head, trying to read the meaning behind the sharp glint in his dark eyes. Had she done something wrong, broken some protocol or tradition? Should she have allowed the intruders to harm or even kill Mandisa and the baby rather than take Themba's rifle without permission?

And then his laughter broke the silence, startling her to the point that she nearly fell backward. Stunned, she regained her balance and watched in amazement as Themba continued to laugh and then reached out and drew her to himself. "So, it seems you have become a fearless comrade as well as my wife—something those poor, unfortunate fools hadn't counted on when they came into my camp to make trouble."

Still holding her to his chest, where the feel of his newly healing wound pressed against her cheek, he turned his head and spat on the bodies that lay at their feet. "They deserved to die at the hands of a woman," he snarled. "They were cowards, and now their miserable lives are over." He held her away from him and looked down into her face. This time she didn't avoid his gaze.

"You've done well, my wife. You killed those who deserved to die. Now we must think of the four who didn't come with them."

She swallowed, though with difficulty. She had done little but think of those four men since killing these three, wondering if and when the others would appear and what would happen when they did. Would they find her and Mandisa alone again? Could she successfully defend the camp a second time?

Themba afforded her a rare smile. "Don't worry, beautiful woman. We won't wait for them to return. We'll break camp in the morning. It's time to move on. We've been here too long as it is."

He rubbed his rough hand against her cheek, his expression serious once again. "I told you I'd protect you, and I will. You're my wife, and you belong to me. So long as I have breath, I will not allow anyone to hurt you. Come, we'll tell the others so they can prepare to leave at sunup."

Relieved at Themba's positive reaction and promising words, Chioma followed him gratefully. After a few steps, he stopped and turned back to her. "You have proven yourself, Chioma. Once we've set up camp in a new location, you'll join me and the others when we go out to fight. Someone else will stay behind with Mandisa and the little one." He nodded, apparently satisfied that she understood. "You've earned the right."

And then his broad back was to her again, as she scurried to keep up.

The words were like a knife to her heart, sharp and searing, flooding her eyes with molten tears.

Chapter 20

EMMA WAS STUNNED AT THE SIMPLE CONDITIONS OF Jeannie and Paul's two-room home, and humbled when they insisted on sleeping on the floor in the room that served as their kitchen/living area so she could have their bed in the privacy of the tiny bedroom.

"I don't need the bed," Emma had argued. "I'll be perfectly fine using a mat on the floor in the main room."

"You're our guest," Paul had repeated. "You're also our elder, and we respect your position. In this country, we might even call you our *tannie*."

Emma laughed, even as her heart squeezed at being referred to as "auntie." Still, she certainly couldn't deny she had more than twenty years on the young couple, and she appreciated their deference to her seniority. It was a point of respect that had no doubt been taught them by their parents, but which also was commonly practiced in the South African culture. And so Emma had yielded to her hosts' good manners and the local custom.

Now, on her first night at the missionary outpost, Emma lay in the small but immaculately clean room that would otherwise be occupied by the young missionary couple, trying to read by the dim light beside the bed. Anana had insisted Emma bring the journal with her so she could finish reading it while she was gone, and then the two of them could discuss it when she returned. Opening to the page that was marked by a ragged piece of white paper, Emma began to read.

I have tryed to beleve in this white man's god, this Jesus, and I mite exept for apartheid. How am I to beleve a messege of love when it is preched by a messenger of hate? Perhaps this Jesus was a kind man as they say, but his folowers are not so. If they were I coud not justify killing them so easly.

The words were like a knife to her heart, sharp and searing, flooding her eyes with molten tears. What had Anana thought when she read these words? And what would Pieter say if he knew his wife was reading and even contemplating what the adherents of apartheid would consider a blasphemous opinion?

Anana was right to be concerned, Emma decided. These words, this sort of thinking, could surely cause trouble between a husband and wife if they didn't see them in the same light. But what was the alternative? Could they continue to ignore this author's legacy and that of so many like him? Didn't they somewhere, some time, have to stop and examine all aspects of the truth before declaring which was the correct path on which they should continue to walk?

She closed the book and laid it gently on the crude table beside the bare-bulbed lamp. She was seldom able to read much from the journal without stopping to think...and pray. Tonight was no exception. As she turned off the light and lay back against the rough, muslin pillowcase, she turned her thoughts to the One who held her in His hand—and the entire world as well. The thought of how big His hand was and how safe she was resting in it brought a smile to her lips. Whatever He had in store for her, she could relax, knowing it was exactly as it should be.

❖❖❖

Anana couldn't sleep. She had tried for hours, but the fear wouldn't turn her loose.

It was ridiculous, she knew. There was no logical reason to believe her sister wouldn't return in a few days, as planned. No doubt her unreasonable concerns were due to the many losses they had experienced in their family through the years. But whatever the reasons, the fear of losing yet another loved one gripped her heart with icy talons, bent on crushing what little life and hope was left inside her.

Pieter also seemed restless, and though he had said nothing since bidding her good night, she doubted he was asleep. Was he, too, concerned about Emma, or was he simply missing Andrew, as they both did, day after day, with little respite?

She turned on her side toward him and reached out her arm to gently touch his shoulder, not wanting to wake him if he truly was sleeping. He responded immediately, rolling toward her and pulling her to his chest.

"Forgive me if I'm keeping you awake," he said.

She shook her head, her voice muffled against him as she spoke. "You're not. I can't sleep, either."

Pieter pushed her back slightly, and she sensed he was looking down at her. "Emma?"

She nodded. "I keep telling myself she's fine, that she'll be back in a few days, but..."

Pieter hesitated before answering. "But you're not convinced," he said at last, pulling her back against him. He sighed before continuing. "I wish I could tell you there's no chance of danger, but you know better. However, it's minimal, and I can't imagine anything will happen to her while she's there at the missionary post with her friends. In just a few short days, our driver will go back to fetch her."

He bent his head and kissed the top of her hair. "You'll see, my dear. Emma will be back safe and sound before you know it."

Anana's heart squeezed with gratitude, but also with doubt. She wanted so desperately to believe her beloved husband, but something told her his words, though well intentioned, wouldn't prove to be true.

❖❖❖

The day was nearly gone before Themba found a spot that satisfied him. "We'll set up camp here," he announced, and Chioma felt the warmth of relief wash over her. They had come across several places that seemed qualified and safe, as far as she was concerned, but always Themba ignored them and pushed on. Chioma wasn't sure why this place was different from the others, but she was pleased they had finally found it.

With little direction, everyone went to work, setting up lean-tos, building a fire pit, stashing weapons and ammunition, and establishing sentry posts. Chioma doubted Themba would ever again leave just one guard on duty, and for that she was grateful. Even if she was now to join the warriors when they left the camp during the day, she shuddered to think of Mandisa and the baby being left behind without adequate protection.

She was still stunned at the way things had transpired the previous day. The fact that she and Mandisa and Sipho had survived unscathed, when a fierce and fearless comrade had been killed while keeping watch, seemed almost too strange to be true. And yet it was. Perhaps the gods had a purpose for her after all, she thought—and for Mandisa and Sipho as well.

Chioma smiled. She had been pleasantly surprised at the outpouring of gratitude she had received from the others in the camp when they learned what she had done. It wasn't so much her bravery they applauded, as life-and-death struggles were an everyday part of their tenuous existence, but the fact that little Sipho had been protected seemed to bring great joy to his communal family. Chioma had come to learn that though the members of this group didn't hesitate to take a life in the name of the cause for which they fought, these same members placed great value on the life of one little child.

A ripple of excitement rolled through her stomach then, as her thoughts moved from the previous day to the next one. Themba had told her she would accompany him and the others when they went out in the morning. As much as she had anticipated this great day, she also feared it, for she didn't really know what it was these brave warriors did when they were gone from the camp. She knew they often came back with blood on their clothing and booty to share with the others. She also knew they were often wounded, and one time two of their people didn't return with the others. But nothing was said of what happened to them, or what they had done to make such a thing take place.

With all those thoughts dancing through her mind as she worked, Chioma wondered what would be required of her when she armed herself and went out to fight. It was what she wanted, what she had dreamed of for a very long time—and yet, she hesitated at the implications. It was one thing to speak of revenge, quite another to carry it out. Would she prove herself worthy of being Themba's wife, or would she put him to shame in front of the others?

She shook her head. No, she couldn't think that way. Failure wasn't an option. She wasn't a coward, after all. Hadn't she already nearly single-handedly taken on three violent men, all stronger and more experienced in warfare than she? And hadn't she prevailed?

Yes, of course she had. And she would prevail yet again. She wouldn't shrink from her responsibility to avenge her ancestors and to show the others she was no coward, that Themba's wife could be trusted in battle.

She lifted her head and found herself looking straight at Themba, who stood across the camp, watching her. When he caught her gaze, he nodded, and his gesture of approval brought a fresh surge of courage to her heart. She would do well tomorrow, and her husband would be proud of her.

For now she would finish her work and fetch him something to eat. She might be on the verge of becoming a true comrade, but Themba would want her to remember that her primary responsibility was to serve as his wife.

❖❖❖

Her first full day at the missionary post had been a pleasant one, as Emma had spent most of the day in the one-room classroom with its twelve young students. When the school day ended that Friday afternoon, she was saddened to discover the children wouldn't return to school for several days, long after she was scheduled to leave the missionary compound. She realized now she should have arranged her visit to be able to spend more time with the children.

But even as she accepted that she wouldn't be able to do so, many of the parents began arriving to collect their offspring. How Emma rejoiced to see the excitement on these parents' faces when they realized that one child per family had been given a Bible to take home. For a single household to have its own copy of the Scriptures was quite a rare privilege, and obviously not one these families took lightly. When Jeannie and Paul explained to the children's parents that Emma was the one who had brought the precious books all the way from America, they thanked her profusely, until Emma became embarrassed at all the attention.

But what a joy it was to watch the families leave the post, carrying their treasured possession with such honor and respect. Emma knew she would never again treat her own copy of the Scriptures with such little regard. She knew, too, she would never forget the humility and gratitude she had experienced that day, nor would she regret having made the trip to this tiny spot on the globe. For whatever purpose God had brought her there and regardless of what happened before she left, the eye-opening, heart-bursting joy she felt at this moment made it all worthwhile.

But a sensation in Chioma's stomach, like the fluttering of paper-thin moths' wings, told her that much had changed.

Chapter 21

AS FRIDAY NIGHT SUCCUMBED TO THE EARLY HOURS OF Saturday, Anana was restless. It was more than her usual sleeplessness when she fought tears and reminisced about her children; it had to do with Emma, and her sense of unease grew as the night progressed.

Oh, Father, she prayed silently, determined not to wake Pieter, who slept peacefully beside her, *am I worrying about nothing? I do that at times, I know, but—*

She sighed, interrupting her own thought. The clock on the bedside stand showed two A.M. It was useless. She might as well get up and fix a warm drink. Perhaps that would help her get to sleep.

Slipping noiselessly from the bed, she slid her feet into her slippers and donned a light robe. Carefully she made her way to the door and was soon safely in the hallway, padding along toward the kitchen. She and Pieter always left a few small lights on throughout the house during the night, so she didn't bother to turn on more until she got to her destination.

Once there, she stood at the sink, waiting for her milk to heat and gazing out into the darkness beyond. If only there were a phone at the missionary post! But, of course, there wasn't. The dear young couple who was now serving there had to depend on a very slow mail delivery service, so there was no point in Anana's trying to get a message to her sister, who no doubt would be back from her journey before the message arrived. Anana would simply have to wait—and trust God.

"Keep her safe, Father," she whispered. "Please! I couldn't bear to lose my sister, too."

But the sound of the ticking kitchen clock was all she heard in the otherwise silent house.

❖❖❖

Chioma decided there were advantages to living as they did, simply and without any comforts beyond the bare necessities of life. Moving one's residence was as easy as packing up a few belongings and then unpacking them again upon arriving at the chosen destination. As she lay beside Themba in the darkness of their lean-to, it was as if they had never left their previous location. The sounds and smells of nighttime in the bush were almost exactly the same as they had been twenty-four hours earlier, and several miles away.

But a sensation in Chioma's stomach, like the fluttering of paper-thin moths' wings, told her that much had changed. Her husband now approved of her and had given her permission to fight alongside the others. Was it excitement or fear that caused the turmoil inside her? Both, she imagined. It was natural to be excited—and prudent to be fearful. Chioma could only guess at what went on during the times that Themba and the others left the camp. She had overheard comments and conversations, yes, but that was not the same as being there. Even Mbhali told her little of their experiences except to assure Chioma that she would find out soon enough.

What exactly did that mean? Chioma wondered, even as she considered the words her friend did not say equally with those she did. Was she about to embark on a journey that would take her even further from her previous existence than when she became Themba's wife?

A shiver passed over her, and she found herself wishing she could sneak away to read from the holy book that lay in the pocket of her clothes beside the sleeping mat. But there was no moon tonight, so reading would be difficult. Besides, Themba had made it clear he expected her to remain by his side throughout the night. Her reading would just have to wait.

She sighed and rolled away from her sleeping husband, pressing her eyelids together and wishing she could will herself to sleep. Chioma was determined to be alert and ready when daybreak arrived, but for now sleep continued to elude her.

❖❖❖

It would be at least a couple more hours before the first silver tinge of light broke on the horizon, signaling the beginning of another day. Sitting at the kitchen table, the milk in her half-empty cup now cold, Anana wished she knew what the day would bring. Then again, perhaps she didn't.

She closed her eyes, envisioning the car as it pulled away with Emma in the backseat and her precious cargo of Bibles in the trunk. "I'll be back in a few days," Emma had called through the open window, "and we'll have *boerekoffie* and a *lekker kuier* together."

Now, in the very early hours of Saturday morning, Anana prayed it would be so. Though she did her best to leave her sister in God's capable hands, she knew she wouldn't rest until Emma was safely home, sitting beside her and regaling her with stories of a brave and selfless young couple, serving God at a lonely missionary outpost, far from their own home and loved ones.

Forgive me, Father. I know I should be more trusting. And yet... Oh, please, God, don't tear out another piece of my heart, as I have so little left to spare...

❖❖❖

Pieter couldn't be sure whether it was the emptiness within him or the emptiness of Anana's side of the bed that woke him, but suddenly he was alert, staring into the darkness and wondering what had kept his wife from sleep this night. Always, he knew, she grieved for their children, but now her worries for Emma seemed to be consuming her, overshadowing all else. Pieter wanted to protect Anana, to reassure her that no more pain or loss would come to her, but he couldn't. He hadn't been able to prevent it before, and he certainly couldn't do so now.

Why, God? Why, if You're truly the great and mighty Lord of the universe as the Scriptures say You are, if You're everywhere and can do anything, and if You love us as You claim to... then why? Why do my children lie dead and buried in the ground? Why does my wife grieve and long to hold her babies just once more? I couldn't protect them or save them, but You could have. Why didn't You, God? Why?

His heart constricted as the words from a familiar Scripture passed through his memory: *For God so loved the world that he gave his one and only Son....*

World. Why did that word stand out from all the others? World. Everyone in it? Equally? If God was indeed trying to speak to him, what was the message He wanted Pieter to understand?

Frustrated, he threw back the blanket and sat up, hanging his legs over the side of the bed and slipping his feet into the familiar, worn slippers. Enough of this prayer and philosophical reasoning for one night. He had a wife who needed him, and he would go to her, convince her to come back to bed with him and rest before the morning dawned upon them and another day began. Yes, that was the right thing to do, the common-sense thing. Prayer and Bible verses were best left to weekly services. The rest of life needed tending to, and he had never been a shirker, nor would he be one now.

Throwing a robe over his shoulders, he headed for the door, determined to comfort his wife and reassure her that all would be well.

❖❖❖

"Get up."

Chioma stirred. Where had the words come from? Themba. Yes. Her husband. She opened her eyes and slowly discerned his outline in the darkened lean-to, as he stood above her, already dressed and preparing to leave as he slung his battered AK-47 over his shoulder.

"Get up," he repeated. "We must go before daylight."

Chioma forced herself to a standing position and commanded her senses to arise as well. How long had she slept? An hour? Two, perhaps? Since the first hints of dawn hadn't yet lightened her surroundings, she knew it couldn't have been much more.

And yet, strangely, now that her mind was beginning to focus, she didn't feel tired at all. Today was the day she was to become a comrade-in-arms, a fighter for the cause that had claimed the lives of her family, her ancestors—and, indirectly, others she loved as well.

Themba thrust an object at her, and when she took it from him, she realized it was the rifle she had used to kill the three intruders. Its stock felt cold and hard in her hand, and she wondered if she would once again be required to use it to end someone's life.

"Don't waste your time thinking or wondering," Themba cautioned. "Just do what you must. It's you or them; remember that."

Had he read her mind? Did he already know her so well? Or was he simply relaying the words he knew from his own experience that she needed to hear? Whatever the reason, she was grateful for the advice and imagined she would need to fall back on it before the day was over.

Themba stepped outside, and Chioma followed, surprised that nearly everyone in the camp stood ready and waiting. Where were they going? What did Themba have planned for them—and for those they would meet before the sun went down again? Did the others already know what the day would hold? Did they care, or was she the only one with questions and concerns?

A shudder ran down her spine, and she was glad it was not yet light enough for the others to see her clearly. She took deep breaths, willing away the now-familiar sensations of fear and excitement that danced in her stomach. This is what she had wanted...wasn't it?

Themba's touch on her arm brought her back to the present. They were moving out, earlier this morning than usual. Why? What was different about this day? And how would she be changed as a result of it?

For a brief moment she envied Mandisa, staying behind with little Sipho. Chioma was certain, after the events of the previous day, that Themba had assigned at least two or more others to stay behind and guard the camp, so Chioma knew Mandisa and the baby would be all right. Still, a part of her longed to stay behind with them.

No. Her place was at her husband's side, fighting for the cause that would one day liberate her people and grant them their rightful place in the land. If it meant extracting revenge and restitution along the way, so be it. She would remember Themba's advice and focus only on what needed to be done. Then she would be successful. Her husband would be proud of her, her ancestors would be avenged, and her descendants would be assured a safe and secure homeland, where their voice would at last be heard and respected.

She struck out behind Themba, determined to keep the pace and fight honorably, whatever the day might bring.

She tried to speak, but could manage only a muffled grunt.

Chapter 22

EMMA HAD HOPED TO SLEEP IN A BIT ON SATURDAY, as she'd had a difficult time getting to sleep the night before. But it was not to be. Jarred from her sleep before dawn by a loud crash and what sounded like angry voices, she threw herself from the bed and raced to the doorway that separated her from the young couple in the main room.

Before she could grab the handle, the door burst open, nearly knocking her to the floor. Struggling to keep her balance, she felt her head jerk back painfully, as her hair was grabbed from behind, then a large, rough hand covered her mouth, stifling her scream. The scent of sweat, blood, and fear mingled to make her head swim. She struggled to breathe against the hand that held her mouth. What was happening? Who was this person who held her captive? She tried to speak, but could manage only a muffled grunt.

"Shut up," growled the man who held her, pushing her through the door and out into the main room where Paul and

Jeannie sat huddled together on the floor, leaning against the wall, as a tall, shirtless black man stood over them with an automatic rifle pointed in their direction while another black man, shorter though appearing equally as strong, busied himself wrapping cords around the captives' wrists and ankles. Blood oozed from a gash over Paul's right eye, but they appeared otherwise unharmed.

"Sit down with the others," growled the man who had briefly held Emma captive, continuing now to push her from behind. "And keep your mouth shut unless I tell you to speak. Understood?"

Emma didn't understand much of anything, but she knew enough to nod her assent and quickly join the young couple, who looked up at her fearfully. She had no sooner sunk down beside Jeannie than the man who had been tying up the couple yanked another cord from a nearby wall plug and began tightening it around Emma's wrists. Within moments all three were trussed up, sitting silent and terrified in the presence of three men and a young woman, each now brandishing weapons and very angry expressions.

How had this happened? What did they want from them? Paul and Jeannie were simply two poor missionaries, with little or no money or worldly goods. Why would anyone attack them or take them hostage? And Emma, though undoubtedly well off enough to pay a small ransom, had none of her money with her. What would be the point of killing or kidnapping them? Did their captors know the young couple and Emma were Americans and think they could somehow obtain a large sum of money from their families or even the United States government? Doubtful, Emma thought, but at this point, anything seemed possible.

She closed her eyes. She knew she should pray, but her thoughts wouldn't focus. *Father,* she cried silently. *Father! Help us!*

As if by direct instruction, Emma opened her eyes and immediately found herself captured in the glare of the dark-eyed beauty who accompanied the three men. Emma opened her mouth, though she had no idea what she would say. Before she could utter a word, a flash of compassion and doubt invaded the young woman's eyes, but it was quickly replaced by hostility, as she jerked the rifle in Emma's direction. "Keep quiet," she ordered, and then transferred her gaze to the tallest of the three men, who nodded back at her.

"Watch them," he ordered. "If they move or say a word without permission, kill them."

Turning toward the door, the man who had just pronounced their death sentence and whom Emma had begun to suspect was the leader of the group strode quickly outside, where she overheard him talking, though she could not make out his words. That meant there were more than just these four. How many? And why had they come? *Dear God*, she pleaded silently, *please don't let them hurt this precious young couple!*

She noticed then that Jeannie was crying, though it was obvious she was trying to conceal it. But Emma was leaning up against her, and the young woman's lithe body shook with silent sobs. *Mercy, Lord*, Emma prayed. *Their life together has just begun...*

Emma wanted to speak to Jeannie, to comfort or pray with her, but she had heard the man's instructions to the woman who now stood with her rifle trained on them: "If they move or say a word without permission, kill them." In the few short moments since their lives had been invaded by this incomprehensible terror, Emma had seen nothing to make her think the man had not meant what he said, or that the young woman wouldn't obey his command, despite the fact that attacks against what many blacks considered "religious people" were uncommon.

Keep us quiet and still, Lord. Give us Your wisdom and Your peace, even in the midst of this evil.

The familiar words came to her then, echoing from the deepest recesses of her heart and flowing courage through her

233

veins: *Even though I walk through the valley of the shadow of death, I will fear no evil, for you are with me; your rod and your staff, they comfort me.*

She felt herself relax. Whether God delivered them or took them home to be with Him, they wouldn't be alone. Their heavenly Father was with them, and that was enough.

❖❖❖

As Pieter sat in his office on Saturday morning, thankful that Anana was still sleeping when he got up, he considered what he would preach about that evening when he served as *dominee* to the gathering of his servants. Since Andrew's death, he had found it more and more difficult to open the Scriptures and attempt to teach them with any sense of authority. Was it simply grief over the loss of his son and the indirect involvement in that tragedy by one of his former servants that caused his unease, or was it because he questioned the very words he was called to proclaim?

Pieter stared at the open book, lying on the desk in front of him, yet nothing registered. There seemed to be no message, no meaning, no purpose in what he was preparing to do. He was well aware the servants attended only because the meetings were mandatory; given the chance, they would all choose to do something else. So why did he bother—particularly given the fact that he, too, would prefer to do something else?

Romans 10.

More clearly than any words spoken to him in his lifetime, these two reverberated in his heart. Was it a message from God, a direction for the evening's sermon?

Vaguely familiar with the passage, Pieter turned to the designated chapter and began to read. When he reached verse 12, he stopped, stunned, reading the verse over three times:

For there is no difference between Jew and Gentile—the same Lord is Lord of all and richly blesses all who call on him.

He was sure now God was, indeed, speaking to him, but he was still not clear why. He sensed the words of this verse were tied in with the words from the Gospel of John—"For God so loved the *world*"—that he had pondered the previous night. But the specific purpose continued to elude him, the depth of it dancing just around the edges of his understanding.

Going on to the next verse, he read slowly: *Everyone who calls on the name of the Lord will be saved.* It was obvious God was reinforcing His call to all people everywhere to repent and return to Him. Pieter understood that. Whatever else he might not be clear on, he knew God's call to salvation was universal, though some within the Afrikaner faith denied that, claiming blacks had no souls, a doctrine Pieter had never been able to accept. Didn't he reflect his belief in a universal call to repentance by faithfully preaching the gospel each Saturday evening to those who worked for him, despite knowing they didn't want to listen to him?

The thought struck him then that after all the years he had been delivering his weekly sermons, not one of his listeners had visibly responded. Was he that ineffectual or incompetent in his preaching? Should he stop preaching altogether? His eyes fell on the next verses, and he had his answer.

How, then, can they call on the one they have not believed in? And how can they believe in the one of whom they have not heard? And how can they hear without someone preaching to them? And how can they preach unless they are sent? As it is written, "How beautiful are the feet of those who bring good news!" But not all the Israelites accepted the good news. For Isaiah says, "Lord, who has believed our message?" Consequently, faith comes from hearing the message, and the message is heard through the word of Christ.

Pieter knew in that moment he had no choice. He must preach the gospel, whether anyone believed his words or not. And yet...

Was it possible, though his words were a message of good news, his attitude didn't reflect the same? Could it be his listeners hadn't believed the gospel because his attitude and actions toward them didn't confirm his faith? Was God trying to tell him the unthinkable—that His love for blacks and coloureds was equal to His love for whites because they were indeed...equal?

As if a crushing weight had descended upon his shoulders, he buried his face in his hands, fighting a nearly uncontrollable urge to cry. "Oh, God," he whispered, "how I have failed You! How I have failed Your people! Forgive me, God. Forgive me!"

❖❖❖

As Mariana slid into her nightgown and prepared for bed that Friday night, her mind turned to Jeannie, and she smiled. *Mom's probably there now, visiting with her and Paul*, she thought, laying her right hand on her ample stomach as her baby moved within her. *How I wish I could be there with them! What a lovely visit that would be...*

She glanced at Eric, already curled up in their king-sized bed, the blue comforter pulled up nearly to the top of his head, leaving only his short blond curls visible on the pillow. Mariana smiled again, pulling down her side of the comforter and climbing in beside him. What a wonderful father Eric would be! She hoped their son would look just like him, though she would also like to see a hint of his grandfather in the child's face.

Her heart squeezed at the thought. How she missed her father, and how much more she would miss him as she watched

her child grow up without the benefit of knowing his grandfather.

"Everything okay?"

Mariana started. She had been daydreaming again, caught
up in her thoughts about her father, her baby, her family in
general. She seemed to be doing that a lot these days.

Turning to Eric, who had lowered the edge of the comforter
and peeked out at her, she said, "Everything's fine. Sorry if I
woke you."

"I wasn't asleep. Just lying here, waiting for you."

She reached up to the lamp on the headboard and flipped
the switch, plunging the room into darkness. Then, a bit clum-
sily because of her growing bulk, she lay down beside her husband, snuggling up in the spot where she felt most safe and
secure.

"Well, here I am. You can go to sleep now."

"I'd rather talk awhile. I know you've had a lot on your mind
lately, especially with your mother at Pieter and Anana's."

"Actually, if Mom is sticking to her schedule, she's at the mis-
sionary post now, visiting with Jeannie and Paul." She sighed.
"I was just thinking how I wish we could be there with them.
Wouldn't that be wonderful? It's been years since I've been to
'sunny South Africa,' as Mom loves to call it, and even though
I wasn't born and raised there, I feel such an attachment."

"That's only natural. You've heard your mother's stories
hundreds of times over the years, and you know how much of
her heart has always remained loyal to her homeland."

"True. She must have loved Daddy very much to leave it
all behind and come and start a new life with him here, so very
far from everything she knew and loved."

Eric nuzzled her hair and whispered, "But aren't you glad
she did?"

"Yes. I can't imagine my life without you in it." She paused,
once again laying her hand on her belly. "Or without our
baby."

Eric's hand joined hers as it rested on her abdomen. When the little one responded with a kick, they laughed. "Sorry about that," Eric said, withdrawing his hand. "Too much weight all at once, I suppose."

"Could very well be," Mariana conceded. "Whatever the reason, this little one has a mind of his own, that's for sure."

"Like his mom. Your dad always said you were that way, even when you were a baby."

Mariana hesitated before speaking again. "Do you think I'll ever get over missing him?"

"I don't know. I doubt it. But I'm sure it won't always hurt as bad."

"I hope you're right." She sighed, her mind once again drifting to South Africa. It was Saturday morning in that far-away land, and as Mariana tried to picture her mother at a small, remote, and undoubtedly primitive missionary post, a twinge of fear passed through her. "Honey, could we pray for Mom? I don't know why, but... I'd just feel better if we did."

Eric's hold on her tightened. "Of course we can. Maybe that's exactly what God wants us to do at this very moment. No one can ever have too much prayer."

❖❖❖

The lingering pain in Chioma's throat since the assault a couple of days earlier was finally beginning to dissipate. Even the sound of her voice was returning to normal. Nothing else, however, seemed normal at all.

She glanced at the three captives, leaning on one another and occasionally dozing fitfully or moving slightly in what she was certain was an attempt to find a more comfortable position. Chioma wondered why she had to keep them in that same spot for so long. After all, Chioma and her group had all the weapons; the three whites had none, and their wrists and ankles were tied. What could it hurt to let them stretch a bit or go to the bathroom, even if just one by one?

But Chioma was not about to suggest it—to Themba or anyone else. It wasn't her place to do so, and if there was one thing Chioma continued to learn, it was exactly what and where her place was. Right now that meant she was to serve as Themba's wife and obey his commands. He was a fair leader, but a fierce one as well, and he brooked no disloyalty. Mbhali had told Chioma of more than one occasion when Themba had shot one of his closest comrades on the spot, simply for questioning his decisions.

Chioma's glance settled once more on the woman who had been sleeping alone in the other room when they first arrived. Her eyes were shut. She was older than the other two, old enough to be their mother or auntie. Could that be their relationship? It struck Chioma that the woman had a vague familiarity about her, as if they had met somewhere before.

She squinted her eyes, trying to distinguish something that would help her identify the woman, but nothing came. Perhaps it was just her imagination. After all, it was sometimes difficult to tell these whites apart, with their pale skin and washed-out hair and eyes.

An image of Andrew flashed through her mind, and she felt her cheeks grow hot at the memory, realizing that he, too, had the same pale complexion and faded features, and yet she couldn't deny that she had been drawn to him. Before she could dwell on the thought, Themba stomped into the house, jarring her back to the present.

He jerked his head toward her, beckoning her to join him. She crossed the room in a few short steps and stood submissively in front of him, waiting.

"Look at me, wife."

She raised her head, the practice of gazing directly into someone's eyes, even her husband's, still an uncomfortable sensation for her.

Themba studied her. "I must go away for a while. I've decided it isn't safe to leave Mandisa and the little one back at the camp, so I've sent Mbhali and two others to fetch them and bring them here. They should be back before the sun goes down. You'll stay here tonight—and tomorrow if necessary. Until I return. Certainly no later than Monday."

He paused, and Chioma longed to ask where he was going, but she knew better.

Apparently satisfied that she understood his directions, he continued. "I'm taking all but you and Kefentse with me. He'll stay to protect you and to help you guard these three until I return. While I'm gone, untie them only to relieve themselves, and then only one at a time. Do you understand?"

Chioma nodded, not pleased to be left behind, particularly with Kefentse, whose ferocity frightened her. But the choice wasn't hers. "Yes, Themba," she answered, hoping he wouldn't be gone long.

He hesitated, and Chioma wondered if he was considering whether or not to confide in her about his mission. His decision would tell her much about where she stood in his eyes. At last he spoke.

"I've heard about a wealthy home, only a few hours' walk from here. I have it on good information that the family will be gone for the next few days, and that those who oversee the estate can easily be bought off—or eliminated. The money and possessions are ours for the taking, if we hurry. And there are other houses of equal value in the area. If it's as I've been told, this one raid could fund our operations for months to come."

He cast a quick glance at the huddled trio on the floor and then looked back to Chioma. "When I get back, I'll allow you to help eliminate these foreigners who poison our young people's minds and turn them from the cause. We must drive others like them from our land by making an example of these three." His eyes flashed with something Chioma sensed was close to pride. "After what you did at the camp two days ago, I know I can trust you to guard them until I return."

Chioma swallowed, her throat complaining less than it had since the man had tried to strangle her. "Yes, my husband. You can trust me."

With a quick squeeze to her shoulder, Themba turned and left the house. Other than Kefentse, Chioma was now in charge.

Emma had overheard bits and pieces of what the man who was their leader had told the young woman.

Chapter 23

SLEEP WAS IMPOSSIBLE FOR THE THREE CAPTIVES, though they managed to doze for a few moments now and then.

Emma had overheard bits and pieces of what the man who was their leader had told the young woman, who was apparently his wife. It seemed he and the others were leaving for a while, going somewhere they expected to find more financial gain for their efforts than here at the poor mission post. She also heard him say something about eliminating the "foreigners" when he returned. Apparently this leader was not concerned about the local taboo against harming or killing religious people. Despite her reassurance that God was with them, their immediate future didn't look promising.

Emma watched the young woman, who appeared to be the leader's wife. She was quite attractive, though obviously young—fifteen or sixteen, Emma imagined. What could happen in such a few short years to turn someone to such a violent life? Did Emma dare hope the young woman had a soft spot and might help them somehow? It was becoming more and more obvious to Emma that if they didn't escape, they would, indeed, be added to the long list of Christian martyrs that had grown throughout the centuries. It was not that she so much minded for herself, though she knew it would be devastating to Mariana, particularly right after losing her father. But Paul and Jeannie—they were so young! She glanced at the two of them, their heads leaned together and their eyes closed, with dried blood running a thin streak down the right side of Paul's face. They had come here with such pure hearts, such noble intentions. Was this how their lives were to end, almost before they had begun?

Emma glanced at the fierce-looking man who stood guard at the inside of the door. It seemed he never separated himself from the automatic weapon slung over his shoulder or the large hunting knife strapped to his waistband, so even if she could convince the young woman to help them, they would never get past that behemoth. Each time she considered asking if they could move around a bit or use the tiny bathroom off the room where Emma had been sleeping, their male captor made some sort of antagonistic gesture in their direction, and she thought better of it.

At last the man spoke to his companion and informed her he was going to take a look outside and make sure all was well. He reminded her of their leader's command to kill any of the captives who made a move or spoke without permission, and then he left. Though the woman had said little to him in return, Emma noticed the man called her Chioma.

"God is great." A common name here. Anana mentioned that one of their former servants, the one who was involved with Andrew, had that name as well. These people don't name their children lightly. Does this beautiful girl with the gun at her hip have any idea what her name implies?

"Chioma?"

The word was out before Emma realized she was about to say it. The girl whirled on her, the rifle aimed at Emma's head.

"You are not to speak," Chioma commanded.

Emma swallowed. Where had she found the courage to say that one word? Dare she say more?

Before she could decide, the girl spoke again. "How did you know my name?"

Taking the question as permission to continue, Emma answered, "I heard the man say it, before he went outside."

Chioma nodded, her eyes squinted and focused on her prey.

Emma waited, but when the girl still didn't speak, Emma took a deep breath and plunged in, reflecting on the words of Queen Esther in the Bible when challenged to risk her life to save others: *If I perish, I perish*. What was the worst that could happen? Chioma would shoot her, and Emma would go to be with Jesus...and with John. Her only concern was that the girl not take out her anger on Jeannie or Paul.

"God is great," Emma said. "That's a very beautiful name. Your parents must have loved you very much to give it to you."

The flash in the girl's eyes caught Emma off guard, but she scarcely had time to notice it before Chioma smashed the butt of her rifle against Emma's cheek, knocking her head back against the wall. Lights flashed before Emma's eyes, as the searing pain launched itself from her head down through her body. She was unsure if she had cried out, but even as the pain swirled around her and something warm and sticky began to drip down her face, she became aware of Jeannie, sobbing openly now beside her, though the ringing in Emma's ears muted the sound.

"Shut up!" Chioma's command penetrated Emma's haze, and even as Emma sensed Jeannie trying to stifle her sobs, the fear Emma detected in Chioma's strained voice denied the fierceness the girl tried to portray.

Emma was certain now. Even with the throbbing of her head and cheek, and her slowly clearing vision, she recognized Chioma's soft spot and understood the blow she had delivered was meant to be a substitute for obeying the command to kill the captives if they moved or spoke without permission.

Chioma had a gun and could easily have killed her. That she hadn't was the first ray of hope Emma had seen since her heavenly Father's reassurance that He was there with them. Perhaps they would make it out of there alive after all.

❖❖❖

Anana woke to the sound of a baby crying. She sat up and listened, but the sound had already faded. When she looked to Pieter's side of the bed to see if he had heard it, he was gone.

Anana sighed. After the earlier instances when she had heard the baby's cries, she had dismissed it as her overactive imagination and her longing for her own babies, now gone from her until she joined them in heaven. And she hadn't heard it again…until now. The haunting cry had returned while she slept, leaving an aching in her heart that went beyond missing Gertie and Andrew.

Was it some sort of sign, a promise or even a warning from God, of something to come? Whatever the reason, the memory of the plaintive wail made her loneliness even greater.

Rising from bed, she hurried to find Pieter. She wasn't sure if she would tell him about what she had heard in her dream, but she knew she needed to be near him right now.

She stopped and peeked in the open doorway of her husband's office, her heart reassured when she saw him sitting in his usual place with his Bible open on his desk. But why was his face buried in his hands? Was he praying? Crying? Either would be very much unlike him.

Tiptoeing toward him, she stopped at his side and waited. When he didn't move, she gently laid her hand on his shoulder. After a moment, he lifted his head, his eyes wet and red-rimmed. So he had been crying after all! Suddenly Anana was frightened. Pieter didn't shed tears lightly. What had happened to bring him to such an emotional state? Had he been thinking of Andrew? She shivered at the next thought that popped into her mind. Had he heard something about Emma? Had something happened to her only sister?

Pieter reached up to her then and gathered her into his arms, pulling her down to sit on his lap. "My sweet Anana. I'm so glad you've come. I need to talk with you."

Anana's heart nearly burst from her chest, as a cry of dismay escaped her lips. "Is it Emma? Did something happen to Emma?"

Pieter's eyes widened with surprise, then softened. "I'm so sorry, dear wife," he said, reaching up to brush back a lock of hair from her face. "I didn't mean to frighten you. No, nothing has happened to Emma. I'm sure she's fine. But—" He paused, smiled slightly, and then said, "But something has happened to me. And I really must tell you about it."

❖❖❖

Chioma tried to put her violent act behind her, but hitting the woman with the rifle butt had bothered her more than killing the men who had invaded their camp. The incident with the men was self-defense, but she was struggling with justifying what she had just done to the defenseless woman who sat tied up on the floor, next to the young couple who was obviously very much in love—all of whom Themba had promised to allow her to "eliminate" when he returned. Though she had long desired to fight for the cause her father had told her about for years, to help bring justice and equality to their people, she had no desire to murder helpless human beings simply for having the wrong color skin or for being in the wrong place at the wrong time.

She might better be able to accept the fate of these people if they were rich, like the ones Themba had said he was going to rob. But those people wouldn't even be hurt, since they were likely not home. For a brief moment, it occurred to Chioma that any servants left behind to care for the house or the grounds would be black or coloured and would undoubtedly be bribed—or killed. If she had gone with Themba and the others instead of staying here to guard these three captives, she would have been expected to help kill those unsuspecting servants. So why should she hesitate to kill these white people who had never done anything for her except steal her heritage and destroy her homeland?

Perhaps it's because I'm here with them—seeing them up close, smelling their fear, and sensing their pain. I mustn't let myself get close to them or begin to care for them in any way. I must distance myself from them.

She glanced around the house. Maybe, if she rummaged around a bit, she would find something of worth in this modest home, though it was doubtful. Still, if she did, she was sure Themba would be pleased.

Yes, that's what she would do. That would keep her from thinking about these three people who were her sworn enemies—and whose lives were in her hands. But first, Themba had told her it was all right to let them relieve themselves, one at a time. She would start with the young woman who sat in the middle.

❖❖❖

When Chioma came toward her, Jeannie was terrified. She knew she shouldn't be afraid, as God had promised never to leave or forsake her, regardless of the circumstances. But, though she knew that in her mind, her heart was having a hard time believing it. Why was this young girl, whom Emma had called Chioma, untying the cord around her feet and not her hands? And why wasn't she doing the same for the others?

"Come with me," Chioma ordered, prodding Jeannie with the rifle stock.

Jeannie felt Paul stiffen beside her and then, even with his hands tied at the wrist, reach out as best he could and grab her arm. "Don't go. She might kill you."

The words were scarcely out of his mouth before Chioma whipped the rifle barrel away from Jeannie and planted it firmly in Paul's face. "I'll kill you first," she hissed, "if you make one more sound."

Jeannie caught her husband's eyes, pleading silently for him to be quiet and let her go. She could see the struggle warring across Paul's features, but at last he released her. Tears coursed down his cheeks as he slumped back, transferring her, Jeannie knew, from his hands into God's. It was obvious Paul felt like a terrible failure as a husband, and Jeannie wished she could communicate to him that he had done the right thing and she understood.

Walking ahead of Chioma, who prodded her forward with the rifle, Jeannie realized the girl was taking her into the bedroom area. Why? And then she understood—and was grateful. Chioma was allowing her to go to the bathroom, which Jeannie had desperately needed to do for several hours now.

With her hands still tied in front of her, Jeannie struggled to use the toilet, feeling particularly uncomfortable because Chioma stood in the open doorway, watching her every move. When she was finally done and ready to return to the others, she waited for Chioma to move. Instead, the girl glared at her and finally asked, "Is he your husband?"

Jeannie swallowed and nodded. "Yes," she said, afraid to say more.

"How long?"

"Just a few months. Not long before we came here."

Chioma's face hardened. "And why did you come here?"

Jeannie searched her mind for the right words, but could find none. "To help," was all she could think to say.

Chioma sneered. "That's what they all say—those who want to take our land from us, and our culture and our ways." She spit on the floor beside Jeannie's bare foot. "That's what I say to your help."

Jeannie had no idea how to respond, so she stood still, her head bowed slightly, praying God would somehow get them through this and help this angry young woman in the process.

"Are you with child?" Chioma asked suddenly, her voice only slightly less harsh than before.

Jeannie snapped her head up, astonished the girl had asked such a personal question. How had she known? Was it that obvious? If so, why hadn't Paul noticed?

"Yes," she said, her voice barely above a whisper. "At least... I think so."

Chioma's eyes softened for a moment before returning to what Jeannie imagined was a practiced hardness. "This is a bad time to have a baby," she said, then stepped aside and motioned for her to walk through the doorway.

Neither of them said another word as they returned to the other room, but when Jeannie had squeezed back in between Emma and Paul, trying to telegraph to her husband with her eyes that she was fine, she noticed Chioma wasn't quite as rough when she retied her feet—and the cord wasn't as tight.

❖❖❖

250

The servants had gathered for the service, as they always did on Saturday evening. Pieter looked out at them, and for a moment he thought he would break down as he had earlier with Anana. How had he not seen this before? How had he looked at these people and not realized their worth in God's eyes, and therefore their equality with the white race? Some had been with him for years, and yet he knew little more about them than their names.

They were waiting. It was time to begin. When the door creaked open and Anana walked in and came to stand at his side, his heart nearly burst with gratitude. No one knew him as did his beloved wife.

He looked out once again at those who were gathered to listen, and it was obvious they were uncomfortable at the unusual occurrence of seeing the *dominee's* wife in attendance. No doubt they wondered if they were about to receive some unwelcome news.

"Our service tonight will be very different," Pieter began, making a concerted effort to keep his voice gentle but even. "It will also be quite short, as I don't plan to give you a message other than this one." He dropped his eyes and breathed a silent prayer before continuing. "I have sinned...as have we all. But I the more because God has given me so much, and I have abused His great gifts." His voice cracked, and he paused to collect himself. Swallowing, he began again. "I must ask your forgiveness. I haven't treated you as our heavenly Father would wish me to. His love for you is so great—and I haven't shown you that love. Tonight I not only ask that you forgive me, but I pledge that things will change around here. Beginning immediately, your wages are being doubled, and your living quarters are going to be refurbished. I'll still expect a hard day's work from each of you, but I'll see that you are fairly compensated."

He stopped again and studied the room full of silent faces, few making eye contact with him but all appearing stunned and even frightened to some extent. And why wouldn't they be? This was certainly not the type of treatment they were used to receiving. And he had no one to blame but himself.

"That's all," he said, his voice gruff as he once again fought tears. "You may go. We'll speak of this more later."

For a few moments, no one moved. Then, slowly, a barrel-chested man with calloused hands and wounded eyes stood to his feet, raised his hands toward heaven, and began to sing praises to God. Within seconds, others had joined him. What began slowly swelled to a joyous roar, multiplying and reverberating throughout the room, as Pieter stood before them, arm-in-arm with his wife as tears streamed down their cheeks. Even as the singers began to make their way outside, the praise continued, until no one was left but Pieter and Anana, listening to the joyful sounds of praise and thanksgiving as the servants returned to their quarters.

"Thank you," Pieter said, pulling Anana into his arms. It seemed the only words he was able to say.

The missionaries were bound, and Chioma
had a rifle.

Chapter 24

THE SUN WAS BEGINNING TO SLIDE BELOW THE horizon, but the tiny two-room house was still stifling. After a light meal, prepared by Chioma and shared against Kefentse's objections with their three captives, Kefentse had moved outside to take up his post under a nearby acacia tree where he could watch both the compound grounds as well as the road. Chioma imagined, too, that it was the coolest spot around, since a slight evening breeze stirred the branches above Kefentse's head but didn't blow strong enough to reach the room where she and the others remained. Still, she was glad Kefentse was gone. The man made her uncomfortable, and she didn't need him anyway. The missionaries were bound, and Chioma had a rifle. The situation was well under control as night approached, and she had no reason to anticipate any problems before Themba returned.

But what will happen when he does? she wondered yet again. The captives were religious people, and killing them might anger the gods, if indeed there were any. And yet...that possibility didn't seem to bother Themba.

Chioma frowned, confused. Though she understood that Themba had brought her the white man's holy book, along with the other two books, simply as a gift he thought would please his new wife, she also thought it odd—and more than a bit frightening—that he thought nothing of killing religious people. The books had undoubtedly been stolen from just such people, possibly even after the people were murdered by Themba himself. The contradiction in this very act seemed to highlight the contradiction of character within this fearsome leader who could take a life one moment and in the next, express tenderness toward his wife or concern for an orphaned baby.

Whatever Themba's reasons for the things he did, would he make good on his threat to eliminate the captives when he returned? Worse yet, would he truly expect Chioma to help him in such a deed? The cold flush of fear that clutched her throat confirmed that he would most certainly do both, and any objections or arguments on her part could result in her own elimination as well. Her position as Themba's wife afforded her respect and protection only so far as she exhibited unquestioning loyalty to her husband.

Pushing the thought from her mind, she remembered her resolve to search the missionaries' house to see if she could find something of worth to present to Themba when he returned. As unlikely as it seemed that such people would possess anything of value, it couldn't hurt their chances or hers if she found something Themba could use to fund their cause.

Calling up her fiercest demeanor, she cast a piercing look at the three captives, who still sat huddled together on the floor, bound with electrical cords and fear. She hoped her angry look reinforced that fear, even as she tried desperately not to show concern over the swollen discoloration of the older woman's face where Chioma had hit her with the rifle. Turning away from them and taking her weapon with her, she decided to start her search in the back room and work her way forward.

Chioma switched on the feeble light on the table beside the unmade bed, where less than twenty-four hours earlier its occupant had slept, peacefully unaware that her life was about to change—possibly even come to a violent end. But Chioma wouldn't allow herself to consider that now.

Other than the bed, the crude table was the only piece of furniture in the room. On it sat the lamp with the dim light, casting a faint glow on a couple of books sitting next to the lamp. The one on top was similar to the holy book Themba had brought Chioma—quite obviously nothing that would be of any use to her or their cause. She was about to turn away to check the lone piece of luggage that rested in the corner when a snatch of something nostalgic tugged at her heart.

She looked back at the two books on the table. Why did the one underneath the holy book seem familiar? Her heart rate increased as she stared at what little of the second book she could see, peeking out from under the one on top. Trembling, she lifted the top book . . . and gasped, nearly crying out in surprise and joy. Her father's journal! How had it gotten here? What explanation could there possibly be? And yet, even before she picked it up to confirm what she already knew, she had no doubt what she would find. She would recognize that precious treasure anywhere! How many hours had she lain awake, wishing she hadn't left it behind that fateful night and wondering what had become of it since?

Hot tears blurred her sight as she set her rifle down on the bed, and then tenderly lifted the tattered tome and pressed it against her breast with both hands. She closed her eyes and let the tears slip down her cheeks. It was as if she were holding her father close, as he had held her so many times when she was young. For the first time in far too long, his voice was clear to her, telling her the stories of Sharpeville and the cause for which their people must always fight. Oh, how the gods must be smiling upon her to allow her to once again find the journal that tied her to her ancestors!

Or was it the God of the whites who had reunited her with the book? The thought rocked her, as her eyes snapped open and immediately fell on the holy book on the table. What was the connection? Why did these two books seem so intertwined in her life? And why would the God of the whites want anything to do with her? Hadn't she ignored Him all those years when she had been forced to listen to her *baas*, *Dominee* Vorster, as he preached about this God and His so-called love for all people? If such a deity did indeed exist, Chioma doubted His love extended to her or her people. So why did His book seem to speak to her as if it were alive?

She shook her head, dismissing the thoughts. Those were not the questions she needed answered at the moment. What she wanted to know now was how and why her father's book had ended up in the possession of these religious people at this remote missionary compound.

With the restored journal in her left hand, she snatched up her rifle with the other and spun on her heel, determined to get the answers she sought—whatever the cost.

❖❖❖

Saturday night and Sunday loomed long to Anana, as she sat in the wicker chair on the veranda and continued to reassure herself that Emma was fine and would be back in less than forty-eight hours. If only she could know that for sure! But without a phone at the compound, it simply wasn't possible. More than once she had considered asking Pieter to have their driver take them out there so they could check on her sister and the young missionary couple, but always she stopped herself before mentioning it. Where was her faith? Why did she pray if she didn't believe God would answer? Surely the Lord knew where Emma was, and He loved her more than Anana did and could care for her better than anyone else. Anana would simply have to rest in that truth and leave Emma's safety in the capable hands of her Savior.

Sighing, Anana turned her thoughts from Emma to the incredible scene that had played out less than an hour earlier when her husband had made his humble announcement to the assembled servants. He had told Anana before the meeting what he planned to do, but neither of them had known what to expect from his listeners. The response, Anana thought, was so typically South African. From the depth of their hearts, the congregation had burst into song, giving thanks and glorifying God. Rather than questioning or grumbling, they had expressed gratitude and praise. Afterward, Anana had returned to the house on her husband's arm, amazed at what she had learned about pure, childlike faith from the very people she and Pieter had presumed to teach through the years.

Now, as Pieter once again sat in his study, going over his books, Anana stared out at the darkening velvet sky, even as the stars blinked to light one by one, and wondered at the grace and mercy of a God who would give His life for such as she. There was so much about His awesomeness and majesty that she would never understand in this life! For the first time in months—perhaps even years, since before Gertie's tragic death—Anana found herself at peace in God's love for her. Maybe that was all she needed to know. Maybe there really was nothing else that mattered.

With that, she rose to go inside before Pieter came and scolded her for being outside alone after dark.

❖❖❖

Emma was ashamed at the level of fear she first experienced when the young woman named Chioma burst back into the front room, brandishing her rifle and the book from Emma's bedside table, demanding to know who had stolen her father's journal. After all, Emma's face still throbbed from the impact of her captor's rifle butt. Yet, at the sudden realization that this was, indeed, the same Chioma who had worked for Pieter and Anana, and with whom Andrew had apparently been so smitten, Emma relaxed. A sense that God had orchestrated the situation in which she now found herself and that He was still in control washed over her, warming and calming her, even as the angry young woman jammed her rifle first in Emma's face, and then in Jeannie's and Paul's, demanding an explanation.

With Jeannie whimpering beside her, Emma breathed a silent prayer before she spoke. "I brought it here...from the Vorster farm."

The jerk of the rifle from Paul's face back to hers didn't frighten Emma. She was too busy watching Chioma's expression morph from anger to shock. Emma's words had hit a nerve.

After a brief instant of what appeared to be confused hesitation, Chioma's eyes blazed. "The Vorster farm? How do you know that place? And how did you come to be there?"

Though it was apparent the young woman was still angry, the slight tremor in her voice showed there was a stronger emotion brewing in her heart. *Help me, Lord,* Emma prayed. *Give me the words to speak, and give her the heart to listen.*

"I was there, visiting my sister," Emma said, measuring her words yet knowing they flowed with God's direction. "Anana Vorster." She paused, and then lowered her voice slightly as she added, "I am Andrew's aunt."

❖❖❖

Chioma's head filled with the swirling words. The woman in front of her, who sat huddled and bound with the young missionary couple, was the aunt of the white man who had died trying to save Chioma's life—the one whose heart still held claim on her own, though she knew it was wrong.

"I don't believe you," Chioma spat, knowing even as she spoke that she truly did believe the woman but desperately needed to hear her admit she was lying. How was it possible that she, the daughter of a loyal ANC martyr and the wife of a rebel leader, had come to this place, to be in the same room with a blood relative of her former *baas*, the man who had sat beside her on a rock, holding her hand as their feet dangled in the cool water, until—

She jerked herself back to reality. The last time she had allowed herself to get caught up in feelings to which she had no right the situation had ended in death. There was no reason to think it would be any different if she yielded to her feelings now. She must focus on the things her father had taught her, the things he had recorded in the journal she had finally recovered, and the things Themba had reinforced by demanding complete loyalty to him—and to the cause. For she knew at that very moment that if she lost her focus, she would pay the ultimate price.

"It's true," the woman said, her voice soft and alarmingly similar to the voice of Anana Vorster. Hadn't she seemed familiar, even from the first time Chioma laid eyes on her? Was it because she looked like her sister... or her nephew? A dart of pain stabbed Chioma's heart, as she remembered the photo on Andrew's dresser. How many times had Chioma cleaned that room, even dusted that very picture of the smiling family, visiting the Vorster farm from a faraway land called America? The woman in front of her appeared a bit older than the one in the photo, but Chioma knew they were one and the same.

"I'm Emma," the woman said, once again confirming Chioma's thoughts. "I'm here from America, visiting my sister and her husband." Their gaze locked briefly, and the familiar blue of Emma's eyes added fire to her next statement. "I came to comfort my sister after the loss of . . . her son."

The words crushed Chioma's heart, smothering the air in her lungs. She tried to call up her strength, to harden herself so she could pull the trigger and stop the woman Andrew would have called Auntie Emma before she spoke another word. But Chioma's hands trembled, and her will refused to obey. Then, without explanation, she heard words from the holy book echoing in her heart: *For he himself is our peace, who has made the two one and has destroyed the barrier, the dividing wall of hostility . . .*

She recognized the words immediately. They were, in fact, words she had returned to, time and again, though she couldn't understand why they drew her. What did they mean, and why would she think of them now?

Summoning what little strength she had left and forcing herself to treat Emma roughly, she untied the woman with eyes like Andrew's and ordered her to the back room, prodding her unnecessarily with the rifle stock in her back until the woman stumbled through the door and onto the bed. For a flash of a second, Chioma considered shooting her in the back of the head before she could regain her equilibrium and sit up to face her. Instead, Chioma breathed deeply and blinked away tears, as Emma turned over on the bed and then sat up on its edge, lifting her face to her captor's. The softness Chioma saw there both angered and unnerved her. As overjoyed as she was at regaining her beloved journal, a part of her wished she had never found it.

Jabbing at the chest of the kind-faced woman with the point of her weapon, Chioma demanded, "What are you doing here? And how exactly did you come to possess my father's journal?"

Chioma was ready to listen now, and as the woman named Emma began to speak, the story that unfolded seemed to flow through the hard places in Chioma's heart like warm honey. More than once the armed girl tried to turn away, but she couldn't. And so the woman continued to speak, explaining that she had come to the compound to bring Bibles for the families whose children attended the missionary school, and then going on to explain how she had come to be in possession of the book.

"Anana and I spent many hours, sitting together and reading from your father's journal," she said, the look on her face affirming the truth of her words. "We discussed his entries, and we thought and prayed about them as well. Anana has already read the journal through many times, so she allowed me to bring it along to finish while I was here." Emma took a deep breath and continued. "He was an amazing man, your father."

Chioma wanted to punch her or hit her, to slam the rifle butt into her face as she had done before, to scream at her, "How dare you speak of my father?" But instead she stood quietly, waiting and listening, wondering where this stunning conversation would take them.

When Emma said no more, Chioma surprised herself by saying, "You're right. My father was amazing. He was brave and kind, fierce and loyal." She stopped, sensing her voice would break if she continued. When she regained her composure, she said, "He is my hero. I wish only to be like him."

Emma smiled and nodded. "I felt the same about my own father. He's dead now too."

Chioma felt her eyebrows draw together. Was it possible to have something in common with this woman? She doubted it, and yet the woman had indicated they both loved and admired their now dead fathers. Chioma was certain, however, that Emma's father had not died in the violent manner of Chioma's father, and that difference stood as a vast divide between them.

For he himself is our peace, who has made the two one and has destroyed the barrier, the dividing wall of hostility... Even as the words resurfaced, Chioma fought them. What did they have to do with her and this woman who knew nothing of the life Chioma and her ancestors had lived? She must stop this slide into sentimentality before it undid her.

"You have no right," she announced, forcing a hardness into her voice, "no right to read my father's words. The book belongs to me."

Emma appeared unfazed by Chioma's harsh tone. "You're right, of course. But when Anana found the journal that night when . . ." Emma's voice trailed off, though Chioma could easily have finished the sentence for her. Instead, she remained silent, waiting.

Andrew's aunt cleared her throat before continuing, ignoring her previously interrupted statement. "My sister kept the journal with her, treasuring it because of the time and manner in which she found it. She meant no disrespect when she read it, nor when she showed it to me. We . . . learned much from the words we found written within its pages. I'm glad, though, that it's finally been returned to its rightful owner. It's quite obviously no accident that God has brought about all that's happened here for His purposes."

Chioma frowned again. God? His purposes? No doubt the woman referred to the God of the white man, but what purpose would He have in returning to Chioma the book that contained the writings of her father, now long dead and gone to be with his ancestors? As for this God of the whites, why would He allow His own people—such as Emma and these missionaries—to be treated so badly, possibly even killed? If He was as loving as He was rumored to be, why hadn't He stopped this attack on their compound?

No wonder Chioma couldn't understand the words in the white man's holy book, for the God it spoke of was impossible to understand. But now she would no longer have to struggle over those words, for she could instead read the words of her beloved father, written by his own hand and recorded in his own journal, and be reminded of why she lived ... and why she fought for her people.

Yes. Circumstances had indeed come together as they should—whether the white man's God had anything to do with them or not. For now, Chioma had learned what she needed to know. It was time to return Andrew's aunt to her companions before Kefentse came in and accused Chioma of shirking her duties. That was not a report she wished Themba to hear upon his return.

Amidst muddled voices, a baby's cry broke through, followed by the bleating of a goat.

Chapter 25

CHIOMA SCARCELY HAD TIME TO REJOIN EMMA to the others when she heard a commotion outside. Amidst muffled voices, a baby's cry broke through, followed by the bleating of a goat, and Chioma realized Mandisa and Sipho had arrived. However, despite her initial pleasure at the thought of having Mandisa there to keep her company until Themba returned, Chioma sensed her friend's presence would somehow complicate the situation.

"Chioma?"

Mandisa stepped into the doorway at the same moment she spoke Chioma's name. The baby, as always, was in the sling that hung from her neck, fussing and flailing his arms in obvious frustration over not having his needs met quickly enough.

At the sight of them, Chioma's apprehensions at Mandisa's arrival melted, and she rushed to her friend and gathered her into her arms. "Welcome! I'm glad you've come. But where are Mbhali and the others who brought you?"

"They went on to join Themba," Mandisa answered, her familiar smile warming Chioma's heart. But Mandisa's smile was interrupted when she looked past Chioma and spotted the three people, tied together with cords, sitting on the floor against the wall. "Who are they?" she asked, instinctively pressing Sipho more tightly against her and evoking a wail of protest.

Chioma turned from the new arrivals to glance at Emma and the young couple, who stared back at them in wide-eyed curiosity and possibly relief that it was a young woman and a baby who had entered the house and not the tall leader of the group or even the fierce guard with the AK-47.

"These are...missionaries," Chioma said, turning back to her friend after making a quick decision not to mention Emma's identity. "But they're no concern to you. Come, you and little Sipho must be hungry after the journey. I'll fix you something while you feed the baby."

Mandisa nodded and sank into the only available chair, immediately pulling out her makeshift bottle and popping it into the struggling infant's mouth, calming him as he sucked the life-giving liquid.

"You're right," Mandisa said. "I'm very hungry. Tired too. It seemed a very long journey, but I'm glad to be here. I didn't like being left behind without you."

Chioma smiled as she prepared a plate of food for the young mother. Mandisa had become very dear to her, more like a sister than a friend. *The only family I have left*, Chioma thought, then quickly corrected herself. *Except Themba, of course.* The image of her husband, looking down into her face just before he left, flashed through her mind. She wanted him to be proud of her when he returned, to know he could trust her and depend on her. That left her no choice but to do what he asked.

She sighed, blinking back tears and steeling herself against the emotions that raged inside her. This was no time to go soft. It was a season of testing, and she mustn't fail, for she sensed that if she did, there would be no second chance.

❖❖❖

Anana awoke with a start. Blinking her eyes against the dark and gathering her thoughts, she confirmed that Pieter slept peacefully beside her. Eyes wide open now and ears attuned for anything unusual, she lay without moving, waiting. All was quiet.

She felt herself relax. Whatever had awakened her had obviously been nothing to be concerned about. And yet…there was still the question of Emma's safety. Perhaps God had prodded her awake to pray for her sister, or for…

A picture of Chioma swam into view, and Anana frowned.

What is it, God? You haven't put this young girl's face into my mind without reason. Am I to pray for her? Is that the reason You awakened me? Is she in danger? Oh, Lord, I don't know where she is or what's happening in her life since she left here that awful night, but You know. You know exactly where she is and what's going on with her—in her life and also in her heart. Help her, Father. Protect her. Help her to make wise decisions. And above all, draw her to Your heart. Show her the truth of Your great love for her, Lord. Please, Father…

A sense of peace washed over her, and Anana sighed. Yes, that had been the reason God had awakened her—to pray for Chioma. Anana wondered if she would ever see the young woman again, but she knew it wasn't important. In her heart she sensed she would one day see her in eternity, and that was all that really mattered.

❖❖❖

After Sipho and Mandisa had filled their stomachs, Chioma escorted them to the back room, insisting they sleep in the home's only bed. The young mother and her child were asleep before Chioma closed the door behind her.

Chioma's eyes, too, felt heavy, and she knew she could easily fall asleep if she gave herself half the chance. But she wasn't about to leave the three captives unattended, and she certainly didn't want to call for Kefentse to come and relieve her. Instead she decided to make a strong pot of the coffee she had spotted in the missionaries' cupboard and do her best to keep herself vigilant and alert throughout the night.

She glanced at the three nestled together on the floor. It appeared they were trying to sleep, so she went ahead with her plans. By the time she had a steaming cup of coffee in hand, she noticed Emma was watching her.

"Do you want some?" Chioma asked, telling herself the small kindness on her part didn't mean she was weak. After all, Themba hadn't told her she couldn't feed their captives.

"I'd like that," the woman answered, her voice soft though noticeably weary.

Chioma filled another cup and took it to her, then lowered herself to the floor where she could watch her charges while enjoying her drink. As she studied the little group, she couldn't help but remember the young woman's confession that she believed she was pregnant. Though Chioma had tried not to dwell on that possibility, she had to admit it made the thought of "eliminating" the threesome even more discomforting. Perhaps Themba would consider letting the pregnant one live, though she doubted it. Besides, to be such a young widow with a child on the way would be no easy life.

Many of my own people have suffered such losses ... and more. Why should I care about this one white woman? Or the one sitting next to her, for that matter?

Her eyes fell again on the older woman with the bruised face, holding the cup between the palms of her bound wrists, watching her with Andrew's eyes. Chioma hated her for that, but her heart also softened at the sight. How much easier Chioma's life would have been if she hadn't run into this woman, this reminder of the past, who watched her as if she had a choice other than to follow Themba and fight for the cause. The woman might not realize there was no other life for Chioma, but Chioma knew it, and there was no point in considering anything else.

"Stop watching me," Chioma grunted. "It's rude."

Emma dropped her eyes. "I'm sorry. You're right, of course. I didn't mean to stare. I just..." Her voice trailed off, and Chioma saw the woman's chest rise and fall as she took a deep breath. "You're such a lovely young woman. I know my nephew thought very highly of you, and...I can't help but wonder why you..." Her voice trailed off again, as if she had run out of words, even as Chioma's anger resurfaced.

"Why I what? Why I ran away from the farm to join this group of freedom fighters? Why I'm married to the group's leader?"

Emma's eyes raised briefly before lowering again, and Chioma felt her cheeks flame—with anger or embarrassment, she wasn't sure. Either way, the woman had no right to judge Chioma's actions.

"I did what I had to do to survive," Chioma hissed, silently chiding herself for feeling she had to justify her behavior. "I couldn't stay on the farm after...what happened to Andrew. I would have been blamed. Or those pigs who killed him would have come after me and killed me, too. So I ran and joined up with this group—with Themba. I became his wife because...because he chose me. And they all protect me and take care of me because we're comrades, fighting for the same cause. We're loyal to one another...to the death."

Emma's eyes raised again, but this time she didn't lower them. "You'd die for them then? For Themba?"

Chioma's heart skipped a beat, and she hesitated briefly before answering. "Of course I would—as he would for me."

After a moment, Emma nodded. "As Andrew did... for you."

Like a bolt of jagged, searing lightning, Emma's words ripped through Chioma's heart, and she nearly cried out with the pain of it. Slamming her cup down on the floor, Chioma grabbed the rifle and leveled it at Emma's face, right between the blue eyes that reminded her of Andrew. "I should kill you for that," she growled, her finger on the trigger.

"You could," Emma said softly. "But it wouldn't bring Andrew back—or your parents or brother either."

The words hung in the air between them, even as Chioma realized the missionary couple was awake, watching the life-and-death struggle playing out before their eyes. Chioma was torn, wanting to kill them all and knowing the rifle in her grip gave her the power to do that—yet sensing some large, unseen hand holding her back, forcing her to face the truth of Emma's words.

At last she lowered the weapon, feeling the fight drain out of her as hot tears filled her eyes. What would she do now that she had acknowledged the words of this white woman who had stolen Chioma's resolve to fight? What good would she be now to the cause, to the group, or to Themba? What point was there in living...and what chance that Themba would even allow her to do so now that she had betrayed her ancestors and all they stood for?

Defeated, Chioma laid her rifle on the floor beside her and let the tears flow down her cheeks, as Emma reached out with her bound hands and pulled the young woman against her chest, holding her close and whispering to her that all would be well and God would take care of them. Chioma desperately wanted to believe her, but she knew better. Themba would soon return...and then all four of them would die.

"I don't know what to do," Chioma said, her voice strained from crying.

Chapter 26

JEANNIE WAS STUNNED, AS SHE LEANED AGAINST HER husband and watched the young woman named Chioma sob on Emma's shoulder. It was obvious God was doing something here; she had been sure of it since Chioma asked Jeannie if she might be pregnant. Though Jeannie was still nervous and unsure about what lay ahead, she was at peace with the certainty that God had everything under control.

Paul squeezed her hand, interrupting her thoughts, and she looked up at him, returning his smile at the emotional scene they were witnessing. When Paul leaned down and kissed her on the forehead, she nearly wept for joy that the two of them were here together, sharing this amazing experience. Hadn't they given their lives to God's service, pledging to follow Him and minister to anyone they met along the way? How would God use them now, in this young woman's life as well as in the lives of others? Whatever happened, Jeannie felt certain she and Paul would be an integral part of it.

Chioma sat back then, drawing Jeannie's attention. Their captor's face was streaked with tears, and her eyes mirrored a depth of sadness that spoke of a suffering Jeannie could only imagine. She understood why Emma had reached out to Chioma and held her, just as Jeannie herself wished she could do at that very moment.

"I don't know what to do," Chioma said, her voice strained from crying. "Themba will return soon—perhaps tomorrow, or Monday for sure." She shook her head. "I don't see how I can save you."

Jeannie's heart leapt at the thought. Chioma obviously realized that her husband, the group's leader, planned to kill them, just as the three captives had suspected. But now the young woman wished to help them, though Jeannie couldn't imagine how that would happen. The tall, muscular man with the AK-47, who Jeannie was sure still waited and watched outside, would surely not hesitate to kill any or all of them without a second thought. Now there was the added complication of the other young woman and her baby, sleeping in the back room. Even if the three of them plus Chioma were willing to take the risk to try to escape, they couldn't put the baby and its mother in danger.

"It's all right, Chioma," Emma said. "God has a plan. With Him, nothing is impossible. If it's His purpose that we get out of here alive, then it will be so."

Chioma hesitated, raising an eyebrow questioningly. "And if not?"

Emma smiled. "Then we'll die and go to be with Him, which is far better anyway."

Chioma looked doubtful, but Jeannie relaxed at Emma's words. Though she wished her friend's mother hadn't been here when this happened, she couldn't deny that her presence afforded great comfort.

"How do you know it would be better?" Chioma asked, her tone skeptical. "I want to believe it's better on the other side, with my ancestors and their gods, but how can we know that for sure?"

Emma smiled again. "You can know the true God who waits for us on the other side. Chioma, can you go into the bedroom and get my Bible from the table? I'd like to show you something."

Chioma hesitated, then reached into her front pocket, pulled out a small, worn book, and held it out to Emma. "I have my own holy book. Themba gave it to me. Many times I've heard the *dominee*—your sister's husband—read from his holy book when I was working on the farm. But... I don't understand what it says. It's very confusing to me."

Jeannie felt herself smile, even as Emma took the book from Chioma. It was obvious God was drawing the young girl to Himself, and it was exciting to realize they were about to witness the greatest miracle imaginable.

At that moment Jeannie caught Chioma's eye, and was surprised when the warrior-child returned her smile—tentatively, gently, even shyly—as Jeannie felt hope mingle with the joy in her heart.

"Are you... all right?" Chioma asked, nodding at Jeannie.

Jeannie raised her eyebrows in surprise. "Yes. I'm fine. Thank you, Chioma."

For a moment Jeannie couldn't read the emotions that seemed to war on Chioma's face. Then the young woman spoke again. "Your baby. It is also well?"

Jeannie felt Paul stiffen beside her, even as she herself came to attention, sitting up a little straighter and groping for the right words. "I... Yes, the baby is fine also." She turned to look up at her husband. "I should have told you, but... I wanted to be sure first. Now, somehow, I am."

Tears formed in Paul's brown eyes, even as a smile formed on his lips. "A baby?"

Jeannie nodded. "A baby. Yes."

"Oh! A baby!" Emma's voice broke through then, and Jeannie turned to the woman sitting beside her. "How wonderful!" Emma exclaimed.

Jeannie nodded, amazed that even in these dire circumstances, the promise of new life brought a joyful response. Surely God hadn't brought them to this point to snuff out a life that hadn't yet seen the light of day.

But when she looked at Chioma, the sadness in the young woman's eyes twisted Jeannie's heart, wrestling with the hope that rested there.

❖❖❖

Emma's heart ached with joy at the thought that Jeannie and Paul were expecting a baby, but it wasn't something she could allow herself to dwell on at the moment. They were scarcely in the best of predicaments to celebrate such an announcement, so they would simply have to leave the details of the impending event in God's capable hands. For now she had a more pressing birth to attend to.

Show me, Lord. Take me to the right page, the perfect verse...

She opened the Bible to the second chapter of the Book of Ephesians. Verse 14 seemed to jump off the page, but before reading it aloud she prayed, *Father, am I hearing You right? This is a wonderful verse, but not the one I would have imagined.*

The verse continued to call her, so she cleared her throat and read it, directing the words at Chioma: "For he himself is our peace, who has made the two one and has destroyed the barrier, the dividing wall of hostility."

When she heard Chioma gasp, she looked up at the obviously surprised girl who stared back at her. "How...how did you know? How did you know to read me that one, out of that entire book?"

Emma smiled. "I didn't. But God did. He wants you to know that He's speaking to you right now—you, Chioma. Out of all the people in the world, He's speaking to you, calling you to His heart, telling you of His great love for you."

Chioma's eyes once again filled with tears. "I've heard the *dominee* say that many times—that the God of the whites loves us all. But I haven't believed it." She swallowed and then, her voice trembling, asked, "Is it possible? Does the God of the whites love me also?"

Emma's heart broke with love for the young woman. "Oh, Chioma, He's not the God of the whites only. He's the God of everyone who has ever lived or ever will live. And He loves each one equally. This verse I just read to you means He's our peace—yours and mine. Everyone's. He has made peace between Himself and us, and He enables us to have peace with each other as well. Everything that has separated us—sin, evil, pain, death, even skin color and race and culture—has been done away with by His great sacrifice for us. In Him we are one—one race, one people, with one Father."

Chioma frowned, and Emma knew the young woman was remembering something. "The *dominee*, I've heard him speak of a sacrifice, of a cross, of great love. But I didn't understand the words he spoke."

Emma nodded. "It's impossible to understand—until God Himself opens your understanding. Do you want to understand, Chioma? Do you want to know what God is speaking to you?"

After only a brief hesitation, Chioma nodded, a hint of eagerness in her eyes. "I would like to know. Yes."

Emma laid down the book and reached out to Chioma, taking the girls' hands into her own, which were still bound together. As best they could, Jeannie and Paul reached over and joined their hands as well. Then Emma closed her eyes and prayed. "Father God, You see this willing heart, this broken but eager heart, Lord. Show her, Father, what she needs to see and understand so she can become Your child. Thank You, Lord. Amen."

No greater love...

The words echoed in Emma's heart, and she knew immediately what she was to say to Chioma. Retrieving the Bible and turning quickly to the fifteenth chapter of the Gospel of John, she read, "Greater love has no one than this, that he lay down his life for his friends."

Looking up at Chioma, she said, "When you listened to *Dominee* Vorster read the Scriptures, do you remember when he talked about Jesus being crucified, or killed, for our sins?"

Hesitantly, Chioma nodded. "I remember. But...I didn't understand why One who is called the Son of God could be killed."

"Because He was the only One worthy to die for our sins," Emma explained. "The Bible says that all of us have sinned—you, me, Paul, Jeannie, Themba, everyone. It also says that because we are sinners, we deserve to die and to be separated from God forever. But God loved us too much to let that happen. For the price of death to be paid for our sins, it had to be paid by Someone without sin. And so He sent His Son, because no one but God's Son, Jesus, qualified. He is the only One who has ever lived on this earth without sin. He was a man, because He was born of a virgin named Mary, but God was His Father—and so He, Jesus, is also God. Do you understand, Chioma?"

Chioma nodded slowly, as if a light were beginning to dawn behind the shimmering dark orbs of her eyes. "A virgin for a mother. God for a Father. The only good One, dying for all the bad. In our place," she said, almost as if she were thinking aloud.

"Yes," Emma agreed. "That's it exactly. And because He paid the price for our sins, that means we don't have to be separated from God anymore. We can know Him, feel Him, hear Him, speak to Him—and one day live with Him forever.

There is no greater love, Chioma, than to die that someone else might live."

Chioma was silent for a moment. Then she said, "Like Andrew. He died for me...so I wouldn't have to. That's why...he spoke His name—Jesus—before he died." She swallowed and dropped her gaze, and it was obvious she was fighting to maintain her composure. Then she lifted her eyes and locked them on Emma's. "He's there now, isn't he? Andrew is with God. With Jesus. With the Father."

Emma nodded again, tears of her own streaming down her face. She could hear Jeannie and Paul sniffling as well. "Yes, Chioma. Andrew is with the Father. With Jesus. And you can be sure that you also will be there one day. Do you want that, Chioma? Do you want to be certain that you're God's child and that you'll spend eternity with Him?"

Chioma nodded again. "Yes...I do." The words came out as a sob of joy, and Emma once again took Chioma's hands in her own. "Close your eyes, sweet girl, and pray with me. Just say what I say. All right?"

"Yes," Chioma whispered, squeezing Emma's hands.

"Father God, forgive me for my sins," Emma said, spacing her words so Chioma could repeat them after her. "I'm sorry, Lord, and I need You. I believe You sent Your only Son to die for me—for my sins—on the cross, and I thank You for that, Father. I believe Jesus died on the cross and that He rose again, and that because He lives, I, too, can be forgiven and become Your child and someday live with You forever. Send Your Spirit, Father, to live in my heart and to change me to become the child You want me to be. I receive You now as my Lord and Savior. In Jesus' name, amen."

By the time Chioma had echoed Emma's "amen," they were all crying tears of joy. What would become of them after that moment, Emma had no idea. But their eternal destiny was assured, and with that they could rest in God's provision for whatever else lay ahead.

❖❖❖

Chioma's heart had never felt so light or free. In the past few hours since praying with Emma and the missionary couple, she had alternated between tears and laughter, but now she was trying to stay quiet so her three new friends could catch a little sleep. Kefentse had checked in briefly and then left again with a cup of coffee, while Chioma had decided she was too excited to sleep and didn't need any more caffeine to get through the night.

But even in the midst of her newfound joy, she was troubled. What would tomorrow bring? It was sure to bring Themba and the others. Even if they delayed until Monday, it would be no later than that. Then what? Though it was comforting to know she and the three captives would go straight into God's presence if they died, Chioma also knew that life was precious, and she needed to do whatever she could to try and preserve it. And, of course, there was Mandisa and Sipho.

Emma had told Chioma that nothing was impossible with God, that He could do anything. But would He? Would He intervene on their behalf and somehow deliver them from what she now knew was certain death? Even if He did, what was she to do in the meantime?

Unbidden, the memory of the King Proteas that had splashed the ground with color in the spot where Masozi's head had been smashed against the Acacia Karoo rose up in her mind, whispering to her of resurrection and promise. Protected by the authorities, the flower continued to grow against all odds—despite revolutions or uprisings, or even the ugliness of apartheid. Eyes closed, Chioma prayed, *Oh, Father, what are You trying to tell me?*

No words came, but a warm sense of peace enveloped her, assuring her of God's love—and of the everlasting truth of His promises, even in the face of death. Comforted, she opened the Bible on her lap as she remembered Emma's admonition that God's will was always found in His Word, the holy Scriptures. *It's up to You, God. I'll do what You want me to do, but You'll have to show me what it is and give me the courage to carry it out. You already gave Your Son's life for me, and Andrew died for me, too. May I also have such great love when it comes time for You to call my name.*

"The prisoners are secure."

Chapter 27

SUNDAY MORNING HAD JUST BEGUN TO CREEP OVER the horizon when Chioma awoke to a sharp jab to her ribs.

"What are you doing sleeping when you should be standing guard?"

Kefentse's gruff voice was accusatory, piercing the fog of sleep that lingered over Chioma's mind. She hadn't meant to doze off, hadn't thought she would, but she must have—at least for a little while. Still, there was no harm done. The prisoners were tied up, and she held her rifle on her lap...but of course, that wouldn't be an acceptable excuse to Kefentse, or Themba either, for that matter.

She pulled away from the wall and sat up straight, determined not to show fear or weakness. "I was resting my eyes for a short time," she said, looking up at the giant who stood over her. "The prisoners are secure."

Kefentse grunted, casting a disgusted look at the now-stirring captives, whom Chioma had wisely left bound, though she had wanted to release them from their uncomfortable ties. Not knowing when someone would walk in on them, however, she had realized she must leave things as they were.

Stomping toward the corner that served as a kitchen for the tiny home, Kefentse cursed when he discovered there was no coffee. Before he could turn on her to complain, Chioma jumped up and hurried to get the hot beverage going. She hoped the offensive man would then take his brew and go back to his post outside.

Sipho's first cry of the morning pierced the uncomfortable silence, as Kefentse glared at Chioma, watching her every move. As the baby's cries escalated, Chioma heard Mandisa's comforting coos, vainly attempting to quiet her tiny charge. It wasn't long before the anxious mother and wailing baby joined them in the main room.

"He's hungry," Mandisa said apologetically, ducking her eyes when she spotted Kefentse, even as she continued to walk the baby, who had finally stopped crying long enough to recognize and receive the nourishment his mother urged upon him from the makeshift bottle.

By the time the coffee was hot, it seemed Kefentse couldn't escape quickly enough. Steaming mug in hand, he hurried from the house, grumbling that there wasn't enough sugar for his drink. Chioma breathed a sigh of relief, grateful for Mandisa and Sipho's presence, which seemed to unnerve the otherwise fearless man.

"Did you sleep well?" Chioma asked her friend.

Mandisa nodded. "Yes, thank you. And you?"

Chioma dared a peek at her three friends, and then looked back at Mandisa and smiled. "Very well. It was a wonderful night."

Mandisa raised her eyebrows at the somewhat overly enthusiastic statement, but said nothing. Sipho was once again demanding her attention, having finished his meal and now fussing over a gas bubble or two. The dutiful mother placed him over her shoulder and began to pat his back before returning to the other room to remove his wet diaper.

When Mandisa had closed the door behind her, Chioma moved quickly to sit down beside Emma. "I'll prepare something for you to eat soon. And when Mandisa is finished with the baby, I'll release you one by one to use the facilities. But then we must think about what to do before Themba returns. With Kefentse outside, it won't be easy to escape. Even if you get past him, how will you get to safety before he discovers you're missing and tracks you down? And Mandisa...I don't know if she'll help us, or...make it worse."

Emma nodded. "I understand, Chioma. And I've been praying most of the night. I believe God will provide the way of escape, and that He'll show us what to do when the time comes."

"I, too, have been praying," Paul added, "and I have a peace that God has a plan. We must be patient."

Chioma frowned. Did these people not realize how bad things could get once Themba returned? "We haven't much time," Chioma cautioned. "Themba and the others could return at any moment, though it may be as late as tomorrow."

Emma nodded again. "God knows that, my dear. Don't worry. Just pray...and wait. He'll show us when the time is right."

When Chioma opened her mouth to protest again, Emma held up her bound hands, palms open toward Chioma. "Don't worry. God is never late."

In spite of her inner turmoil, Chioma felt herself relax. If God could reach her by speaking through one spot in the entire holy book, He could certainly deliver them all from this situation.

He can...but will He? That was the question that still echoed in her mind. She laid her hand against the bulge in her front pocket that now contained not only her Bible but her father's journal as well. She would simply have to wait to see what God would do.

❖❖❖

As the sun rose to its full height, stretching hot over the land, Chioma waited...and prayed. No answer came. The only words she heard, wending their way through her thoughts and emotions, were "no greater love."

She knew, of course, what the words meant. The woman called Emma, Andrew's aunt, had read to her from the holy book about the greatest gift ever given, the greatest love ever shown, when Jesus, the only Son of the true God, willingly gave His life for others. She knew that now—but how was that to help any of them when it came to escaping the certain death that drew closer with each passing hour?

Mandisa and the baby had joined them in the main room for most of the day so far, and Chioma had made good on her promise to feed the captives and take each one to use the facilities before retying them. As the afternoon sun baked the house, making them all drowsy, Chioma pulled her holy book from her front pocket and tried to read.

If only Mandisa weren't here, I could ask Emma and the others to explain these words, to help me understand. But I can't let Mandisa see me being too friendly with them—not until I know what we're supposed to do to escape...and whether or not I'm to go with them.

She closed the book, and then her eyes, as Emma had instructed her to do. *Soon, God,* she prayed. *Can You please show us soon what we're to do? Emma says You're never late...but could You perhaps be just a little early this time? I'm afraid my faith is very weak...*

No greater love was all she heard in return. *No greater love...*

❖❖❖

By late afternoon Chioma had nearly given up. If they were to die, so be it. At least she and Emma and the young missionary couple would go to be with God, and according to Emma that was truly all that mattered. Maybe that was what God was trying to tell her as well.

As Chioma prepared the simple evening meal from the meager ingredients she had found in the missionaries' cupboards, Kefentse stormed inside, his ever-present AK-47 slung over his broad shoulder. "I'm hungry," he announced.

Chioma nodded. "The food's nearly ready."

Kefentse grunted as he lowered himself to the room's only chair, his already bad mood seeming to have taken a turn for the worse. No doubt he was tired of waiting for Themba's return. He wasn't used to being assigned guard duty over women and children or missionary captives, and it was obvious he didn't like it. As he waited, eyeing the prisoners through slit eyes, Chioma noticed with alarm that he lifted his gun and pointed it at Paul. What was Kefentse doing? Was he toying with them, trying to frighten them, amusing himself at their expense?

Then Chioma noticed Mandisa. She, too, was watching Kefentse, her eyes wide with fear. Was she frightened only for herself and her baby, or did she sense that the impatient man was about to go over the edge?

Chioma's heart raced. What was to stop Kefentse from killing Paul—or any of the captives, for that matter? Hadn't Themba left orders to kill them if they moved or spoke without permission? If Kefentse told Themba the prisoners had tried to escape and he therefore had to kill them, how would Chioma convince her husband otherwise?

The longer she observed Kefentse and his increasingly antagonistic stance toward Paul in particular, the more certain she was that she had to do something quickly.

"The food's ready," she announced, a tremor in her too-loud voice. But her words got the man's attention, and he turned from Paul to Chioma.

"Bring it to me."

Obediently Chioma prepared a plate of food and presented it to Kefentse, who received it with a grunt. Her heart sank when she realized he planned to eat it in the house, rather than taking it back outside. But at least he was no longer glaring at Paul.

From behind Kefentse, Chioma looked over his head to Emma and the others, who returned her glance warily. It was apparent they, too, realized how close they had come to a fatal encounter with this angry man who now sat stuffing food into his mouth, his eyes on his plate and his weapon once again slung over his shoulder.

Did the man never put down that gun? Chioma wondered. If he did, she might be able to take it, and—

No, it was suicide even to think about it. But then...it could be suicide not to, she reminded herself. Perhaps after dark. Surely he had to sleep sometime. Yes, that was it. She would wait until he was asleep and then steal his gun, or at least try to get the drop on him with hers. As darkness once again began to spread across the land, it seemed their only chance.

❖❖❖

Chioma's heart beat so hard it felt as if it would burst from her chest. She had considered trying to sneak up on Kefentse, but there was no way she could know until she got close to him whether he was awake or asleep. If he was awake and spotted someone trying to approach him without warning, he would certainly shoot first and ask questions later. She would have to call out to him and approach him openly, getting as close as possible and then using the excuse that she didn't feel well and needed him to watch the captives for a while. He would no doubt ask why Mandisa couldn't cover for her, but by that time Chioma hoped to have her rifle in Kefentse's face.

Stepping from the house and taking her first tentative steps toward the tree under which she knew Kefentse sat, she sent up a silent prayer, glad the others had promised to do the same while she was gone. Then she called out to the surly guard, immediately evoking an angry bellow in response.

"What do you want?" he demanded, as she continued to approach his post.

"I need to speak with you," she said, forcing her feet to move as quickly as she dared without alerting him to her intentions.

She was within a few feet of him when he ordered, "Stop. You can talk to me from there. What do you want?"

Pulse racing and mouth dry, Chioma answered, "I'm not feeling well. Is it possible for you to come inside to watch the prisoners while I rest?"

The snarl coming from the dark space beneath the tree exhibited the contempt Kefentse felt for such a sign of weakness. "You wish to abandon your duties so soon? Themba won't be pleased."

He was right, of course. Chioma knew that, so she could offer no argument to the contrary. "I just need some air. I've been in the house since we got here. I'm sure I'll feel better if I can remain outside for a while."

Kefentse was silent for a moment, and then suddenly he emerged from the shadows, his weapon over his shoulder and his scowl deeper than usual. Less than five feet away from her, he loomed in the moonlight as a terrifying specter. Fear of what she was about to do nearly buckled her knees beneath her, and then she heard the words once again: *no greater love*.

She swallowed. "Thank you, Kefentse. I won't be long. Just a little air, and I'll be fine."

The man grunted and pushed past her, just as the lingering promise of the words she had heard in her heart catapulted her into action. "Stop," she ordered, even as she jammed the barrel of her rifle into his back. "Don't take another step. Slowly drop your weapon and kick it away." When he stood, unresponsive, she demanded, "Do it now!"

Slowly the muscles in Kefentse's back began to ripple as he slipped the AK-47 from his shoulder and lowered it to the ground. Chioma, her own muscles tense and her eyes fixed on Kefentse's weapon, was not prepared for the man's sudden spin and lunge, as he simultaneously snatched his knife from his waistband, kicked at her, and knocked her to the ground. The next thing she knew she was lying on her back, watching this crazed giant of a man leap toward her, his knife blade gleaming in the darkness. With her rifle still in hand, she jerked it up to meet his chest and fired just as his body began to fall toward her. The only thing she saw after that, as the rifle recoiled against her, both from the shot and from Kefentse's weight, was the wide-eyed shock of the man's dark eyes. And then he was upon her, landing with a nearly bone-crushing blow...heavy, but motionless, his knife plunged into the ground beside her.

The problem of Kefentse's presence was no longer an issue...but now Chioma bore the added burden of having killed once again.

Now what?

Chapter 28

FOR A FEW MOMENTS, CHIOMA LAY MOTIONLESS, stunned and terrified, beneath the dead weight of the man she was certain would have killed her if she hadn't managed to kill him first. Telling herself she'd had no choice helped a little, but her heart still grieved for the necessity of what she had done. At the same time, the realization that she had indeed stopped her assailant with a bullet from the hard rifle that now lay uncomfortably between herself and Kefentse's body finally spurred her to struggle against her entrapment, pushing with all her strength in an attempt to roll him off of her. When at last she succeeded and Kefentse fell to the ground beside her, she gasped for air, sucking in the welcome oxygen and trying to regain her senses.

Now what? It was obvious she had killed yet another man in self-defense, but would that explanation work with Themba? How would she justify being outside with him when she was supposed to stay inside and watch the prisoners?

Would he believe Chioma had come outside to ask Kefentse to relieve her, and that she had left Mandisa in charge for the few minutes she was gone? Would Mandisa go along with that story?

Even if she did, Chioma decided, Themba would not likely believe her explanation of the events—or her reasons for doing what she did. Therefore, she had little choice left but to help the three captives escape, and to leave with them. But again, the question of Mandisa and the baby weighed on her heart. Would her friend leave with them and return to the farm where they used to work, not knowing what the consequences or outcome might be, particularly for little Sipho? And if Mandisa refused to accompany them, what would they do then? Chioma couldn't leave the young mother and her child behind to face the wrath of Themba alone.

Sitting up slowly, she heard Mandisa's voice, frantic and trembling, calling to her from the house, unaware of the dangerous plan that had sent Chioma out into the night.

"Are you well, Chioma? What happened? Where are you?"

"I'm here," Chioma called back. "I'm fine, Mandisa. Don't worry."

Then, using her rifle to support her still shaky legs, she managed to rise to her feet. "I'm coming," she called into the darkness. Then she began to make her way back to the little house, where Mandisa and her baby, as well as the missionary couple and the woman called Emma, no doubt waited anxiously for her return.

❖❖❖

By the time Chioma had related her story, with Emma, Paul, and Jeannie nodding in understanding and compassion as she talked, Mandisa was nearly hysterical.

"What have you done?" she cried. "You've betrayed Themba! He'll kill us all! Why, Chioma? Why would you do such a thing?"

Chioma watched her friend through eyes of compassion, knowing it would be nearly impossible to make her understand, but praying somehow she would. The future of each one of them might very well depend on it.

With the baby asleep in the other room, Mandisa paced, tears flowing down her cheeks, flailing her arms as she spoke. Chioma had never seen the girl so distraught, not even when they had run away from the farm to escape the men who killed Andrew.

Approaching her gently but firmly, Chioma attempted to gather her friend into her arms, but Mandisa pushed her away. "No, no," she sobbed, still pacing as she spoke. "I can't go along with this. What you've done is wrong, Chioma. You've killed one of our own people!"

Chioma's voice was low but determined. "It was self-defense, Mandisa. If I hadn't killed him first, he would have killed me."

Mandisa stopped for a moment, fixing her tear-filled eyes on Chioma. "He wouldn't have tried to kill you if you hadn't left your post and stuck a rifle in his back." She shook her head slowly as she spoke. "No, Chioma. You've betrayed the cause, and you've betrayed your husband." Her dark eyes flashed before they softened, along with her voice. "He'll kill you. You know that. Themba won't let you live when he knows what you've done." She glanced at the three captives and then back at Chioma. "He'll kill us all—every one of us, including my son." Her momentary composure crumpled once again. "Oh, Chioma, what have you done?"

Hysterical again, she resumed her pacing and weeping, as Chioma wrestled with Mandisa's words. She was right, of course. Chioma had, indeed, betrayed the cause, as well as her husband, and now they would all die—unless they escaped before Themba returned. Surely she could convince

Mandisa to leave with them, if for no other reason than to save Sipho's life.

Yes, that would have to be the source of Chioma's appeal to the young mother. They must all leave together—quickly—or remain where they were and die. There simply were no other options.

❖❖❖

As the hours of darkness crept by and Chioma continued to beg Mandisa to come with them for Sipho's sake, Mandisa became more obstinate, more resolute to remain behind. "I'd rather die—both me and my son—at the hands of Themba than to return to the white man's farm and betray our people. I can't do that, Chioma! Don't ask me."

And then she had stormed off to the back room to be with her child, refusing to discuss the matter again.

Chioma was amazed to realize the level of loyalty that had developed within Mandisa during their short time with Themba and his group. She was also surprised to recognize the personal conviction that now complemented Mandisa's otherwise sweet personality. Those changes, however, finally convinced Chioma that the rest of them would have to move ahead with a plan to escape, with or without Mandisa.

The first thing she did was to untie Emma and the missionary couple, as the four of them began to explore ideas for the best way to put as much distance as possible between them and the compound before Themba returned. They knew, too, that even if they convinced Mandisa to accompany them, Themba would immediately come after them. But at least if he returned to an empty house, he wouldn't realize Chioma had killed Kefentse and then escaped with the captives she was supposed to be guarding. He would, instead, believe someone else had come into the camp and killed the only guard, then kidnapped the others. At least then he would be pursuing them with rescue in mind. If Mandisa stayed behind, she would certainly tell Themba what had really happened, and he would set out to find Chioma—and the others—with vengeance in his heart. And there was little doubt he would find them before they could make it to safety.

As Emma rubbed her now unbound wrists, she cleared her throat. "We need to pray before we do anything. It's only the mercy of God that Themba and the others haven't returned already. But as you said, Chioma, he'll be here today for sure. Morning is fast approaching, and we need clear direction from God."

Paul and Jeannie murmured their agreement, and now that they were all untied, Emma took one of Chioma's hands in her own, while Jeannie took the other. With the four of them joined together in a small circle where they still sat on the floor, Paul began to pray.

"Father God, You see us here, coming together to ask You for direction and for help. We believe You have a perfect plan for us, Lord, and we're asking You to show us what it is. Whatever it is, God, we promise to follow it. But please, make it clear to us, and go ahead of us that we might execute Your plan faithfully. We know we can't do anything without You, Lord, and we'd be foolish to try. So show us, Father, and give us the strength and courage to do what we must. We trust You, Lord, and we thank You that You've promised never to leave or forsake us. We're Your children, and we'll follow You wherever You lead—in life...or in death. We ask this in Jesus's name, amen."

Chioma swallowed what felt like a lump of hot food stuck in her throat and then chimed in with an "amen," as the others had done. There was much she didn't yet know or understand about this God who had so recently invaded her life, but she sensed above all that she could trust Him.

"I have an idea," Paul said as he stood to his feet and then turned to help Jeannie and Emma do the same. Chioma had already risen to join them, and she felt her heart leap with his words of hope.

Paul turned to Emma before continuing. "Didn't you say your driver would be arriving today? Before noon, right?" When Emma nodded and affirmed his words, he said, "There's always the chance he'll get here before Themba, but we can't count on that. We need to get out of here quickly — the sooner, the better — and find a safe place to hide where we can watch for the car and hail it before it passes. Though the children are on holiday and won't be coming for school today, I'm sure one of their families who lives near the road would help us." He shook his head. "But we can't put anyone else at risk. If Themba discovered us in one of their homes, he might kill the entire family, and even their neighbors. At the same time, the homes of our students are probably the first places he'll check. He has no idea a car is coming for you today, Emma, so he won't necessarily think to watch near the road. In fact, if Mandisa comes with us and he thinks the guard was killed by intruders and the rest of us abducted, he might assume our captors would purposely keep us away from the road."

He took a breath and looked again at Chioma. "We must convince your friend to come along. If she stays behind, even if Themba doesn't harm her, she'll tell him of your involvement in our escape, and Themba might then realize we'd be sticking close to the road. We have a better chance to make this work if the young woman and her baby come along."

Chioma nodded. She knew the man was right, but she had little confidence Mandisa would agree to leave this place and return to the farm with them. Still, Chioma knew she must try once again to convince her.

"There's a place I know of," Paul said then, "not far from here, though beyond the homes of most of our students. It's an old building, long abandoned and nearly hidden among the tall grass, where we can have a clear view of any approaching vehicles—or pursuers, for that matter. If Themba is diverted, even for a little while, we just might make it. We could spot Emma's driver, flag him down, and have him deliver us all safely to the Vorster farm."

Though Chioma wondered if the farm would truly afford her any safety, she decided the plan might work for the rest of them. And even her chances at the farm were better than remaining here to face Themba.

Now all she had to do was change Mandisa's mind. Chioma sighed, praying silently that God would show her what to say and that He would cause Mandisa to agree to their plan.

With that in mind, she left the others to gather their things and went to the back room to talk with the girl who had become like a sister to her.

❖❖❖

It was no use. Mandisa refused to listen, and instead grew more adamant that she and Sipho must stay behind. She also pleaded with Chioma to do the same, promising she wouldn't tell Themba of Chioma's complicity in Kefentse's death and the captives' escape. But Chioma knew once Themba fixed his dark, piercing eyes on the girl, she would be terrified, and would quickly crumble and tell him the truth.

And yet, the more Chioma thought about it, the more she realized it would be better for the others if she stayed behind with Mandisa and the baby. At least it would buy some time for Emma and the missionary couple to make it safely to the abandoned building, as Themba would undoubtedly be busy for a while, taking out his wrath on his unfaithful wife. Chioma knew how it would end, but she also knew if she didn't remain behind, Themba would be much more likely to catch up to the others before they made contact with Emma's driver.

The decision was made. She would tell the others she couldn't accompany them because she had to stay with Mandisa and the baby. She would assure them Themba would be upset but would not kill her, as she was his wife. Perhaps they would believe her. If not, she would insist they leave anyway.

With her heart racing and a fear so palpable she could nearly taste it, Chioma returned to the main room to tell her three friends what she must do.

"Chioma! Where are you?"

Chapter 29

CHIOMA WAS SURE THE HEAVINESS IN HER HEART reflected in her face, but she couldn't help it. Ever since finally convincing Emma and the others to leave without her, she realized how desperately she had wanted to go with them. Knowing she had done the right thing to help ensure their escape didn't take away the pain or fear of what lay ahead.

As she waited, slumped on the floor where the three captives had spent so many hours bound together, a seemingly unending stream of tears trickled from Chioma's eyes. They had been flowing for so long she no longer tried to wipe them away. On occasion, when Mandisa and the baby entered the room, Chioma sensed their presence but refused to speak. What was left to say? She had stayed because Mandisa had stayed. If the girl hadn't been so stubborn, they might all be safely hidden away in the vacant building by now, watching for the approaching car that would carry them to safety. Instead, they were stuck here in this empty home that would no doubt soon become Chioma's tomb. She had accepted that, but she hoped and prayed Mandisa would be spared, if only to care for the baby.

She closed her eyes, remembering how Emma and the others had pleaded with Chioma to come with them, almost refusing to go without her. But at last Chioma had convinced them that if for no other reason, they must go for the sake of the baby Jeannie carried within her. Paul had then propped up Kefentse in a sitting position against the tree outside, his AK-47 resting in his arms, in an attempt to postpone Themba's discovery of what had happened at least until he got inside the house.

Then, at last, Chioma and her three friends had parted, amidst fervent prayers and many tears.

❖❖❖

Themba was tired, though he would never show it in front of his followers. They had been gone far too long, though their monetary take had made the journey worthwhile. But he longed to get back to Chioma. He missed the comfort of her sleeping beside him, of having her prepare his food and look to him for protection. There had been many women in his life, but none like Chioma. She was beautiful, yes. But so were the others, each in their own way. Chioma was different. She had fire and courage, but she was learning to respect his leadership. As the missionary house came into view, shimmering in the mid-morning sun, he smiled, anticipating his reunion with his wife. His followers knew to lag behind and give their leader the privacy he required.

"Chioma?"

He called to her as approached the entrance, wanting her to come and welcome him. When she didn't appear and the only sound he heard was the fussing of little Sipho, he called again, louder this time, as he stopped and stood in the open doorway.

"Chioma! Where are you?"

His eyes quickly adjusted to the muted light inside the house, and he was surprised to see his wife sitting on the floor, slumped against the wall, her head down. Was she ill? Had something happened to her? Then he realized the captives were gone.

"Chioma!" He hurried to her, reaching down to pull her to her feet just as she lifted her head. Her tear-streaked face and sorrowful eyes set off alarm bells that told him the prisoners had escaped. But how could that be? How could she have allowed this to happen? And why had Kefentse not stopped it?

Before he could speak or yank her to her feet, he heard Mandisa behind him, sobbing in accompaniment to the crying baby. He stood and whirled around, causing Mandisa to shrink back in obvious terror. What could have happened in his absence to cause such behavior from these two women?

Themba turned back to Chioma, who by this time had drawn herself to a standing position, though her head was bowed before him. His initial reaction was to pull her into his arms and assure her that he was here now and all would be well. Yet he sensed there was more to the story of what happened than he wanted to hear.

"What is it?" he asked, forcing a sternness into his voice, determined not to show any weakness or compassion until he understood the entire situation, yet praying to gods he didn't believe in that his suspicions were wrong. "What happened, Chioma? Tell me!"

He grabbed her chin in the palm of his hand and jerked her head up until she was forced to look at him. Even before she spoke, he sensed the guilt in her eyes.

"They're gone, Themba. They...escaped."

Mandisa's sobs increased in intensity then, as did the baby's wailing, but Themba stopped his ears to all but the words that passed between himself and Chioma.

"What have you done?" he demanded, his voice low and menacing, as he squeezed her face until he knew he had caused her pain, hoping the suffering in her eyes would drown out the agony he felt in his heart. "Tell me what you've done!"

Chioma's eyes were nearly wild with terror, sending a thrill of power through Themba's veins, even as his heart broke at the realization that his wife had betrayed him, as well as the cause to which they had pledged their lives. This was going to be the most difficult execution he had ever performed, but he knew even before she spoke another word that he would have to carry it out. Honor demanded it. There was no room for disobedience or betrayal among their ranks.

"I..." The woman he considered so beautiful now struggled to speak, as he held the lower part of her face in a vise grip, but he refused to lessen his hold. Let her suffer as she tried to explain. It would make no difference in the ultimate outcome.

"I let them go," she whimpered, even as her eyes pleaded for mercy. Did she not understand that mercy had never been shown to him and he therefore had none to give?

Instead he squeezed tighter, leaning toward her until his face was mere inches from hers. "Why?"

Chioma closed her eyes, and he could feel her trembling beneath his touch. Good. The more she suffered, the better. And when he was through with her, he would kill the other one and give the child to someone else. What did it matter who raised him? He was, after all, Themba's child, though no one in the camp ever spoke of it and Themba doubted that either Mandisa or Chioma suspected it. As the leader's child, Sipho would be raised to be a mighty comrade who would fight to the death for the cause Chioma had now betrayed. It didn't matter that Themba scarcely remembered the name or the face of Sipho's mother, for until now, Chioma had been the only woman Themba had ever cared for. He wouldn't make the same mistake again.

"Because...they didn't deserve to die," Chioma whimpered. "They're good people. Religious people. They were here to help the children — "

Her voice trailed off, as Themba, in his rage, squeezed her jaw until she could no longer hold back her cries of pain. "They don't come here to help our people," Themba growled. "They come here to take from us what is rightfully ours, and to turn our young people against us." He spat in her face and watched her try to recoil as the slime dripped down from her forehead. "And you, my faithless wife, have helped them. You and your cowardly friend, with her bawling brat — and Kefentse as well."

Despite Themba's hold on her face, Chioma's eyes sprang open and she managed to shake her head no, as she struggled to speak. "It was me, Themba. Not Mandisa. She tried to talk me out of it. She begged me not to do it. She said it was wrong. She refused to go with them. That's why I stayed. And Kefentse is dead. I...shot him."

Themba glared at her before answering, determined not to show the depth of pain he felt over her betrayal. "So you admit you killed my guard," he said at last, "a loyal comrade who fought valiantly at my side. And you also admit that if not for Mandisa's loyalty, you would have run off with those white devils. It wasn't enough to betray me or the cause by letting them go; you would have joined them if Mandisa hadn't insisted on staying behind."

With a rough shake of his hand, he released Chioma, nearly toppling her to the floor in the process. Then he turned to Mandisa. "You did well by refusing to join in this treason and by trying to convince Chioma of her wrongdoing. I'll let you and the little one live. Now get your things. We're returning to the camp as soon as I finish my business here."

Though Mandisa had stopped crying by then, she stood unmoving, staring wide-eyed at Themba, until he bellowed, "Get moving! Or must I deal with your disobedience as well?"

Mandisa's eyes opened even wider, as she shook her head quickly. "No, Themba. I won't disobey you. I'll be ready right away." With the baby pressed tightly against her, she scurried to the back room and returned within seconds, her scant belongings in hand. "I'm ready, Themba."

Themba nodded. "Wait for me outside."

With only a furtive glance at Chioma, Mandisa lowered her eyes and hurried out the door, hushing the baby all the way.

And then they were alone. Themba returned his attention to his treacherous wife, who still cowered in front of him. "I should make this slow and painful," he said, watching her reaction. "But you can be thankful I'm in a hurry to leave. And though I take pleasure in killing a traitor, I don't take pleasure in killing my wife. Do you understand that?"

Chioma raised her eyes to his. Though her lashes were still wet, the tears had stopped streaming down her face. "Yes, my husband. I understand."

"And do you have anything to say for yourself before you go to be with your ancestors?"

He saw her swallow before she answered. "Only that... I'm sorry for betraying you. I would rather not have done so. But a greater love compelled me, and... I had no choice."

Themba felt his jaws clench. How dare she speak of love and betrayal in the same breath? Though he would miss her, he couldn't let her live. Perhaps the young woman Mandisa, who already cared for his infant son, could warm his bed as well. At least she had proven her loyalty, and though she might lack the fire and passion that he so admired in Chioma, he now knew Mandisa could be trusted. He wouldn't marry her, but he would protect her and allow her to serve him for as long as he needed her. Time would take care of the rest.

With that, he retrieved the rifle that leaned against the chair beside them, the rifle Chioma had used to kill the intruders at the camp, and also a brave brother who was loyal to the cause. Leveling it directly at his wife's heart, he looked into her eyes one last time.

"I go to God with a prayer for your soul on my lips," Chioma said, her voice soft but surprisingly strong.

Steeling himself, Themba fired and watched her drop. With her spattered blood still warm upon him, he noticed two books on the floor beside her already lifeless body. Picking them up, he realized one was the holy book he had given her weeks before. The other appeared to be a journal of some sort. Jamming them both into his waistband, he turned from his dead wife and walked out the door to join those who waited for him, thinking that maybe, one day, he might read the books she had left behind. Perhaps they would help him understand this woman who had so captured his heart—and then smashed it into little pieces.

With that, he set out to lead the others back to camp, unconcerned with what had happened to the missionaries. Now that he had taken out his vengeance on Chioma, the rest no longer mattered.

In the distance, Anana imagined a baby's cry, drifting to her on the night breeze.

Epilogue

ANANA SAT, AS SHE HAD SO MANY TIMES BEFORE, in her favorite wicker chair on the sweeping veranda of their home, watching the glorious South African sunset splash its majestic hues across the expansive veld. She thought of Emma, probably dozing now as she leaned back in one of the passenger seats of the massive airline that carried her away from her first homeland and back to her second, the one where she and her husband had made their home and raised their family. But Anana knew Emma would arrive in America with a fresh love and appreciation for the country of her birth.

They had sat right there on that very veranda, she and Emma, after her sister and the others had returned on Monday afternoon—exhausted, frightened, and disheveled, with a story to tell that was nearly too bizarre to be believed. And yet, because of the integrity of those who told it, Anana knew every word was true.

She closed her eyes now and leaned her head back, listening to the soft, familiar sounds of the approaching night. Had it really been less than a week since Emma told her of all that had taken place in the humble missionary home, and then relayed to her the harrowing story of their escape? The thought of her sister, as well as Paul and Jeannie, running for their lives, hiding in a broken-down building, praying they wouldn't be discovered before they were able to spot the car and hail Emma's driver nearly made her sick inside each time she thought of it. But they had done it. The car had arrived on time, and they had escaped, overjoyed at God's deliverance yet mourning those they had left behind.

Now Emma had begun her journey home, while Paul and Jeannie remained at the farm until their missions committee decided what they should do next. In the meantime, Anana was enjoying the company of the young couple, even as they, too, shared with her about "the great conversion," as they called it, of the young woman named Chioma.

And where are you now, sweet Chioma? Anana sighed as she thought of the possibilities, knowing there was little chance the girl still walked the earth, yet rejoicing to know that if she had died as a martyr, giving her life to save others, she was now safely home with the God she had so recently come to know.

And with Andrew, she thought. *And Gertie, too. Yes, I imagine you've seen them both by now, if indeed the situation turned out as we imagine it must have.* Anana smiled. *Such great love. How grateful I am, wherever you are, dear Chioma, that you found such love in your lifetime. For there truly is none greater...*

In the distance, Anana imagined a baby's cry, drifting to her on the night breeze. Was it the memory of her own little ones, Gertie and Andrew, now gone from her until she joined them at the end of her own life? Could it be the promise of the little one carried within Jeannie's womb—or Mariana's? Or was it possible it was the cry of little Sipho, the one Emma and the others had told Anana about — the one with the same name as the baby Anana had heard in her dream so many nights before?

No matter. The cry of a baby was always the cry of hope, wrapped in mercy and given in love. And with that thought, Anana was finally at peace.

The End

❖❖❖

About Apartheid

Apartheid was a tragedy of humanity, a mockery of divinity, a fallacy of purity—in black and white. It was the political system that governed South Africa from 1948 until 1994, 46 years that saw the subjugation of the majority at the hands of the minority. Its overthrow did not come quietly or gently, as evil does not yield power without a fight. It came at the cost of bloodshed, not just by those who lived in South Africa during that nearly half a century but also by One who lived nearly 2,000 years earlier and whose purpose was to bridge the otherwise impassable chasms of sin wrought by mankind's pursuit of selfishness.

More than Conquerors

Book 2 in the "Extreme Devotion" Series

Prologue

PASTOR HECTOR MANOLO RODRIGUEZ SIGHED WITH relief, as his dilapidated, once-blue station wagon crawled and chugged through the final inches of the hourlong event known as a border crossing. The international station between San Diego and Tijuana saw the heaviest traffic of any crossing in the world, with about 300,000 people making the trek every day—some to work, some to play, some to shop or visit relatives, and some to conduct illegal activities of various kinds. For Hector, it was strictly a venture of love, one he made regularly and yet was relieved when it was over.

It wasn't that Hector didn't appreciate the beauty and modern conveniences of his sister city to the north, but he preferred the slower, quieter pace of his humble home on the outskirts of Tijuana, even now in 2008 when crime increasingly encroached on the peace of their existence. He had lived there his entire thirty-eight years, the middle child in a family of nine offspring, and had later married the beautiful Mariana Lopez, who had grown up right next door to him. That she had even noticed Hector never ceased to amaze him, and that she had agreed to marry him was nothing short of a miracle. Now, still living in the same neighborhood where they grew up, they did their best to feed and clothe the three children God had given them, as well as minister to the fifty or so members of their beloved *Casa de Dios* congregation. To supplement their income, Hector worked part-time in his younger brother Jorge's shoe repair shop. Though their financial situation did not allow for luxuries, it did provide a roof over their heads and food in their bellies.

It was a good life, Hector thought, as he coached and prayed the twenty-five-year-old car through the undisciplined crush of traffic on Avenida Revolucion, the main drag in this burgeoning city of nearly one and a half million people. As always, Hector was anxious to break away from the city's hub and escape to a quieter, more navigable thoroughfare. Though the quality of the roads would deteriorate the farther out he went, he would be glad to leave the hustle and bustle of the Tijuana tourism trade behind.

He would also be glad to leave behind the sadness that seemed to cling to him each time he crossed the border. And yet he knew his need to continue making the trip would end far too soon...

He shook the thoughts from his mind, turning on the radio, scanning for today's news.

"Many adherents believe recent earthquake tremors are another sign of a final countdown to the 2012 apocalypse the Mayan calendar predicts..." Hector clicked off the radio with dismay.

Then, of course, there was the situation in Chiapas, which seemed to grow more desperate and dangerous by the day. And his sixty-three-year-old mother, Virginia Correo Rodriguez, was living right outside San Juan Chamula, right in the middle of it all.

New Hope® Publishers is a division of WMU®, an international organization that challenges Christian believers to understand and be radically involved in God's mission. For more information about WMU, go to www.wmu.com. More information about New Hope books may be found at www. newhopepublishers.com. New Hope books may be purchased at your local bookstore.

If you've been blessed by this book, we would like to hear your story. The publisher and author welcome your comments and suggestions at: newhopereader@wmu.org.

 WorldCrafts

You can join other caring people to provide income, improved lives, and hope to artisans in poverty around the world.

Own handmade items produced by people in fair-trade, nonexploitative conditions.

Show your passion for South Africa. Purchase WorldCrafts South African products with this book:

African Candle Set
H094155 • (South Africa)
$19.99

Star Wall Décor
H094156 • (South Africa)
$24.99

Beaded Bee Purse
W024149• (South Africa)
$10.99